A CHRISTMAS CONFESSION

"Look at me," Alan demanded. "What do you see?"

Gen blinked, stiff in his grip. "I . . . I don't know what you mean."

He gave her a gentle shake. "No, of course you don't, because you refuse to look beyond the end of your aristocratic little nose. Well, try, just this once, to see the man beyond. A man who'd give his life for you." He gave a wry snort of laughter. "A man who's already lost everything he holds dear for the chance to win your love."

She stared up at him, arrested, and a last tear slid down her pale cheek. Her eyes were misty, her lips parted. With a groan, he pulled her to him and kissed her.

His anger melted immediately, even as she melted against him. He had dreamed of holding her like this for so long, and for once the dream did not disappoint. She was soft in his arms; he could feel the curve of her pressed against his chest. As he pulled her closer, his heart pounded against his ribs as if trying to reach hers. He could feel her heart's answering rhythm. And he knew in that instant that he would do anything, anything, to have her by his side forever

Books by Regina Scott

THE UNFLAPPABLE MISS FAIRCHILD

THE TWELVE DAYS OF CHRISTMAS

Published by Zebra Books

THE TWELVE DAYS OF CHRISTMAS

Regina Scott

Zebra Books
Kensington Publishing Corp.
http://www.zebrabooks.com

To the Babe in the manger, without whom there would be no Christmas, no gifts, and no book; and to Larry, Teddy, and William, the greatest gifts I ever received.

ZEBRA BOOKS are published by

Kensington Publishing Corp.
850 Third Avenue
New York, NY 10022

First Printing: December, 1998
10 9 8 7 6 5 4 3 2 1

Printed in the United States of America

Prologue

Milford Carstairs, senior partner of the firm Trent, Macy, and Carstairs, Solicitors, London, eased his craggy frame back against the beige-striped Sheraton chair in the satin-draped drawing room of Wenwood Abbey and regarded the Munroe family assembled about the wrought-iron tea cart. The Widow Munroe rested on the matching Sheraton chair nearer the white-marble fireplace, her slender back straight, iron gray head erect. His friend Rutherford Munroe had always said he'd married her because she carried herself better than most of the titled ladies in Society. He rather thought her well-known reserve had been a challenge to the outgoing Rutherford. Lord knows, the only time Carstairs had ever seen her smile was in her husband's company. There had been precious little to amuse her since the man died; it would only get worse when she knew the whole of it.

She inclined her head toward him as she passed him his tea in the gilt-edged bone china cup, and he accepted it with a nod of thanks. Condescending to the lesser mortals again, he noted as he took a sip, wrinkling his long nose at the steam. Thank goodness the daughters had only inherited her aristocratic good looks.

He glanced at the youngest, Allison, trying to sit on the nearby gold-threaded sofa with as much dignity as her mother, but only succeeding in looking uncomfortable. She caught his glance and arrested her fidgeting. Too much energy in that seventeen-year-old. A shame she had been too young to come out before Rutherford's untimely death. Even with her flaxen blond ringlets, vibrant blue eyes, classic features, and slender form, they'd be hard pressed to find a husband willing to take her in their current situation, especially here in Somerset.

His gaze was drawn to the oldest, Genevieve, seated next to her sister on the sofa, and he had to suppress a smile. Now, there was a lady. She'd inherited her father's sense of humor and lively intelligence, along with her mother's considerable physical assets. As she was smaller than her mother, her curves were all the more noticeable. Where her mother's hair had turned to iron, Gen's was the color of pure gold. Where her mother's aristocratic features were frozen in propriety, Gen's always reflected her thoughts, which were generally enthusiastic ones from what he had seen. It was little wonder she had been the toast of London the two years before her father died. She could have whistled up a fortune had she wished it. But she hadn't; she had made that point abundantly clear to him.

She also caught his eye on her and gave him a wink as she accepted her cup of tea from her mother's hand. He felt himself relax. At last, the girl was going to do it. He'd made the offer to do it himself several times, but it showed her courage that she had chosen to inform her family of their financial difficulties. A pity the girl had to take on such an onerous task when she hadn't yet reached her twenty-first birthday. But the mother had refused to even discuss the matter with him. He remembered her quiet disdain.

"Women should not interfere in financial matters, Mr. Carstairs," she had informed him, gazing serenely out the window of their London town house as if she were contemplating a formal garden instead of a busy London street. "It isn't proper. My husband retained you to see to these affairs. I'm sure you will continue to serve us with your usual thoroughness."

He had been at his wit's end as to how to get her to make the decisions necessary to pay their mounting debts when Gen had taken him aside to ask him about their finances. In her, he had found a quick mind and an inventive conspirator. He wondered if the Widow Munroe even realized that she had already signed away the London house, all its furnishings, all but the four horses that had carried them to Wenwood, the two in residence here, and a single carriage. If Gen hadn't taken the initiative, he shuddered to think what would have happened to the family. The Widow Munroe would have been hard pressed to maintain her reserve when faced with debtors' prison.

Gen cleared her throat, and he focused on the current situation. They had been ensconced in Wenwood Abbey, their small country estate, for several days now. Although Rutherford had mentioned the place several times, Carstairs had never seen it. He was surprised to find it a rambling, single-story structure set in a small clearing in a stretch of woods. True to its name, it even had a chapel at one end. With the trees towering on all sides, the dark wood of the house, and the small, infrequent windows, it had seemed to be brooding over dark thoughts. The inside made one feel a little less oppressed, thank goodness, with most of the small rooms having white-plastered or satin-hung walls and flagstone floors. He had to own the place possessed a quiet dignity, not unlike the Widow Munroe.

He and Gen had concocted a story about spending the first holiday since her father's death in more quiet surroundings than London, and he had to agree that the Abbey fit the bill. Despite an initial reluctance to the idea, both Allison and the widow seemed to have settled in well. It didn't hurt, he supposed, that the villagers seemed so glad to see them, stopping by for little visits and showering them with gifts of cakes and jams. The country air had already put the bloom back into the girls' cheeks. They had obviously begun to feel the Christmas spirit, as they had decorated the small drawing room with evergreen boughs over the mantel and a kissing bough of holly, ivy, and mistletoe atop the doorway, as for any proper Christmas celebration. Just yesterday, the widow had announced she was ready to allow them to put off the black they had been wearing since Rutherford's death six months ago. Accordingly, Allison was wearing a sky blue kerseymere gown with a white tucker and cuffs, and Genevieve wore a darker blue wool crepe with embroidery along the hem. Even the widow wore a fitted gown of gray silk which showed that age had not detracted from her willowy figure. He was sure they found his long coat and breeches outmoded in the extreme, but he was comfortable in them.

He shifted in his chair, waiting for Gen to speak. They were contented here. All but her mother's tea was poured; the widow even now was reaching for the pot. There would be no better time. He held his breath as Gen opened her mouth.

"I've invited the Pentercasts for Christmas Eve dinner and festivities," she announced.

He frowned, puzzled, and let out his breath. Then he jumped as the widow dropped the silver pot onto the table with a clatter. Allison gasped, paling, and fell against the back of her chair as if she were going to swoon. He stared at them in surprise.

"Genevieve," the widow murmured, allowing a frown to crease her brow, "that is a poor joke to play on your family."

"That was cruel in the extreme," Allison agreed more heatedly. "Sometimes I think you have quite changed since Father's death. How could you be so unfeeling!"

"I don't think it's unfeeling," Genevieve shrugged with a smile. "And I don't think Father would mind. I think he also found it ridiculous to keep up an enmity that began over a trifle a hundred years ago."

"A trifle?" The widow's frown deepened, and her blue-gray eyes were like slate. He wondered what could possibly be so awful that she would show this much emotion. Heaven knows she hadn't frowned like this when he had come to tell her that Rutherford had been killed in a carriage accident on the way home from his club. He wracked his brain to think of where he had heard the name Pentercast before. Hadn't that been the name of the local fellow Rutherford had had watch the property while they had been living in London these last six years?

"I do not believe," the widow was continuing, "that you can call evicting us from our home and usurping our rightful place in the community a trifle."

He glanced at Genevieve, who was sipping her tea with composure. Eviction? Usurping? What was this? Had he inadvertently sent the family into some kind of danger?

"Not to mention all the infamous things they've done since," Allison put in with a shudder.

"Those are stories," Gen maintained, reminding him of her mother in her cool reaction to their obvious concern. "By all accounts, Alan Pentercast and his family are well respected in the area. You heard the villagers when they came to visit the last few days—they all call him Squire. They've never done that with any of the other Pentercasts."

"What the villagers choose to call him is hardly our concern," the widow sniffed, succeeding in pouring her own cup of tea at last. He noted that her hand shook slightly on the handle of the ornate pot. "Pentercasts are Pentercasts. And we do not associate with Pentercasts."

Gen set her cup down on the carved mahogany table beside the sofa and leaned toward her mother. "But surely Father would have wished us to make amends. Didn't he have Alan keep an eye on Wenwood Abbey while we were away?"

"Mr. and Mrs. Chimes have been our caretakers," her mother insisted, refusing to meet Gen's defiant gaze. "I doubt Mr. Pentercast could have provided much assistance."

"Nevertheless, if we are going to live here at the Abbey,

surely we must learn to get along with the Squire and his family."

Carstairs allowed himself a private smile. There was method in the girl's madness after all. She was going to get them all excited over this Pentercast fellow so that when she made her announcement about their living here in near penury, it wouldn't be such a blow in comparison. Smart chit, hadn't he always said so?

"Genevieve," the widow chided, with a glare at him that surprised him with its heat, "I do not know *where* you get these ideas. I agreed with you and Mr. Carstairs that a change of scene for the Christmas holidays might be refreshing. In truth, I've missed some of our country traditions since moving to London. However, I hope you do not think I plan to take up residence here. We have Allison's come-out to plan for next Season, after all."

Gen leaned back casually. "Actually, I was going to suggest that we have her come-out here."

Oh, the girl was a master. Had she been a man, he would have hired her immediately.

"What!" Allison cried, leaping to her feet. Her cup of tea thumped to the floor, and he was forced to swing his long legs to one side as the brown stain spread across the Oriental carpet. He caught Gen's frown and knew that, like him, she was calculating how much it would cost to repair the damage.

"Moderate your tone, Allison," the widow sighed. "See what comes of immoderate temper? Sit down. As for you, Genevieve, I think we've had quite enough of your announcements at this tea table. Mr. Carstairs, I blame you for this outburst. I told you how I felt about young ladies and financial matters. It quite fills their heads with nonsense."

He opened his mouth to protest, but Gen beat him to it. "I think Father would be proud of what Mr. Carstairs and I have been able to accomplish. Someone had to manage the estate."

And better than Rutherford had, Carstairs amended silently. The man had been the most congenial of fellows, but he had had absolutely no sense for finances. Every bit of his inheritance, frittered away on fripperies to amuse the children, the refurbishment of the Abbey with such unlikely things as a functioning bell tower and a flock of black swans, and the entertainment of his many friends. The man ought to be thanking God daily in his place in heaven for an intelligent daughter who knew the cost of a good meal and a warm roof over her head.

"Your father was always proud of both his daughters," her mother replied. "I simply make the point that you have gone too far, Genevieve. For you to even think about extending an invitation without consulting me . . ."

"You would never have done it," Gen protested.

"Precisely, and with good reason."

"You talk as if this were a reality!" Allison interjected, clearly annoyed. "Gen, did you really invite those Pentercasts to dinner tonight?"

Gen put out her small chin. "Yes, I did. Furthermore, they have accepted. They will be here tonight at seven, along with Vicar York and young Mr. Wellfordhouse."

The widow set her cup of tea on the cart, rose, and shook out the skirts of her gray silk gown. "Well, then, it seems that we will have to make the best of this situation. Allison, come with me. We must find you an appropriate dress and consult Bryce on hairstyles. Genevieve, since you have taken it upon yourself to act as mistress of this house in my stead, I shall leave the entire event in your hands. Whatever happens tonight is on your head. Mr. Carstairs, I wish you well on your trip back to London. I hope you understand when I say that Genevieve will not be spending time with you there when we return. Come, Allison."

Grimacing, the girl followed her mother from the room.

"Well," Genevieve sighed, rising. "That went remarkably badly."

"I thought you had them before your mother stormed out, in her own quiet way, of course," Carstairs admitted, rising to join her. "That business about the Pentercast fellow was an excellent diversion. I take it he isn't the blackguard they made him out to be."

"Hardly," she replied, gazing toward the fire. A smile played on her lips, and he wondered what she was seeing. "His family has a somewhat unsavory reputation, but he was something of a hero when I was a child. My father once said there wasn't a man in London who could match him."

Carstairs raised an eyebrow. "Your father always did see the best in people. Still, that does seem unaccountably high praise, even from him."

"You wouldn't say that if you'd seen him save the Mattison twins from drowning. I'm afraid I must agree with my father's assessment. Certainly none of the gentlemen who courted me were anywhere near as impressive."

He knew at another time he'd find that remark intriguing. Now he felt it incumbent upon him to return to the point. "Be that as it may, my dear, you realize you must tell them the truth."

She wandered closer to the fireplace, holding out her long-fingered hands to the fire even though he doubted she could be cold in that fetching confection of wool crepe she was wearing.

"I've been trying, Mr. Carstairs, truly I have. It's just so much harder than I expected. How can I tell Mother she must give up her town house? How can I tell Allison she'll never have a come-out? The future we offer is too bleak, I fear."

"But it is a future nonetheless," he insisted. "My dear, we've done everything we can. You know as well as I do that the only way for your family to stay together is to attempt to live quietly here at the Abbey. We had agreed it was the best course."

She sighed. "I know. Are you absolutely sure we didn't overlook anything? There truly is no other course?"

"None less daunting. Unless of course you've reconsidered . . ." He hesitated to bring up the subject, for her reaction had been so strong the first time he had mentioned it.

"No," she snapped. Then she shook herself. "I know I should consider all the alternatives, Mr. Carstairs, and I know I'm being selfish. But I cannot trade my own happiness for their ability to maintain a more opulent lifestyle. We can all make sacrifices here in the country, and I believe we can all find some measure of happiness." She sighed again. "I can explain it so logically to you. Why do I find it so hard to tell them?"

He offered her his most supportive smile. "You will find a way, my dear. I have complete faith in your diplomacy. You're Rutherford Munroe's daughter."

She started to smile, then sobered. "Yes, I am."

He patted her on the shoulder and turned toward the door. "I'm sorry to have to miss the entertainment this evening, but I promised to return to London within the se'ennight, and I don't want to miss Christmas with my own family. Write to me when the deed is done, will you?"

"Yes, of course," she nodded. "Thank you, Mr. Carstairs, for all your help. And happy Christmas."

He turned back to her, standing with the fire a golden glow behind her, outlining the curves of her silhouette and turning her hair to flame. If he had been thirty years younger and unmarried, he'd have offered for her himself. "Happy Christmas, my dear." As he moved out into the hallway, he thought he heard her answer.

"I will do everything in my power to make it so."

One

Prelude, Christmas Eve

Genevieve Munroe paced the wide wood-paneled entryway of Wenwood Abbey, listening for the sound of carriage wheels on the drive. Even with her back to him, she knew Chimes, their man of all work, was watching her from his spot, propped up on the parson's bench on the opposite side of the space.

"Settle down, miss," he chided. "They'll be here soon enough."

She let her pacing turn her toward him and winked. "Settle down yourself. You're as anxious to see this fight end as I am."

"Now there's a true statement," he allowed, folding his hands over his pot belly and stretching his long legs out in front of him. "It would make my life a great deal easier if you Munroes would learn to get along with them Pentercasts. I wouldn't have to be near as particular which side of the wall the game was on. And the Squire, now, is too fine a man to be treated like he was the dirt beneath your mother's slippers."

A tingle of excitement shot through her. She could not let Chimes see it. No one could see it. "We are in agreement there as well," she replied calmly enough, but she couldn't help adding, "Has he changed much since we left, Chimes?"

The servant's sharp black eyes lit up, and she struggled not to look too interested in the answer, afraid she'd given away the game. "Since you and Miss Allison and Mr. Geoffrey went to the curate's school together? Not all that much, I suppose. Still interested in the Squire, are we, Miss Gen?"

She wandered closer to him, letting him see how casually she gazed at her reflection in the gilded mirror beside him. She tucked a stray curl back into the golden coil at the nape of her neck. The woman who gazed back at her was cool and confident, the champion of many a London fete. Satisfied, she turned from the reflection to face him with a gracious smile. Somehow, she knew she wasn't fooling him for a second.

"I remember how you used to look up at him when you was just a little gel and Alan would come to take Mr. Geoffrey home on his horse," Chimes continued as she resumed her pacing. "Right fine figure of a man is the Squire. I heared tell he was interested in courting Mary Delacourte."

"Did her eyes ever uncross?" Gen asked sweetly.

"Now, they were never really crossed. That right eye of hers just tends to wander since she was kicked in the head by that cow all those years ago. If I didn't know better, I'd say you were still sweet on him."

She snorted, and the unladylike sound echoed against the polished wood walls. "I was never sweet on him, Chimes. It was an infantile adoration. I was only fourteen when we left; he must have been, oh . . ."

"Twenty-two. Which would make him just a year or two shy of thirty these days." He scratched the bare spot on top of his graying head. "Good age for a man to marry and settle down."

She scowled at him, determined to put that idea from his mind. "I hope you remember how to keep that mouth of yours shut when Mother arrives."

"Takes more than a pretty frown to scare me, gel," he winked at her, tapping the crook of his long nose. "And don't you worry about your mother. She never did think I was good enough to be the butler, but she can't live without my Annie's cooking." His merry smile faded. "Especially now. Carstairs says you haven't told them yet."

That pulled her up short. Twice now she'd underestimated Chimes's ability to see to the heart of matters. What a pity her father hadn't taken him with them to London. She'd have given much to have him point out the shallowness of her beaus before she could even think of engaging her heart. And a word from Chimes might have kept her father from allowing a drunken friend to take the reins. She blinked away the unhappy thought. Still, she couldn't let her appreciation of his abilities deter her now. "I do not wish to talk about it further," she informed him, hands on hips. "I warn you, Chimes, I will brook no arguments on this. They deserve one last happy Christmas."

He held up his gnarled hands in surrender. "Very well, miss. You can count on me to stay mum." He lowered his voice. "Are we still hunting tomorrow morning?"

She relaxed, the two topics she feared most now past. Lowering her voice as well, she nodded. "Yes. I've convinced Mother that letting me plan the Christmas dinner is excellent practice. Do you think we can still find some good birds for Annie to cook?"

"Good birds, bad birds, my Annie will make them sing in your mouth. Hark, there's the carriage now."

She was surprised at the flutter of excitement in her stomach, even more surprised at the lowering of disappointment when Chimes shrugged himself into his coat to find that it was only their vicar, Thaddeus York, and his curate, William Wellfordhouse. She chided herself for her lack of enthusiasm. William had been her father's protégé; she had known him for years. He deserved better than her disappointment. She pasted on a smile of welcome as the grooms led the horses away and Chimes showed them in.

"Good evening, Miss Genevieve," Wellfordhouse smiled, taking her hands. "I must say you're looking quite well."

She grinned up at him, noting that his sandy hair was as immaculately combed as ever and that his gray eyes sparkled. Before she could return his greeting, the vicar broke in.

"Quite well indeed, under the circumstances, quite well," grumbled York, running a hand over his balding pate as Chimes hurried off with their coats and hats. "There are many who question the proper time for mourning. Three months? Six months? A year? Respect for the dearly departed is the key, I find. Your father has been gone a mere six months, has he not?"

She bit back a smile at his faux pas. Her father had ever delighted in baiting the poor vicar into just such a statement. "Yes, Vicar," she said aloud. "How kind of you to remember." She focused on the young man who had become like a brother to her. "William, you look thinner than when we saw you in London. I hope the vicar isn't working you, too hard."

Wellfordhouse opened his mouth to respond but the vicar coughed into his meaty hands. "Hard work, Miss Munroe, is the best road toward heaven, the very best."

"Then dear William must be nearly there," she replied, allowing the smile to show. She noted that Chimes had returned and signaled him forward. "Chimes, please make these kind gentlemen comfortable in the drawing room and inform Mother that they have arrived. I will wait here for our other guests."

Wellfordhouse, who had been looking rather uncomfortable, brightened. "Oh, are we to have other company as well?"

She winked at him. "Yes. The Pentercasts."

"Bravo, Miss Gen!" he exclaimed.

The vicar grunted. "It is the true penitent who knows the worth of peace, the true penitent indeed."

Gen's smile was threatening to become a laugh. "Chimes," she prompted. She was relieved he led them away.

She really should try to remember Vicar York's position, she scolded herself as she resumed her anxious pacing. He had been the head of the church at Wenwood since before she was born. Of course, she never felt as comfortable in his company as she did in William's. William was always pleasant, always kind. He seemed to have taken every lesson in humility and duty to heart. Her father had said he was born to be a clergyman. Somehow she didn't think the same applied to Vicar York, who seemed far more interested in good food and fine wine. The very thought made her feel guilty. She would simply have to try harder to appreciate the man if they were to live here in Wenwood. If only he didn't insist on repeating every other phrase. She remembered when Allison had pointed it out to their father.

"Don't let it annoy you," her father had replied with that telltale twinkle in his eyes that meant he was never less serious. "He only repeats himself to show how very little he has to say, how very little indeed." She could hear Allison's answering giggle. Yes, she'd have to work very hard if she were to be suitably serious with Reverend York.

She had crossed the wide entry twice more when her mother and Allison appeared from the corridor that led to the family wing. She nearly groaned out loud. While she had gone out of her way to pick a simple gown of watered green silk with a modest neck, she saw that her mother had decided to show the Pentercasts who they were dealing with. The lilac satin gown was more suited to a royal ball than a country dinner, with its full skirt, lace overdress, and silver embroidery at the lowered neck and high waist. The puffed sleeves required long gloves, but Gen knew it wasn't modesty that had caused her mother to include the two amethyst rings or the matching stone that glinted from the folds of her silver turban. Allison, not yet out, should have been more simply dressed. The white gown she wore was as plainly cut as Gen's, but it too boasted a silver lace overdress sprinkled with beads that reflected the candlelight. With a pang, Gen noted the Munroe diamonds, one of the few pieces of jewelry she had refused to sell, sparkling at her sister's throat and wrist. The tiara, usually reserved for the eldest daughter or daughter-in-law, nestled in her flaxen curls. Her mother was obviously making a statement. Standing next to them, Gen felt like a poor relation.

They had no time to talk as the sound of a carriage came again, and Chimes bustled forward to receive their guests. Her mother uttered a short sigh at his rumpled coat, but he opened the arched double doors with proper ceremony. Trying to ignore the fluttering in her stomach, Gen put up her head and pasted another smile on her face.

Mrs. Pentercast entered first. She was shorter than Gen remembered, reaching only to Gen's shoulder, and much rounder. Gen could only hope her face didn't show her shock as Chimes took the woman's black velvet evening cloak to reveal that she was wearing a lilac satin gown with a lace overdress and silver embroidery. It was obviously a copy of the London gown, done somewhat less grandly and looking much less impressive on the short, squat figure than on her mother's tall, spare frame. Even the silver headband with its purple ostrich feather she had elected to wear instead of a turban failed to give it the proper polish. Nevertheless, the Widow Munroe's forced smile of welcome froze on her face.

"Clear the way, Mother," an annoyed voice demanded, and Mrs. Pentercast scurried forward so fast that Gen's mother was forced to step back to keep the purple feather from lodging in her nose. Geoffrey Pentercast, looking much as Gen remembered in his many-caped brown tweed greatcoat that called attention to his broad shoulders, clumped into the entry, trailing mud, decayed leaves, and a six-foot log in his wake.

"Thought you wouldn't have a proper Yule log," he announced, dragging the massive stump by a chain into the center of the entry. Gen tried not to think about what it would cost to repair the scratches he was making in the parquet floor.

She could feel her mother's disapproval. "Why, of course, Mr. Pentercast," Gen answered quickly for her. "How very thoughtful of you to bring it along. We haven't had a Yule log in years, have we, Allison?"

"Yule logs are such quaint customs," Allison sniffed, "for children."

"I like to think there's a still some of the child in all of us, Miss Munroe," a deeper voice said from the doorway. The flutter in Gen's stomach intensified and she swallowed, looking up to find Alan Pentercast regarding her from the door. Her first thought was that he was very different from what she remembered, but she wasn't sure what it was that had changed. Like his brother, he still had the shaggy thatch of brown hair that defied combing and the dark brown eyes that seemed to sparkle with some secret. Unlike his brother, who was shorter and more powerfully built, he stood a good head taller than anyone in the room. His face seemed leaner, his features more sharply planed. He moved with a negligent grace she'd only seen on London dance floors. As Chimes took his many-caped blue tweed greatcoat, she saw that he wore the black trousers, white satin waistcoat, and black cutaway coat of a London Corinthian. Unlike the dress his mother wore, the outfit was obviously no copy. She would have said it had been cut by Weston, although she'd have also wagered there was no padding in the shoulders or calves. The sensitive, brave young man she remembered had been replaced by a confident, authoritative gentleman. She wasn't sure whether to be disappointed or awed.

"As my daughter Genevieve noted, Mr. Pentercast," her mother was murmuring, "we appreciate the thought. Chimes, please see to the . . . er . . . log."

"Mind you," Geoffrey put in as Chimes stepped forward to take up the chain. "I expect to be the first to sit on it, since I brought it."

"I'm sure that won't be a problem," her mother quipped. "I

believe we all know each other. You are all most welcome to our home."

Gen cast a sidelong look at Alan, who towered over his mother. She caught herself standing a little straighter and recognized the ridiculous desire to have him notice her. *Good heavens, you'd think I was being introduced to the Prince Regent,* she thought in disgust. Nevertheless, she kept her head high as his family stepped forward.

Little Mrs. Pentercast was peering up at Gen's mother, squinting as if to focus on the narrow, aristocratic face a foot above hers. "My word, Trudy, I hope you're not going to stay on this high horse of yours all night. I told Alan I thought that invitation was a mistake."

The Widow Munroe glowered down at her, and for a moment Gen thought her mother's reserve would crack. She wracked her brain for a way out of the growing hostility.

"Mother," Alan put in, "I'm sure the Munroes wouldn't have asked us here if they hadn't wished for the company." He made a bow over her mother's hand. Some of the lines around her mother's mouth eased. "And on such an important occasion. We are honored."

His mother sniffed and Geoffrey rolled his eyes, but her mother offered him the closest thing to a smile she had seen since her father died, and Gen began to relax. "Perhaps it is time to put our differences behind us, sir."

He smiled a genuine smile in return as he straightened, and she found herself wishing he'd smile at her that way. "Nothing would please my family more, I assure you."

"Except, perhaps, for something to eat," Geoffrey interrupted, causing her mother's eyes to narrow once again. Gen sighed in vexation. "This was an invitation to dinner, was it not?"

"Chimes?" her mother snapped, and their man scurried forward from the back of the house, dusting off his hands. "Please escort our guests to the withdrawing room."

Chimes motioned them down the corridor that opened to the left of the wide entry. Alan offered his mother his arm, and Geoffrey fell in behind, muttering something about wanting to withdraw himself. Her own mother followed with stately steps. Allison walked beside her at the end of the procession.

"I don't know why you wanted these people in our home," she whispered to Gen. "They are every bit the rudesbys we have been warned about for years."

"Shhh," Gen warned. "I haven't been overly impressed with your own manners, miss."

Allison tossed her head.

Gen hoped things might go better when the company was all gathered in the drawing room. Reverends York and Wellford-house rose as the procession entered, their voices raised in greeting, and her hope seemed justified. Then Mrs. Pentercast disappointed them, especially Vicar York, by giving the reverends the briefest of nods before turning to try various chairs in the room. After several were proclaimed unsuitable, she deigned to sit in the Sheraton chair nearest the fire. With a shrug that seemed to indicate he'd been through this before, Alan went to stand beside her, leaning against the fireplace mantel. As the chair she had taken was Gen's mother's favorite, her mother had no choice but to take the matching chair in the corner nearest the door, making it look as if she wanted nothing more than to escape. Allison threw herself down on the chair next to it. Geoffrey glanced around the room with a shake of his head, grumbling about the tastes of females in general, then clumped over to slump down in the chair nearest his mother. The reverends resumed their places on the sofa across the back of the room. Gen forced back a sigh as she sank onto the chaise longue on the other side of the door. She knew she wasn't the only one to notice that the Pentercasts and the Munroes were now effectively lined up on opposite sides of the room.

Silence stretched. A log settled in the fireplace. She could hear the clink of silver next door as Chimes and their footmen put the finishing touches on the table. This was maddening! What had she been thinking to arrange this? Despite her father's admiration of Alan, no Munroe had been seen in the company of a Pentercast for a hundred years. What had made her believe she could get them to change their behavior now? So what if it was Christmas, time of peace on earth and goodwill toward all? The all must not have included the Pentercasts and Munroes.

If only she could help her mother and Allison realize how important it was that they get along with their neighbors . . . But she was the only one who knew why it was so important, and she had promised herself to remain silent. She felt like a prisoner in her own handmade cell. Looking up, she caught Alan's gaze, and to her surprise, he grinned at her. She blushed, looking away, afraid of what he might think should he see the frustration in her eyes.

"You are looking exceptionally lovely tonight, if I may say so, Mrs. Pentercast," York rumbled, breaking the silence. "That color is the perfect shade on a lady of your influence in the community."

Her mother's eyes snapped fire. Mrs. Pentercast blushed prettily, patting down her skirts. "How very kind of you to say so, Vicar."

"All the ladies look lovely if you ask me," William put in with a nod to all the corners of the room. "We gentlemen are most fortunate to be in their company."

"Well said, William," Alan agreed heartily. "If I may compliment our hostess, this room is particularly festive. It's been a long time since Wenwood had a proper Christmas with the Abbey open. Your neighbors have missed you." He said the last with a pointed look at Gen, and the fluttering in her stomach began again.

"Hear, hear," William nodded agreeably.

Her mother inclined her head in acknowledgment. "It is good to have Christmas in the country once more."

"Will you be coming with us to see the Thorn tonight?" Alan queried.

Her mother looked thoughtful. "I haven't done that since I was a child. Is it still alive?"

"Very much so," William assured her. "Tom Harvey spotted the bud this morning, I'm told. I expect the entire village will be there tonight to see if it blooms."

" 'Course it will bloom," Geoffrey grumbled. "That's what the damn thing's for, isn't it?"

Her mother stiffened, and Allison widened her eyes, looking shocked at his language. His own mother glared at him.

"Well, if you ask me, we must be very careful how we treat these trappings of Christmas," York grunted. "There is entirely too much reverence paid to this Wenwood Thorn, entirely too much. And these boughs and that ivy over the door are pagan customs that once would have had no place in a good Christian home, no place at all."

"How very thoughtful of you to remind us," her mother all but snarled.

"My duty, madame, my duty," he nodded, patting his sagging belly with complacency.

"I don't know but I rather like them," Geoffrey insisted. He leered at Allison. "Especially the kissing bough."

"What a pity there aren't any proper gentlemen on whom to use it," Allison replied with a toss of her flaxen curls.

"Chimes!" her mother fairly shouted. The beleaguered servant bumped through the door leading to the dining room, rubbing a stain off his already dirty black trousers. "How soon do you expect dinner?"

"I'm quite happy to report, madame, that dinner is served."

She rose, and the rest of the company rose with her. Gen suppressed her disappointment as Alan made to take his mother's arm again. To her surprise, Vicar York, his considerable bulk quivering, fairly leaped from his seat to offer Mrs. Pentercast his arm. Alan raised an eyebrow, but stepped aside. Geoff snorted as they moved past him. When Alan made no move to claim the hostess, William, looking awkward, offered her mother a tremulous smile. "Mrs. Munroe?"

She inclined her head, accepting his arm. He sighed visibly, and Gen bit back a smile at her childhood friend's difficulty playing the gallant. Allison stomped after them, ignoring the grin Geoffrey cast her. He fell in behind her.

"May I?" Alan asked, beside her. The room was suddenly too warm and much too small. She swallowed, unable to meet his eyes. This is what you wanted, she reminded herself. You've been dreaming of his noticing you since you were fourteen. She put out her hand, noticed it was trembling, and scowled at her own timidity. She was no longer that girl of fourteen in the midst of her first crush. She had gone in to dinner with marquesses and earls, danced with royal dukes and princes. There was no reason for her to be so nervous around Alan Pentercast, of all people. She slapped her hand down on his arm. He chuckled.

"I was hoping it wouldn't be quite this difficult," he murmured with a grin, and she wasn't sure if he was referring to her attempt to bring their families back together or her own hesitation in accepting his offer. With a smile that was much too stiff, she allowed him to lead her in to dinner.

The meal was no better than their attempt at conversation in the drawing room. Chimes had done a credible job of making the long, damask-draped table look festive, with a silver epergne of red-berried holly in the center and sprigs of ivy by each crystal goblet. She found herself wondering where he had found the silver serving platters and how much they might sell for at auction. But as the first course, a lovely mulligatawny soup, was served, she found she had other problems to contend with.

Geoffrey continued to live up to her mother and Allison's preconceived notions of the Pentercasts by gulping enormous quantities of food, guzzling glasses of wine, and burping after each course. Allison, seated opposite him, glowered at each infraction and made a point of daintily picking at the various dishes. Mrs. Pentercast spent her time comparing everything to other dinners she had had: it seemed the table was not nearly as festive as her first Christmas Eve dinner with friends, the various courses were not as exotic as what the Regent served, and the large brass candelabra above the table was not nearly as large as the one in the Manor dining room. The only time she paused in her litany was to blush and giggle over Reverend York's incessant stream of compliments. Seated at the head of the table, Gen's mother refused to eat, her conversation dwindling to near nods when someone addressed her directly. Although both Alan and William continued to be congenial, Gen was hard pressed to find topics of conversation that would be entertaining.

The men didn't even stay for their after-dinner port, but repaired with the ladies to the withdrawing room. Geoffrey insisted that Chimes produce the Yule log he had brought, and then uttered a few more curses when there wasn't a brand from the previous log available to light it. Alan managed to turn his tantrum aside with a joke, but she could see that her mother was ready to throw the youth out. She had to think of something safe to discuss, some way to pass the time until it would no longer be rude to send them all home. She considered cards, but she wasn't sure of the vicar's feelings on the matter, and she shuddered to think of the fighting that would accompany any attempt to pair the group into partners. Music was out of the question: she knew she'd never get her sister to perform, and she didn't think her voice or fingers would be steady enough, given the present company. Heaven only knew it was hard enough to focus on conversation when every time she looked up she met Alan's gaze. Another time she knew she would have been thrilled by his regard, but at the moment it seemed singularly inappropriate when the rest of the room was actively feuding. She had to think of something. Her eyes lit on the Christmas greenery over the mantel. Perhaps the season of peace might inspire.

"You mentioned the Wenwood Thorn a while ago, William," she ventured as the flames licked around Geoffrey's Yule log and they had all settled in their places around the room. "That was always one of my favorite Christmas customs. What was yours?"

Ever willing to join in the conversation, he smiled at her, looking thoughtful. "My goodness, there are so many. I suppose one might be the bells calling the villagers to midnight services. It's so quiet then, one can almost imagine what that first Christmas must have been like for the Holy Family."

"I've always liked that old wives' tale that the animals talk on Christmas Eve," Alan smiled. "When I was a boy, I don't know how many times I crept out to the stable to find out. Unfortunately, I always fell asleep before I could prove the tale true."

Gen found herself smiling as well, imagining the dark-haired little boy curled up in the hay. Then her mother surprised her by joining in the conversation. "Rutherford always liked that story as well. He loved all the Christmas traditions. Do you remember, Gen, how he liked to play Snap Dragon?"

Gen nodded. "Oh, yes. I think his grin was brighter than the flames from the brandy."

Allison clapped her hands. "Oh, Mother, may we?"

"Now who likes childish games?" Geoffrey muttered.

Gen ignored him, signaling to Chimes, who left with a wink. At last, she seemed to have found something they could all agree on. She was pleased when a few moments later Chimes returned with a large, shallow silver bowl filled a quarter of the way with raisins. A footman followed him with a bottle of her father's best brandy. Mrs. Pentercast pulled her chair closer to the little table on which he set the bowl, and the others drew around it as well, their eyes shining with expectation. The gentlemen peeled off their gloves and the ladies did likewise. With a flourish, Chimes poured the brandy over the raisins and lit it on fire. Gen wasn't sure who uttered the "Oooh" as the other lights in the room were put out.

"This was your idea, Allison," her mother said quietly. "Why don't you start?"

William's tenor began the song and Alan's baritone joined in.

> "Here he comes with flaming bowl
> Don't be mean to take his toll,
> Snip! Snap! Dragon!"

Allison's quick fingers darted through the flames and she popped her captured raisins triumphantly into her mouth.

> "Take care you don't take too much
> Be not greedy in your clutch.
> Snip! Snap! Dragon!"

William pounced in, then snatched his hand ruefully back, fingers empty. He shrugged good-naturedly.

> "With his blue and lapping tongue
> Many of you will be stung.
> Snip! Snap! Dragon!"

Her mother daintily reached through the blue mist and produced a single, plump raisin, which she ate in two bites.

"For he snaps at all that comes
Snatching at his feast of plums.
Snip! Snap! Dragon!"

Geoffrey had stepped up beside her, darting a hand into the bowl and scooping up a handful while the hairs on the back of his hand smoked. He shoved the raisins into his mouth and licked the brandy off his fingers.

"But Old Christmas makes him come,
Though he looks so fee! fa! fum!
Snip! Snap! Dragon!"

It was her turn. She reached through the blue mist of brandy flames, but before she could reach one of the plump raisins beneath, she felt the heat on her skin and snatched back her hand. Geoffrey snorted in contempt.

"Don't 'ee fear him, be but bold
Out he goes, his flames are cold.
Snip! Snap! Dragon!"

Alan's large hand swept through the flames and brought out a handful of the raisins. With a bow, he offered them to Gen. Shyly, she reached out and pulled two from his palm, popping them into her mouth. Licking the brandy from her lips, she looked up at him, noticing the blue flames reflected in the depths of his dark eyes. Then Chimes stepped forward and covered the dish, extinguishing the blaze.

"That was fun!" Allison exclaimed as the candles were relit. "Let's do another game. How about Forfeits—'The Twelve Days of Christmas'?"

As the others moved back to their seats, Alan blocked her

way. "Sure you wouldn't like some more raisins?" he mur-mured, his large hand open.

Gen shook her head, pulling on her gloves. As before, it was as if the temperature in the room had increased with him so near. She reminded herself again that she was an accomplished lady and squared her shoulders. "You won them fairly," she managed to reply congenially. "I never was all that good at these kinds of games."

He popped the remainder into his mouth. Then he cocked his head, regarding her even as he pulled on his own gloves. By the light in his deep brown eyes, she would have sworn Chimes had never extinguished the flames. "I've heard you were very good at other games, however. What do you say to a friendly wager?"

She frowned at him, feeling a bit unsteady. "What do you mean, sir?"

"I wager you'll not be able to remember the gifts in 'The Twelve Days of Christmas.' "

"What must I do if I lose?" she asked, trying not to eye the nearby kissing bough.

"Marry me," he replied.

Gen stared at him, growing cold all over. She could not have heard him correctly. But the intent look on his face told her she had.

"La, sir, but I do not understand," she murmured, lowering her eyes and praying he would confirm it as a poor joke.

"Surely I'm not the first to propose to the incomparable Miss Munroe," he quipped and she was forced to look up, surprised by the touch of bitterness in his tone. His expression, usually so open, seemed guarded. He watched her as intently as Chimes had. It made her no more comfortable.

"If you truly are sincere, you will understand when I say this is rather sudden."

"Ah, but we have so little time. You return to London after

Epiphany, do you not? I fear I must make my mark while I can. Come now, Miss Munroe, have we a wager?"

She stepped back from him, the sharp look in his eyes, the implacable line of his jaw, the perfect cut of his coat combining to focus her thoughts to the sharpness of a spear point. She had struggled to understand the change in him: now it was clear. The self-assurance she had admired had inflated into arrogance, an arrogance that was all too familiar from her time in London. Another wretched Corinthian. How she despised the breed. They lived on a shallow plane. To them, a female was only to be coveted for her pretty exterior; the woman beneath held no interest. To think she had always thought he was different, more noble, better. He was the standard to which she had held all others. She marveled at her own naiveté. She felt as if a favorite statue had fallen and shattered at her feet, a statue of a hero, no doubt. With two words he had destroyed the last of her childhood illusions. Illusions that had been destroyed one by one as she had learned of her father's other life.

"Only a Pentercast would wager something so important on a trifle," she heard herself sneer.

That she had stung him was obvious by the look that quickly came and went in his eyes. For a brief moment, she thought she had misjudged him. Then his face stiffened. "Apparently the good Reverend Wellfordhouse has been remiss in his duties. He should have warned you that what the Pentercasts set out to get, they achieve. Whether you take my wager or not, by Epiphany you will agree to be my wife."

She could have cried at his arrogance. "Then he should have warned you as well that we Munroes are not to be had so easily."

She was surprised to see the return of his former grin. "I never expected it to be easy. But I will prove to you that we are meant to wed, if I have to play the devoted lover and bring you the twelve gifts myself."

"How typical," she snorted, shaking her head. "Do you honestly think you can buy my love as easily as your ancestor bought my home?"

"I won't spend a penny," he replied with a twinkle in his eyes. "If I can do it, will you marry me?"

She ought to slap his face for daring to ask. Better, she ought to order Chimes to throw him out, him and his entire rude family. Her mother had been right—Pentercasts were not to be trusted. What a shame she'd had to bring her own family here to live near them. And she had so hoped they might be of assistance. Perhaps they still could. She eyed him, mentally calculating his chances of success as Carstairs had taught her to do. The exact nature of the gifts eluded her at the moment, but surely at least a few of them were rather obscure. If he somehow had to gather them without purchasing them, it would make winning harder still. She had twelve days to outwit him. With his arrogance, it shouldn't be all that difficult. Perhaps it was time the Munroes put the Pentercast arrogance to good use. Perhaps this time, the wager would turn out differently. "If you fail, will you renew the harvest tithes—ten percent to my family in perpetuity?"

"Now who's after money?" he countered.

Gen blushed, but stood her ground. She knew how difficult the change in finances would be for her mother and sister. Life at Wenwood would be easier if they could count on a steady source of food. "Come, sir, you cannot expect me to play if there is nothing to my advantage. Have we a wager?"

Alan cooked his head. "If I succeed in giving you the appropriate gift for each day of Christmas according to the old Forfeits game, without spending a penny, you will agree to be my bride. If I fail, I provide your family with ten percent of the harvest from my land and ensure that future generations do likewise. That's it?"

"That's it." Gen peeled the glove from her right hand. "I

believe you Pentercasts follow the traditional way of wagering."
She spat on her palm and held it out to him. "Is it a wager?"

Alan grinned, peeling off his own glove. He spat on his palm.
"A wager it is."

He clasped her hand and she felt the strength of his grip, his
warm fingers curling around the back of her hand until his
fingers touched his thumb. She pulled away much more quickly
than she had intended. Turning to hide the blush she could feel
staining her cheeks, she felt him catch her arm. "Oh, no. I
suggest we enter the wager tonight with a neutral party."

She frowned, and he released her. "We are not in London,
sir. There is no betting book at Wenwood as there is at White's."

"No," he smiled, "but there is the Reverend Mr. Wellfordhouse."

Gen glanced over at William, who was actively helping her
mother through the various verses of the poem, to much laughter by Allison and Geoffrey as he insisted that it was a goose
in the pear tree. Catching her glance, he excused himself and
joined them near the sofa.

"Is there something you need, Miss Genevieve?"

Pulling on her glove, she felt her blush deepening as she tried
to think of a way to phrase what she had just done. William
would of course be shocked at her mercenary wager. She felt a
little shocked herself. But of course, Alan would not win, and
her family would have no need to worry for their food. Perhaps
this Corinthian at least would think twice before making such
an insulting offer again. She put up her head. "Yes, William.
Mr. Pentercast and I wish to enter a wager with you."

He frowned. "A wager?"

Alan grinned, and she knew he was watching her squirm.
"Yes, Mr. Wellfordhouse. Miss Munroe has just wagered her
honor against the harvest tithes from my land."

William choked, and Gen glared at Alan.

"What this odious man is trying to say, William," she explained, thumping him on the back to help him catch his breath, "is that Mr. Pentercast has wagered that he can bring me each of the gifts in 'The Twelve Days of Christmas' poem on the appropriate day without spending a penny. If he cannot, he will owe my family the income his forefather stole from us."

"Uh, uh, uh," Alan tisked with a shake of his finger. "He won a wager, fair and square, as I intend to do. And if I win, Miss Munroe has agreed to become my bride."

William looked back and forth between Alan's confident smile and Gen's equally determined scowl. "I see. What is it exactly you expect me to do?"

"Set the rules of this contest," Alan explained, "and act as judge to ensure that each of us follows them."

"Fairly," Gen amended.

"I see," William said again. "And you are willing to marry Miss Genevieve in full ceremony and treat her as any other wife, Squire?"

Alan nodded. "I so swear."

"And you're willing to marry the Squire and be his obedient wife, Miss Genevieve?" he continued.

Gen glared at Alan. "Perhaps not completely obedient. But, yes, I so swear as well."

William glanced between them again. "Very well. Here are your rules, then. The gifts are fairly well specified in the poem, I believe. They shall be delivered through no direct use of money to Miss Genevieve before the last stroke of midnight on each of the days specified. If the Squire succeeds in this undertaking, I shall be more than happy to read the banns myself."

Gen turned her glare on him.

"Of course should the Squire fail," he quickly added, shrinking back from her, "I will be just as happy to count the harvest tithes myself."

"Done," Alan nodded. "Now, if you'll excuse me, I had best

see to my mother before the vicar quite turns her head with his flattery." He moved off to stand beside his mother's chair.

"I must say, William, that I am bit surprised at you," Gen chided.

He raised an eyebrow. "Why, Miss Gen? I've thought you and the Squire were well matched for years. If this is what it takes to win you, I wish the man well." He hurried off to rejoin the game as she stared at him open-mouthed.

Two

Verse One, a Partridge in a Pear Tree

The Pentercasts left at ten, and all agreed they had had a marvelous time. The Reverends York and Wellfordhouse left shortly thereafter, William promising to return the next day for the traditional private Christmas service in the Abbey chapel.

As Chimes closed the door behind them, Allison sighed. "What a lovely evening."

Gen burst out laughing.

Her mother managed a smile. "You may well laugh, Genevieve. You did quite nicely tonight. I believe Allison and I owe you an apology."

Allison nodded, ringlets bouncing. "Yes, indeed. The Pentercasts aren't nearly as bad as I had feared."

"No, they don't breathe fire or eat small children," Gen teased. All except one particular Pentercast, she amended.

"One might actually find them tolerable," her mother agreed, "in very limited circumstances, of course."

Chimes snorted on his way toward the back of the house. Her mother's eyes narrowed.

"I'm very glad to hear you say that," Gen put in quickly to divert her. In truth it was a relief to know that most of the members of the two families might coexist on easier terms because of tonight.

Allison turned away, wandering toward the family wing with another deep-felt sigh. "I'm just sorry to see it end so soon."

"Who says it has to end?" Gen challenged, putting her hands on her hips. She had worked too hard to put them in a good mood to see it spoiled now. "We have the Twelve Days of Christmas before us."

Allison grinned at her. "Yes, I know. But tonight is over."

Gen shook her head, determined to keep their spirits up. Soon enough, they'd be back in mourning, this time for their lost hopes. "I thought we were going to see the Thorn?"

Her mother's eyes glowed. "Why, Genevieve, I believe that's a lovely idea. It will be cold, mind you. Best we change into warmer clothes."

It took them nearly an hour to change. Bryce, their mother's abigail, bustled between the three rooms buttoning wool gowns and smoothing coiffures into bonnets. Gen barely had a moment to think. By a little after eleven, they were bundled in their woolen cloaks and fur muffs and trudging down to the end of the drive to view the Wenwood Thorn.

As they had done as children, they let Chimes, wrapped in a dark wool hooded cloak, go before them, lantern held high in one gloved hand to light the way. Mrs. Chimes, her tiny figure dwarfed by her dark cloak, came behind with another lantern. It might have been easier to bring the carriage, but by Wenwood tradition, each family came to the Thorn on foot. The trees on either side loomed up as they approached, bare branches raking the stars far above, only to retreat behind them into the darkness. It was quiet in the woods; their voices seemed to hang in the cold air like icicles on the wind. It was almost as if they were alone in the world.

As they neared the foot of the drive, Gen saw other lights begin to glow, and other voices pushed back the cold. They

broke out of the wood into the little clearing that housed the
Thorn and found the village already there, clustered in groups
of friends and families in a rough semicircle around the Wenwood Thorn.

The tree was much as Gen remembered it, standing amongst
a host of smaller trees like the matriarch of the family, a single
bud on a twisted branch like a flower of celebration in her hair.
She remembered her father's pride in the tree, a legacy the Munroes had left the village of Wenwood. His own great-great-
grandfather had managed to get a slip from the famed thorn
that grew at Glastonbury Abbey. Legend had it that when St.
Joseph of Arimathaea had first reached England in those early
years after the Lord's crucifixion, he had climbed the hill at
Glastonbury and where he'd planted his staff the Thorn had
sprung. Gen's ancestor had planted the cutting just off the foot
of the drive to the Abbey and had cared for it until it grew large
enough to sustain itself. Now, each Christmas, like its famous
forefather, it budded on Christmas Eve and bloomed on Christmas Day. Everyone in the village and on farms for miles around
traveled to witness the miracle. She had made the trip to view
it every Christmas until they had moved to London. The last
time she had seen it had been with her father.

Moving into the clearing now, it was as if she had never
left. Mrs. Smitters and the elderly Widow Tate nodded in rec-
ognition of her mother, and Mrs. Gurney and her husband
Henry made a place for them near the front of the semicircle.
The voices around her were hushed but happy, murmuring of
Christmas memories, of hopes for Christmases to come. The
dozens of torches and lanterns brightened the little clearing
with their glow. Tom Harvey had started a fire near the back
of the crowd, and people were taking turns warming themselves by it. Mary Delacourte started a song, and others joined
in in rough harmony, their voices rising through the trees. Children laughed, chased each other around their parents' and

grandparents' legs. Lovers held hands. Despite the chill night air, Gen felt warm all over.

"Couldn't resist, could you?" Alan asked, appearing at her side from the crowd. She couldn't help but stare in surprise. His handsome face was flushed with excitement, his fashionable top hat was askew, and all at once he was the good-natured young man she remembered. If he'd have looked like this when he'd proposed, she realized, she'd probably have accepted. Her heart started pounding unaccountably loudly, and she raised her hand to her chest. Before she could say a word, a laugh rang out from behind them, and looking past Alan, she saw Geoffrey clapping Dutch Mattison on the shoulder, a tankard in one gloved hand. Closer to the front, Mrs. Pentercast shivered but smiled in welcome. Beside her, Gen's mother nodded in reply.

"It wouldn't be Christmas without the Thorn," Alan murmured beside her. "I was afraid you wouldn't come. I'm very glad you did."

"I couldn't have missed this," Gen managed, feeling her spirits rise. "It's the very heart of Christmas to me: the hope that something wonderful can happen, even in the midst of darkness."

As soon as she said it, she regretted sharing such an intimate part of herself. But one look at the warmth in his gaze and the regret evaporated. "Miracles do happen, Miss Genevieve," he murmured. "If we believe in them."

As if on cue, the bells from the village church at Wenwood began chiming midnight, their peals echoing across hill and dale. The children froze in their games, eyes wide. Voices died on the wind. The village youths set down their tankards. As one, the crowd leaned forward, watching. Lanterns were raised as eyes peered through the night. Gen caught her breath as the bud slowly opened to the light.

"Happy Christmas, Miss Genevieve," Alan murmured beside her.

"Happy Christmas, Mr. Pentercast," she murmured back, believing for the first time that it might be just that. Around her, other voices took up the chant, until the wish was a thunder of sound across the clearing, pushing back the darkness, climbing to heaven. The children laughed again. The village youths toasted the day. Lovers embraced. Then, in families and pairs, the villagers and farmers moved off toward the village for services. Geoffrey Pentercast stamped out the fire. With one last smile to Gen, Alan returned to escort his mother. Gen watched him for a moment, bemused. Was this kind gentleman the same man who had arrogantly demanded her hand? She shook her head. It must have been the sense of celebration the tree inspired, the atmosphere all at once peaceful and invigorating. She shook her head again. Surely it was only a momentary aberration. Having only half convinced herself, she turned to go, then saw her mother still standing before the tree. She touched her mother's cloak, and the older woman turned, wiping tears from her eyes. "Your father always loved this," she smiled.

Gen squeezed her gloved hand, tears coming to her own eyes. "I know he did, Mother. And I'm sure he knows we're here."

"He's probably watching us right now," Allison agreed, glancing up at the cloudless sky where a million stars twinkled. "I think he'd be pleased that we're here at the Abbey."

Gen closed her eyes for a moment, pushing back the tears. Allison was right. Her father would be proud of what she was trying to do. If she could just hold out a few more days, perhaps her sister and mother would come to see that the Abbey was the best place for them as well. She had been right in bringing them here after all. As if to prove the notion, her mother reached out and drew her daughters into an embrace. The gesture was so rare that Gen found she couldn't spoil it with words. Together, they turned and walked back to their home.

She thought at first she might have trouble falling asleep that night. All the events of the day seemed to crowd in on her as she lay in the large four-poster bed she had known as a child. All in all, she told herself, she should be pleased with what she had accomplished. Her mother and sister were safely ensconced at the Abbey. True, she hadn't managed to tell them the truth about their situation, but she was going to give them one last happy Christmas and that counted for something. She had also managed to prove that the old Pentercast/Munroe feud was no longer necessary. True, she had her own private feud to continue with Alan Pentercast, but that would likely come out all right as well.

One of her biggest worries in retreating to the Abbey had been food. They had plenty of clothes to wear, and the elaborate furniture crowded into the many rooms would keep them for years to come. The small clearing could hold a garden, she thought, and the woods abounded with game. Yet one couldn't count on either of those as a steady source of food. When Alan lost his wager, that problem would be solved.

That left only one difficulty to surmount: Allison's come-out. She had to be properly presented if she was to have a chance in the marriage mart. Surely Gen owed her that chance. Lord knew, she had already resigned herself to the fact that she herself was unlikely to find a suitable husband, despite Mr. Carstairs' kind words to the contrary. Like Allison, she had once looked forward to her London Season, expecting that she would have dozens of men as dashing as Alan Pentercast vying for her hand. Instead, she had found the gentlemen who pursued her sadly disappointing. Each one cared more for wardrobe and stables than family and friends. Heaven forbid that any of them read more than the *Times* or converse about anything more daring than the weather. And none possessed her father's wit or good humor. She had hoped that here in the country at least Allison might meet men of greater substance. Alan's face came to mind—hair falling over his forehead and curling around his ears, brown eyes sparkling with laughter, generous mouth turned up in a grin. She blinked the vision away. His ridiculous wager ought to prove how little substance he had, yet she could not forget his obvious enjoyment of the Thorn. Sad to admit, but a part of her still hoped the Alan she remembered had not disappeared. She told that part of herself to be silent.

She had barely had five hours of sleep when Chimes tapped on her door the next morning. She crawled out of bed and donned her riding habit, pulling on the boots with a yawn. By eight, she was out in the forest, searching for their Christmas dinner.

Her mother had disapproved of her father's teaching her to hunt, but now Gen had to own it was a useful skill. This morning, however, the animals seemed to have decided to sleep in on Christmas as well, for they found none of the usual grouse, partridge, or quail. She saw a deer, which froze with one tiny hoof in midair at the sight of her, but she found she couldn't bring herself to shoot the delicate little thing. Chimes, coming up behind her too late to get in a shot, chided her on her sensibilities.

"Yer father bought you that Lepage for a reason, gel." He shook his head, clamping his slouch hat more firmly in place against the cold. "Now's the time to use it if ever there was one."

Gen nodded, fingering the inlaid stock of the French flintlock. She remembered her squeal of delight and her mother's compressed lips when her father had given it to her on her sixteenth birthday. Now she wondered at the expense to have the rifle specially made to her slender frame, let alone the firing of the metal to a blue that matched her eyes. Still, it was one of the few gifts from her father that she could put to good use in this new life she was creating for them. She planted the stock back into the boot by her stirrup and nodded to Chimes to continue looking for game.

They saw nothing more that morning, and she was on foot,

ready to settle for a plump, hardy pigeon, when she heard the sound of an approaching horse and sent Chimes to investigate. A moment later, he returned with the Reverend Wellfordhouse.

"Happy Christmas, William," she hailed, and he smiled in agreement. "Is it time for services already?"

"Very nearly, Miss Genevieve. May I say it seems a bit odd to find you hunting on such a day." He regarded Chimes with a frown, and the older man bustled off to bring their own horses forward from hiding.

"We aren't poaching on the Pentercast lands, if that's what's worrying you, William," she assured him. "I know when I reach the wall, unlike some others."

"A rather obvious landmark, to be sure," William agreed. "But perhaps I ought to ride with you toward the house, just to be sure you arrive in time."

Chimes snorted, but he helped Gen to mount and pulled his horse obligingly behind them as she and William rode side by side down the little track through the woods. The air was cool and crisp; frost shone on the few leaves left on the trees. Gen was thankful once again for her father's foresight. The forest green wool hunting outfit he had insisted on buying her last winter was warm and well fitted, with a full skirt that afforded her ample movement on foot or on horseback and a cunning hooded caplet that shielded her eyes from the bright winter sunlight. Beside her, William shivered in his shabby wool jacket and breeches. For his sake, she urged the horses forward.

They rode along the track in companionable silence, making their way out of the wood and traveling a short distance along the low stone wall that divided the Pentercast property from the Munroes'. Through the bare trees of the old orchard on the other side, she could make out the solid brick block of the Manor. Round paler circles on the dark trunks showed where Alan had had them pruned recently. The grass beneath them was neatly cropped. He appeared to be taking his ownership duties more seriously than his forefathers, who had largely let the land run wild as she remembered. Even as she admired the rows across the wall, Chimes shouted and a flock of birds rose from the nearby shrubs.

She grasped her rifle and leveled it at the cloud of feathers. William ducked. The flintlock roared, and she heard the echo from Chimes's gun. Two of the birds fell from the flock. One landed back in the shrubbery ahead of them, the other near the top of one of the trees, on the Pentercast side of the wall. William's horse snorted in alarm, prancing in circles as the reverend sought to calm it. Gen's horse, more used to hunting, only shied.

As he got his mount under control, William shook his head.— "What a shame. You almost had that one."

Chimes dismounted even as Gen pulled her horse to a stop. "I *did* have that one. You saw it, William. It was on my side of the wall, wherever it chose to land."

"That's right, miss," Chimes agreed, going to retrieve his own bird, which he shoved into a game bag at his hip. "I'll fetch it for you." He swung himself over the wall and hurried to the tree. His swift movements and constant glances about him belied his confident words.

Gen watched him from the saddle as her horse lowered its head to graze. Atop his own horse, Wellfordhouse frowned.

"This seems a lot of trouble for a bird, Miss Genevieve," he murmured.

Gen kept her gaze on Chimes, who had begun to climb the tree. "You won't say that when you eat it this afternoon, William. It will be a poor Christmas dinner without it."

His frown deepened. "I find it hard to believe the Munroe hospitality depends on that one bird."

"Believe it," Gen snapped. She pushed back her hood, shielding her eyes from the sun with her hands, and tried to focus on Chimes's craggy form struggling up through the gnarled old branches. She grimaced, sliding to the ground. "He's too big. I'll have to get it."

"Oh, I say, Miss Genevieve," William protested, starting to dismount. "I can't have you climbing trees. What would your mother say?"

Gen swung on him, striding to his stirrup. "Mother mustn't know anything about this. Do you hear me, William? I went hunting because I wanted a certain dish for Christmas dinner. No more than that. Now get back on that horse and let me get on with my business."

He snapped his mouth shut and settled back in his seat, looking decidedly worried. She sighed.

"I'm sorry to be so cross, William. It's been a difficult few months. I must swear you to secrecy on this, just as I've sworn Carstairs and Chimes. We are nearly penniless. Our one hope is that we might be able to live quietly here at the Abbey. I haven't been able to bring myself to tell Mother and Allison yet."

"I . . . I see," William managed, swallowing. "Would you like me to get the bird?"

She laughed at his instant contrition. "Certainly not. I wouldn't want to corrupt a man of the cloth. I've climbed a few trees in my life. It will take but a moment." She swung herself over the wall and hurried to help Chimes.

He was three-quarters of the way to the top, but already the tree was shaking beneath his weight. She could hear him cursing as the branches dug into him. "You're too big for this job, Chimes," she called from below, cupping her hands about her mouth. "Let me try."

Chimes climbed partway back down, puffing in his exertions. "Your mother would have fits if she knew what you were about," he fussed. "I don't hardly see how I can let you do it, Miss Gen. Perhaps we can find another bird after all."

"We've had terrible luck all morning," she disagreed, helping him to the ground. "I don't expect that will change. I'll be up and out in a moment, you'll see."

"Not if I have anything to say about it," Alan Pentercast declared. Gen whirled to find him leaning against the tree behind them, a flintlock not unlike her own propped in one arm. She thought she made out a horse grazing several rows down. "Pardon my interruption. I was returning from the village when I heard the shots. Silly of me, but I thought I might have poachers."

Chimes coughed, and Gen could feel herself reddening.

"They shot the bird from this side of the property, Squire," William called obligingly over the wall. "Unfortunately, it fell on your side of the wall."

"Pity," Alan agreed, moving toward them. "If you'll allow me."

Gen eyed his tall frame, dressed today in rough wool trousers and a long coat. The outdated outfit, combined with his shaggy hair, made him look slightly disreputable, as she had always imagined a highwayman or footpad to look. She somehow thought it suited him "You'll never reach it," she informed him. "You're too big."

"Au contraire, my lady. Mr. Chimes, if you will be so kind as to stand below the tree there, that's right." He braced the rifle in the crotch of the tree and clambered up beside it. Hanging onto one limb, he stretched out his arm, extending the rifle up and out. The limb bobbed, and he swayed with it. Gen caught her breath, her mind conjuring images of him falling and injuring himself.

"Stop this, you idiot!" she cried. "The bird isn't that important."

"Well," Alan grunted, reaching out once more, "it was certainly important enough for you to try climbing up here in that fetching riding habit of yours." Gritting his teeth, he thrust the barrel of the rifle against the higher limb. Gen nearly sagged in relief as the bird tumbled to the ground. Leaving the rifle temporarily in the tree, Alan jumped down beside the bird. Chimes bent guiltily to retrieve it. Suddenly, Alan's arm shot out to stop him. Chimes backed away, and Alan knelt down, frowning. Then he swept the bird up into his hands and moved to Gen's side. Grinning, he handed it to her with a bow.

"Your partridge, my lady," he laughed, "in a pear tree."

Alarmed, she looked up. She could hear Reverend Wellford-house's chuckle from the other side of the wall. "I'm afraid he's right, Miss Genevieve. That is, if my botany doesn't fail me, a pear tree."

"You planned this!" she accused Alan. Alan held up his hands.

"Actually, I had another plan entirely. However, as I told you, we were meant for each other. Fate is conspiring against you to prove me right."

"One gift, sir," she informed him icily, "does not a wager win."

He laughed, dusting off his hands on his trousers. "Quite right, Miss Munroe. Well, I wish you well with your bird. But somehow, I have a feeling it might taste a bit like crow."

Gen spun on her heels and climbed back over the wall. Even as she allowed Chimes to hand her up into the saddle, she had a sinking feeling that Alan was right.

Three

Verse Two, Two Turtle Doves

Christmas dinner was a much merrier affair than Gen had expected, even with their poor hunting of the morning. Annie's cooking made the two partridges seem plentiful as she marinated the bite-size pieces in a honey glaze. Reverend Wellfordhouse was congenial company, and both she and her mother were relieved when Reverend York declined their invitation, eating with the Pentercasts instead. They spent a pleasant evening by the fire, sharing memories of other Christmases, happier times. By the time she went to bed that night, she had to admit that country living was not nearly the sacrifice Mr. Carstairs had feared it would be.

Perhaps it was the stories she had heard that night, but as she lay in bed, more memories arose, memories of Alan Pentercast. Of the two brothers, she would never have thought it would be Alan who turned out to be the personification of the overweening arrogance of all Pentercasts. She had somehow expected more of him. Certainly everyone else had. When she was a child, he had always been touted as the knight errant of the village—climbing a tree to rescue Mrs. Smitters' cat, bringing food to the Harveys when Mr. Harvey had broken his leg during the harvest, chopping wood for Widow Tate. And Gen didn't need anyone else's word for his bravery in rescuing the Mattison twins. She had been present that famous day when he had jumped into the Abbey pond to save the redheaded five-year-olds from drowning.

It had been a wonderful summer day in Somerset. The sky was as blue as the waters of the pond behind the Abbey. Every child in the area who wasn't working in the fields had managed to find an excuse to appear on the shore to either brave the cool waters or lounge in the shade of the nearby trees where songbirds called. Allison had been only ten at the time, even more unrestrained in her behavior than now. Knowing their mother was nowhere in sight, she had peeled off her stockings and pinned up her skirts to wade along the edge of the water. Geoffrey Pentercast, only a couple of years older, had only bothered to shrug out of his jacket and throw off his shoes before stomping in after her. She remembered Allison's high-pitched squeal as she tried to dodge his splashes.

The oldest there, Gen had sat on the grass beside the pond, knees hugged to her chest, giving her nod of consent to the children who begged her to play in the sapphire water. Allison had said she was playing mother again, but she had felt like a grand lady, granting boons to the struggling poor. She herself had nodded agreement when the Mattison twins had managed to get up the courage to ask her to allow them to wade.

What happened next was engraved in her memory. The five-year-old girls had been hesitant at first, holding up the skirts of their pinafores to dip bare toes in the water, but before Gen knew what they were about, they had wriggled out of their dresses entirely and waded into water over their waists. Even as she'd stood to warn them to return to shore, one of them, she thought it was Daisy, had slipped and gone under. The other sister, Maisy, had splashed deeper after her and disappeared as well. The songbirds had fallen silent. Allison had cried out in terror, and Geoffrey, for once in his life, had stood frozen in shock.

Gen remembered running to the edge of the pond, wringing her hands, her legs trembling in fear, the other children rising and crying out around her. She had never so much as waded in the pond, let alone swum in it. She had no idea how deep the water might be, how far the girls might have sunk. She remembered shouting their names, but no red head bobbed into sight to answer. She was bending to untie her own boots when someone darted past her and with a mighty splash, Alan Pentercast made a running dive into the pond.

She had no idea where he had come from, but she couldn't remember ever being so glad to see anyone before. With strokes that seemed powerful and sure to her, he plowed into the pond, caught his breath, and dove under. She counted the seconds, her own breath held tightly in a shaking chest. She hadn't even reached four before he surged up, a twin under each arm. Several kicks got him to shallow water where he could stand. He strode ashore and dropped the coughing, spitting five-year-olds onto the damp grass.

She remembered breathing something reverent about his rescue, but he had only stood looking down at the children, his sodden clothes clinging to his body. He then had wiped away a drop of water from his nose with the back of his hand. His dark eyes had met hers, and for a second, she'd thought he was as frightened as she was. Then Geoffrey had galloped up to his side and caught him in a bear hug.

"That was famous, Alan! You saved their lives."

Daisy had begun to whimper, and Gen had crouched to take each of the girls into her arms. They'd trembled against her, both trying to climb onto her lap at the same time. She'd sat down heavily and they'd cuddled against her chest.

"I'll fetch Mother," Allison had cried, dashing back toward the Abbey. Alan had shrugged off his brother's grip and knelt beside her.

"Are they all right?" he had murmured, not meeting her eyes.

"They're just scared," she had assured him as if she were the older one and knew all about children. "But Geoffrey's right; they'd have been dead but for you."

She thought she'd seen him swallow, but he'd risen quickly. "It was nothing. I'd better go find dry clothes or Father will have a fit. Come on, Geoff." Before she could thank him, he was beyond the trees.

Remembering now, she shook her head. There hadn't been a single villager who hadn't sung his praises that day. All these years, she had thought he deserved them. But what she had thought was humility had surely just been arrogance. Look at the way he had handed her the bird this morning, with that insufferable smile on his face. She shuddered. What a pity. One more of her heroes proven untrue. She knew if she stopped to remember the other hero who had fallen, she wouldn't sleep at all that night. She told her mind firmly to be silent, plumped her pillows, and put her head down so she might sleep.

Her mother awakened her early the next morning, passing quietly into her bedroom to open the shades on a gray winter day. "Good morning, Genevieve. I'm sorry to awaken you so early, but I'll be needing your assistance today with the boxes."

Gen nearly groaned aloud. How could she have forgotten the old tradition of giving all the servants presents on the Feast of St. Stephen? She had yet to tell any of them but Chimes about their predicament—that would mean there would be, good heavens, two grooms, a coachman, a stable boy, three maids, the two men who assisted Chimes as footmen during dinner parties, a gardener, her mother's abigail Bryce, and Mrs. Chimes each expecting a box of gifts today. Her father had been known to encourage the most elaborate of gifts. She remembered once he had given Chimes an entire case of French champagne. Another time he'd hired an acrobatic troupe to perform. And last Boxing Day, each of their servants in town had been given boxes with twelve different gifts, one for each day of Christmas. She remembered how long it had taken the family to wrap and pack them. The potential cost stunned her, and she sank back upon the bed, wondering how she could possibly explain the problem to her mother.

"You needn't look so daunted," her mother murmured with a small smile. "Allison will help too, and I believe we can even prevail upon Mrs. Chimes to assist with the lesser servants. Of course, there are the pensioners on the old estate as well. I thought since we were home again, we shouldn't forget them."

Gen stared at her. "But . . . but, Mother, surely they are the Pentercasts' concern."

Her mother's mouth tightened. "I've never known the Pentercasts to be overly generous. Your father frequently had to make up for their lack of hospitality. Honestly, Genevieve, I do not know what has gotten into you lately. You were never afraid to put forth a little effort for the people for whom you care."

Gen closed her eyes, thinking of all the work she and Mr. Carstairs had done to keep their family together the last six months. "It isn't the work, Mother. I'm just concerned that it might be a little expensive."

Her mother raised an eyebrow. "It seems a bit selfish, my dear, to count the cost of thanking those who have given good service. I will leave you to think on that. When you are dressed, please join us in the music room. I believe there's space there to spread out all the boxes."

"But surely, Mother," Gen persisted, desperate, "we don't have the items here to put in the boxes. You've complained any number of times that Wenwood doesn't even have a market."

"I do not complain," her mother sniffed, turning toward the door. "However, as to the notable lack of shopping facilities in the village, I took care of that before we left London. We have everything we need downstairs."

Gen's heart constricted: another set of bills that Carstairs didn't know about. She was afraid to even ask what her mother had bought. She scurried to the wardrobe and slipped into her lavender kerseymere gown, not even waiting for Bryce's help. Whipping her thick hair up into a bun at the top of her head, she dashed down the corridor to the music room.

She paused in the door, her worst nightmares confirmed. Spread out on the parquet floor, the Oriental carpet in the center, the bench in front of the spinet, and the window seats of the two multipaned windows overlooking the drive were various knickknacks, gewgaws, and tidbits designed to bring a smile to the most overworked and browbeaten of servants. Her mother was obviously trying to surpass last year's event. Allison was untangling a batch of beaded necklaces. Her mother was perched on the sofa opposite the spinet, sorting through various brightly colored mufflers and gloves. Before Gen could protest, Chimes tapped her on the shoulder, taking her arm as she turned, and leading her back into the corridor.

"Don't you fret, miss," he winked. "I have it all figured. We let them pack the boxes and convince them to let me deliver them. Then I just brings them back to the kitchen, and back they go to London to be sold for a profit."

Gen took a deep breath, relaxing. "A wise plan, Chimes. Thank you." Squaring her shoulders, she went back into the room. Chimes, whistling through his wide-spaced front teeth, came in behind her, ostensibly to bring in the pile of ornamental packages in which the gifts were to be boxed.

"Ah, there you are, Chimes," her mother nodded, rising. "I'd like to you assemble the staff at ten this morning to receive their gifts."

Chimes and Gen exchanged glances. "As you wish, madame, though I was hoping to be able to hand out the boxes at dinner this evening."

She frowned. "That is far too late in the day. They will think we have forgotten them. No, it must be ten. Then they can take the rest of the day off. All except John Coachman, of course.

Have him bring around the carriage so that I can go visiting the pensioners."

"Sorry, madame, but the carriage wheel looked wobbly when you came in and I took the liberty of having the blacksmith in the village look it over. Wouldn't want an accident, now would we?"

Her frown deepened, and she shot Genevieve a dark look. Gen tried not to squirm. "Chimes, I believe you're being difficult. I will deliver these boxes today, this morning, with or without your assistance. And if it is without your assistance, I think it safe to say that you may be getting a box from a different employer next Boxing Day."

Chimes coughed, not bothering to hide his own squirming. "Yes, madame."

Gen wracked her brain for some other way to stop her mother. Why, even if Alan lost his wager, she wouldn't be able to pay for these trinkets for months. The Munroe diamonds came to mind again, but she bit her lip in determination. Surely she and Allison deserved something of their family inheritance! There had to be some other answer.

Someone rapped sharply on the front door, the sound echoing through the paneled halls. Chimes excused himself to go respond. A moment later, he ushered Alan Pentercast into the room.

Gen bridled immediately, looking to see what he carried. His hands, covered in black leather gloves, were empty. He tipped his high-crowned beaver to her mother and Allison before allowing Chimes to take it and his many-caped greatcoat. Then he offered her a bow. She nodded in return, earning a warning frown from her mother for her lack of enthusiasm.

"Good morning, Squire," her mother murmured. "To what do we owe this honor?"

"I'm sorry to intrude so early, ladies," he replied, crossing to her side and pointedly ignoring the dark looks Gen cast him.

"But I came to ask your assistance, Mrs. Munroe. I can see you were prepared for Boxing Day, but I'm afraid to admit that my mother is all at sixes and sevens. She has a few gifts put aside, but somehow the things she ordered from London never arrived. To make matters worse, Geoffrey has gone off on some fool's errand, leaving Mother to deal with the packing all by herself. I know you've dealt with Boxing Day for many years, with far more servants to reward than we have. I was hoping to prevail upon you to share your skills in our time of need."

Her mother positively glowed, inclining her head regally at his request. "But of course, Mr. Pentercast. I'm sure we can contrive something."

"Madame, you are too gracious. What I'd like to do, with your concurrence, of course, is to move the entire affair to the Manor, where we have all the room we need, as I'm sure you're well aware. Combining what you have here with what my mother has been able to squirrel away should give us more than enough to—reward all our staffs adequately."

Gen narrowed her eyes at his audacity and her mother's duplicity. Couldn't she see what the man was trying to do? "There is, of course, a matter of funds, Mr. Pentercast," she put in firmly. "These trinkets cost my family a pretty penny."

"Genevieve!" her mother cried. "Squire, please disregard my daughter. I don't know what's come over her lately. She seems to have developed quite an interest in finances, an aberration I assure you will not last."

"I think young ladies who take an interest in their family's well-being should be much complimented, Mrs. Munroe," he replied, smiling. Then, turning to her with a twinkle in his dark eyes, "I assure you, Miss Munroe, I will pay for every trinket in this room. As a service to my mother, of course."

Gen eyed him, trying to determine what his game was. He couldn't be trying to procure his gift for the day—what was it, two turtle doves? Surely he knew that if he bought them so easily, he would be disqualifying himself from the wager. Besides, she doubted there was anything like a turtle dove in this collection of her mother's. "How very commendable of you, Mr. Pentercast," she managed.

"Very commendable, and quite unnecessary," her mother put in. "Now, if we're to accomplish this plan of yours, we'll need to start moving things immediately."

With great misgivings, Gen helped them repack the various presents and watched as Chimes and Alan carried the boxes out to Alan's waiting carriage. His entire story could only be a concoction of lies, but she couldn't understand how he stood to benefit. Chimes had the groom bring round the Munroe carriage, miraculously fixed, and the Munroes climbed in for the drive to the Manor.

The Manor had, of course, once been known as Munroe Manor, and Gen knew the Munroes took great pride in the fact that it wasn't uncommon even to this day for someone in the village to slip and use the old name. While the house was a little over a mile from the Abbey through the woods, it was considerably farther by road, as the Munroes had to follow a curving drive nearly to the main road and the Wenwood Thorn before branching onto the drive that led to the Manor. As they came up through the trees, bare now in the winter wind, Gen saw that Alan had been refurbishing the old place. A square block of brick, three stories high, the house stood in direct contrast to the sprawling single-story wings of the Abbey, but the red brick had been recently washed; she could see fresh mortar in places. The white edging around each of the six rectangular, many-paned windows on each level shone in the gray winter light, as did the Doric columns on the two-story pedimented front porch. The lawns that stretched to either side of it and beyond were brown with winter, but the grass was neatly trimmed. Her mother put a hand on her arm, nodding to where a herd of dairy cows grazed in the pasture almost next to the back of the house.

"That was where the lake used to be," she murmured. "Philistines."

Gen hid a smile. "No doubt they'd have kept the lake, Mother, if our great-grandfather hadn't damned up the stream that fed it." She had to admit, right now she'd have happily released the resultant pond behind the Abbey for a similar herd of cows. Her mother only sniffed.

They drew up to the front of the Manor, and a stately white-haired butler came down the stone steps to usher them in. They ascended the steps to the entry, which was easily twice as big as the one at the Abbey, and much brighter with the many-paned windows on either side of the door, the gilt-edged fanlight over the door, and the crystal chandelier that hung from the high ceiling. Even her mother had to look impressed as the liveried footmen spirited away their pelisses and bonnets and the butler escorted them into the front drawing room.

The room, which boasted several satin-striped sofas and matching chairs, all in shades of rose and dusky green, looked much as the music room had looked when she'd first entered it that morning. Scarves, necklaces, small pieces of pottery, and even a mustache cup were perched on every flat surface, from the credenza under the windows to the mahogany table near the fireplace. There were even suspenders hanging in the greenery over the polished wood mantel. The Pentercasts' generosity had obviously increased. In fact, there were entirely enough articles to give good-size boxes to an army of servants and farmers. She found it difficult to believe that anyone but her family took Boxing Day this seriously. Gen narrowed a glance at Alan, who was standing innocently near his mother's chair, ostensibly engrossed in determining whether a burgundy muffler went better with a gold ring or a silver one.

Looking up, he favored her mother and Allison with a smile,

patently ignoring the frown on Gen's face. "Mrs. Munroe, the Misses Munroe, thank you again for assisting us. As you can see, the job is just too big for so few sets of hands."

"I must admit, it was very kind of you, Trudy," Mrs. Pentercast murmured with a shy smile at her mother. "We used to do Boxing Day so well. I don't know what happened. I think it's so important that we don't forget anyone, especially some of the pensioners in the village. This is the high point of their year."

Her mother visibly thawed. "I couldn't agree with you more. Perhaps if we made a list, we might divide the gifts more evenly and make sure we have the appropriate items in each box."

Mrs. Pentercast clapped her hands. "What a wonderful idea."

They went to work. Gen was surprised at how quickly the time passed. Between her mother and Mrs. Pentercast, the list was calculated, the gifts divided, and the packing begun in short order. They argued a little over the names of the pensioners, farmers, and servants to be included, and her mother had to insist that the servants from each house be given identical boxes, but overall, the process went surprisingly smoothly. At some point, the butler announced the Reverend William Wellfordhouse, who was promptly conscripted to duty. A short while later, Geoffrey Pentercast made the mistake of wandering in, only to have his mother drag him into the middle of the project as well. He flopped down on the foot of the chaise longue where Allison sat and began stuffing anything he could reach into a box. Allison at first shrank back from his hostility, then frowned, and finally leaned forward to take the box from his hands.

"If you can't do it right, Mr. Pentercast," she told him sternly, "perhaps you'd better not do it at all."

Geoffrey looked contrite. "Oh, you're quite right, Miss Munroe. I shall be delighted to sit here and watch you do it for me. It will be a lesson to me in humility."

"A lesson, sir," William put in, watching them as did Gen, "that you sorely need, if I may say so."

Geoffrey scowled at him, but made no more moves to help, and Allison went back to filling the boxes herself. She tried to pretend to ignore him, but Gen caught her casting him dark looks. Geoffrey must have noticed them as well.

"You keep that up," he grumbled, "and your face will freeze that way."

"If it's going to freeze," Allison retorted, "I'd rather I was doing something more pointed." She stuck out her tongue at him. To her obvious dismay, Geoffrey gave a whoop of laughter.

"Less amusement and more activity, if you please, sir," his mother called to him. With a shrug, Geoffrey rose to help Alan carry some of the finished boxes out to the entry for delivery.

Mrs. Pentercast and her mother agreed to finish by noon, take a break for luncheon, and then tour the estates and village together, handing out the boxes as they went. Watching the party working away, Gen couldn't believe how well the two families came together when given a common purpose. William noticed it as well.

"Quite a change from the other night," he murmured to Gen as they finished one of the boxes. "I must say, I'm quite amazed to see your mother and Mrs. Pentercast getting on so well. I had heard they've been rivals since childhood."

"Billing and cooing like two turtle doves," Gen agreed with a shake of her head. "Who would have thought—"

"My word!" the curate exclaimed, turning to her with wide eyes. "That's it! Two turtle doves. You said it yourself."

Gen stared at him aghast. "But that's not right! They're not real doves. It doesn't count!"

William shook his head. "No one said the gifts couldn't be symbolic. If you ask me, having the two most important women, to you and Alan and to this village, getting along is the best gift anyone could have. I'm afraid, Miss Genevieve, that he's done it again."

Gen watched him cross the drawing room to where Alan was stuffing knitted scarves into a box. As William spoke to him, he looked up and offered her one of his most daring grins. She could almost hear his words in her mind. "Only ten more days of Christmas."

Four

Verse Three, Three French Hens

"The man is an odious makebait," Gen insisted, pacing the music room in Wenwood Abbey while Allison attempted a gavotte on the spinet. "Did you see how those poor farmers doted on his every word yesterday when we delivered the gifts, as if he actually cared about them in any small way? He is easily the most overweening, toplofty, arrogant, odious—"

"You've used 'odious' once already," Allison pointed out, frowning at the sheets of hand-copied music before her. "And I believe that makes three times for 'arrogant.' "

Gen paused to scowl at her. "Don't interrupt, if you please."

Allison shrugged. "But I must, for you're being quite unreasonable. Of all the Pentercasts, I find Alan the least objectionable. Why even his mother was being rather likable yesterday, I thought. She and Mother certainly became thick as thieves. You knew she was taking tea over there this afternoon."

Gen stamped her foot. "That's what I mean. You all are being taken in by this . . . this . . ."

"Odious, arrogant makebait," Allison supplied helpfully. "If you want my opinion, I think that description far better suits the younger Mr. Pentercast." She gave the keys an extra thump. "Now, there is a bully and a lout if there ever was one."

Gen waved her hand. "He is all of that and annoying as well. However, he is just young, Allison. No doubt he'll settle down once he finds a proper girl to wed. I find the elder much more objectionable. Why have you stopped?"

Allison quickly returned to her music. "Sorry. Daydreaming. But, honestly, Gen, I don't know what's come over you. I thought you were the one who wanted us to be friends with the Pentercasts."

"I did want us to be friends," she tried to explain to her sister, casting herself down on the sofa opposite the spinet. "But it's all happening too fast."

Allison frowned, keeping her eyes on the music. "What do you mean, fast? Father made friends constantly—he was always bringing home some poor soul he'd found somewhere, and usually they turned out to be quite interesting people."

Gen sighed. "Yes, but that was Father. He always saw the good in everyone."

Allison raised her eyes at last. "You used to be just like him."

Gen hung her head, picking at the fringe on her paisley silk shawl. It was so difficult to explain to her sister. Somehow, she felt Allison should be shielded from the truth she had been forced to confront. "I suppose I did. That was before . . . Well, that was just before. I can't help feeling that something isn't right here. Why does Alan Pentercast want to help us so much? I keep asking myself that."

"And what do you answer?"

Gen shrugged. "I don't have an answer, except that it cannot be a good reason. Perhaps I'm being prejudiced, but I cannot help remembering how we lost the Manor in the first place."

Allison laughed, finishing the song with a trill up the keys. "Now you are being Miss Friday Face. We lost the Manor in a silly wager. No one would be so ridiculous as to make a wager with a Pentercast again."

Gen looked away from her. "No, of course not."

Allison frowned. "Now who's being evasive? Genevieve Munroe, have you done something I should know about?"

Gen fiddled with the fringe. "I cannot think what you mean."

Allison leapt from the bench and threw herself down beside her sister. "You have! Oh, tell, tell! Did you make a wager with Alan Pentercast?"

Gen looked up into her sister's sparkling blue eyes. The temptation to share the story was great, but she'd have to tell the full story, and that she was still unwilling to do. "I told you, it is of no consequence. Pray continue with your practice."

The light in Allison's eyes faded, and she scowled. "Very well, don't tell me." She jumped to her feet and stalked back to the spinet. "But don't expect me to agree with your glum opinions unless I understand the reasons for them."

Gen listened to her vehement pounding of the keys, wishing she could share her thoughts as easily as her sister shared her feelings. She rose to leave. If she had to be isolated, she might as well be alone.

She ought to be more trusting, she scolded herself as she wandered through the corridors of the Abbey. There had been a time when she would have seen nothing untoward in Alan's behavior. But that had been before she had learned the truth about her father—that all his loving gifts had come with a price. And the price had been the future security of his family. He had refused to accept the fact that they must economize, turning instead to gambling to fill his nearly empty coffers. It had only made matters worse. She shuddered when she thought of the men who had loaned him money only to encourage him to drink and gamble some more. Now she was left to explain it all to her mother and sister.

Small wonder she had such trouble believing Alan's gestures were so innocent. In truth, there might be nothing more to Alan's thoughtfulness than wishing to be a good neighbor. She could have believed that, except for his behavior the first night. He hardly had to offer for her! And in such an insulting way! She shook her head. There was more here than met the eye; she was sure of it. She just had to be careful these next few days to ensure that Alan did not win his wager.

But how to ensure that he lost? That she had failed to consider. She had meant from the first to keep him from winning, but she had begun to realize that she had little control over the wager. What was today—three French hens? She pondered how he might bring that about. Did he have some variety of hen on his farm that would qualify? Surely he'd have to give them to her personally? What if she just refused to come down to callers? She smiled. Could it be that simple? She hurried to the kitchens, where she knew she would likely find Chimes.

Mrs. Chimes smiled at her as she entered the wide warm room. She returned the smile, noting that as usual, their housekeeper and cook's round cheeks were as red and wrinkled as the frost-nipped apple she was peeling. As Gen crossed to the center of the room to the huge oak table that did double-duty as Mrs. Chimes' worktable and the staff dining table, she also noticed that the woman's hands trembled ever so slightly. The Chimes had been caretakers of the Abbey for as long as she could remember. She had never stopped to consider that they might be nearing the time of being pensioners themselves. She'd have to look into that soon. She had counted on their support as she and her family made their transition, but it would be unfair of her to expect them to work in their old age. One more problem she would have to contend with. Smothering a sigh, she approached Mr. Chimes, who was seated at one end of the table, a cup of tea at his elbow, a copy of the *London Times* they had brought with them open before him. He, at least, looked as cantankerous as always, going to great pains to pretend she wasn't there when she knew he had to have heard her enter.

"Chimes, I need your help," she announced without preamble.

Chimes grunted, setting the paper across his lap and squinting up it her at last with his sharp black eyes. "With what, miss?"

"I expect Mr. Pentercast will be coming to visit frequently the next few days," she explained, schooling her face to sternness. "I refuse to be home to him. I will not receive him. I will not meet him. I hope I've made myself clear."

He nodded, snapping the paper back open, almost in her face. She stepped back, surprised. "Yes, miss. I quite understand. But he'll find another way to win that wager."

Gen gasped.

"Now, Ben, you shouldn't tease her so," Mrs. Chimes murmured, moving to Gen's side. "Your secret's safe with us, dear. We wouldn't dream of telling a soul."

"But . . . but how did you know?" Gen managed, feeling far from mollified.

Chimes grunted from behind his shield of paper. "I have my ways."

"He overheard you talking with the Squire the other night, of course," Mrs. Chimes explained with a scowl at her husband. It only made her round face look slightly less welcoming, and Gen was sure Chimes would have ignored it even if he could have seen it. "I promise you, he hasn't told anyone but me."

"Fat lot you know," Chimes muttered. Panic was rising in Gen. Mrs. Chimes swatted the paper to the table.

"Benjamin Chimes, if you've broken your promise to me . . ."

He quailed before the fire in her dark blue eyes. "Now, Annie, I was only funnin'. I just want her to know that she's casting aside a perfectly good match."

Now Gen knew her own eyes were sparkling with fire. "I'll be the judge of that, if you please. There hasn't been a Pentercast born worthy of marrying a Munroe, and well you know it."

Mrs. Chimes paled, and Chimes scowled. "Your father would be ashamed to hear you talk so."

Gen drew herself up to her full height. "I am the head of this family now, Mr. Chimes. See that you remember it. And see that you remember I am not at home to Mr. Alan Pentercast. Now, get back to work."

She stalked from the kitchen, blood roaring in her ears. How dare they question her decision! She'd done everything she could these last six months. Even Mr. Carstairs agreed with that. She'd been the first to offer up her jewelry, her clothes, even her beloved horse Spirit. She'd watched as the presents her father had given her left the house, one by one, to be auctioned or sold. When that wasn't enough, she'd forced herself to sell off the unused furniture in the attic of the London house, then some of the paintings. She'd even swallowed her pride and ignored her guilt to raid her mother's jewelry box, having each of the treasures except for the Munroe diamonds replaced with paste. She'd seen every debt settled without the creditors appearing on their doorsteps, even though it had required her to learn about the most unsavory parts of London, where her father had gambled. And she had kept his secret from her mother and sister. The only thing she had kept to herself, the one thing she had refused to sell, was herself. Carstairs was right—apparently her name and beauty still commanded a price in the marriage mart. She just couldn't bring herself to put them on the block.

She slammed the door of her room and cast herself down upon the bed, pounding the feather mattress with her fists. They had no right to ask it of her, any of them! Why did she have to be the sacrificial lamb? Why must her happiness be the one forfeit? Surely she had the right to marry for love. If her father had been alive, he'd understand. But, of course, he wasn't alive. That was what had brought her to this pass.

Somehow, she had thought things would be different at Wenwood. When she had left here at fourteen, it had seemed an idyllic place—warm, peaceful, full of friendly people who honestly cared for her. London, with all its bustle and noise, had seemed superficial in comparison. The girls in her finishing school had only cared for fashion and flirting, and they had ridiculed her when she'd tried to introduce more substantial topics. The men who courted her after her come-out had been no different. She knew in her heart she had been comparing them to her ideal—an ideal personified by her memories of Alan Pentercast. And now even those memories had been shown false.

If she had any doubts about his cavalier behavior, it was in the motive for it. At best, he was looking for a pretty wife to brag over at the village inn. At the worst, he wanted to align his family with one that was higher on the social ladder. If he had cared for her at all, he would have waited to propose. He would have courted her properly, at least made the pretense that he was interested in her more than her family name. And they thought it was an excellent match! She wanted to scream at them all to go away, leave her alone! But of course, she couldn't. Her mother and Allison had no idea why she had changed.

By dinner time, she had calmed sufficiently to join her mother and sister at the dinner table. She noticed that Mrs. Chimes was serving; Chimes apparently hadn't forgiven her for her outburst. She sighed. Since he knew the story, perhaps she should explain the whole to him. Maybe if he understood how she felt about the issue, he wouldn't harp on it. The Lord knew, she needed his support if she were to carry this off.

She picked at the dinner, chiding herself for not making the most of it. The main course was a savory roast chicken in a wonderful orange sauce. She was sure she wouldn't be able to afford it again soon. In fact, she was a little worried how she had been able to afford it now. Chimes was in charge of the provisioning; had he been so angry with her that he had done something rash? Or had her mother been shopping somewhere again? She was almost afraid to ask, but she had to know.

"I thought we were going to have ham tonight," she ventured

to her mother, thinking about what had surely been left over from their meal of the night before.

Her mother frowned. "I don't believe I asked you to plan the meal tonight, Genevieve. Don't you find these to your liking?"

Frustrated, she shook her head. "They're delicious. I just wasn't expecting them."

Her mother managed a smile, picking up a bite of the golden brown flesh. "It was a nice surprise, I must admit. Fancy said Alan was sure you would like the hens this way. It's called chicken à la Provence, and they were served to King Louis XIV."

Gen choked on the meat and dropped her fork. "Are you saying these are French hens?"

Her mother's frown returned. "Well, I suppose you could consider them such. Alan insisted I take three of them, and the way you've been about economizing, I thought you'd be pleased."

"Three French hens." Allison laughed. "And it's the third day of Christmas. Just like in the Forfeits game."

Gen had no appetite for the rest of the meal. Somehow, the chicken tasted even more like crow than the partridge had.

Five

Interlude, Baritone Solo

Alan Pentercast watched the Munroe carriage trundle down the drive and allowed himself a smile. There, if he wasn't mistaken, went his gift for the third day of Christmas. Nine more days until Genevieve Munroe agreed to be his bride. He had to stop himself from rubbing his hands together with glee. The Pentercast forefathers must be rolling in their graves to think he would unite the forever-feuding families.

Let them roll, he thought, returning to the Manor. She was worth any trouble she put him to. He'd known that long ago, but it had taken him time to convince himself that her father would ever agree to allow him to court her. It was surprising how agreeable Rutherford Munroe had been when he'd had the temerity to approach him in London last year. He shook his head. So much time wasted. If only the man hadn't died before telling Gen his plans. With their families' sworn enmity, Alan could hardly waltz in the first day they arrived and announce that her father had given his blessing. They'd have thrown him out on his ear.

Still, he hadn't exactly made a better impression by waiting until Christmas Eve. He winced as he remembered how he'd blurted out the proposal, like a callow youth overwhelmed by his first crush. She may have been the first woman he'd admired, but he'd had his share of flirtations since. He'd even acquired a bit of polish, or so he had thought. Just having her next to him, her hand touching his to pick out the raisins, and he was reduced to a stammering fool. It was little wonder she'd reacted so badly.

He remembered the first time he had realized she was truly a woman. Oh, she'd been a taking little thing since the day she was born, but he'd been much too sophisticated at eight years her senior to pay much attention to a female of the clan Munroe. He'd only become head of his own family a year before her father had decided to take them all to London. And he remembered a distinct feeling of pride that Rutherford Munroe would entrust the safekeeping of the Abbey to him, a Pentercast. Cocky young man that he had been, he hadn't even wondered when he was invited to London to Genevieve's come-out. Her father must have had it planned for some time.

It had been a masked ball. He had wondered at the time why anyone would want a come-out to be a surprise, but Londoners were famed for their eccentricities, and the Munroes were famed among Londoners. He had managed to find a shop that specialized in costumes and arrived at the event dressed in velvet doublet and hose, a redoubtable Romeo. The parallel of the feuding families had been irresistible. Behind his mask, he knew no one in the room would know who the tall, wavy-haired gentleman who arrived fashionably late might be. His anonymity had given him a sense of power over the more sophisticated people of the *ton*.

He had been propped up against one of the Grecian pillars that supported the high ceiling of the huge ballroom, trying to decide how to safely dispose of the warm, flat champagne he had been given, when he saw her. She seemed to have just entered the room and was standing near the door hesitating. In her heavy burgundy velvet with the low waist, tight bodice, and slashed sleeves, she was the perfect Juliet to his Romeo. Just the thing to liven up the otherwise dull event. He set the crystal goblet in the middle of a potted palm and hastened to her side.

She was still scrutinizing the room when he reached her, and for the first time he found himself just a little unsure how to proceed. The dark color of the velvet bespoke a married lady, or at least one with some experience of the *ton,* yet it was only a costume and he wondered if he could trust his first instincts. She was a tiny thing, not much bigger than his mother, but far more slender. He could have picked her up with one hand, he was sure. She seemed completely oblivious to his presence, which he was ashamed now to admit had galled his youthful pride. So, he had decided to do something rather audacious.

" 'If I profane with my unworthiest hand,' " he quoted from the bard, " 'this holy shrine, the gentle fine is this—my lips, two blushing pilgrims ready stand to smooth that rough touch with a tender kiss.' "

He wasn't sure what he had been expecting. She was fully within her rights to give him the cut direct for such impertinence. To his delight, she had raised her vibrant blue eyes to his with a look that was decidedly saucy.

" 'Good pilgrim,' " she had replied in kind, her voice husky and low, " 'you do wrong your hand too much, which mannerly devotion shows in this; for saints have hands that pilgrims' hands do touch, and palm to palm is holy palmers' kiss.' "

If he had thought to take the jest further, he was only slightly disappointed when she held out her gloved hand to him. He had raised it to his lips, holding it entirely too long. The gentle tug from her told him she knew it. He released her with difficulty, finding himself once again tongue-tied. She glanced out into the room, where they were just lining up for a set. "It seems to me that Romeo did not dance. Are you so afflicted, sir?"

"Before such beauty, madame," he told her, offering her his arm, "I could fly."

Her delighted laughter had carried him across the room.

He managed two dances before someone swept her away. He thought she looked disappointed, but with her face behind the mask and him now being across the room, it was impossible to be sure. He returned to his pillar to consider his next tactic. Though he had only been planning on staying in London for a few days, it seemed he might be able to extend his time. He could imagine seeing the sights with her on his arm. But how to get the lady's direction? He knew he had already caused a bit of a scandal, with Mrs. Munroe looking him daggers each time he turned in her direction. Dare he risk a third dance? Surprising how just one evening in the lady's company and he was willing to throw caution to the winds. He no longer cared why he had been invited or which of the various women in the room might be young Genevieve. All that mattered was meeting his siren again.

He cornered her at the refreshment table just before midnight. It was evident the young man who had led her there was scowling at him, even through the sequined mask he wore. He seemed to remember he had been dressed all in pink, and that someone had said he was trying to emulate some exotic bird in the Regent's garden. He decided that ignoring him was the best approach, leaning instead in front of the lady to catch her eye.

"I hear the next dance starting," he murmured for her ears alone. "Come with me?"

He could see her cheeks below the mask reddening in a blush. "You are a most determined Romeo, sir. Alas, my mother would never allow me to dance three times with the same partner."

He stared at her, and the young man in pink managed to put himself between them with a huff. Alan couldn't seem to move as the young man led her farther down the table. She glanced back at him and frowned, as if noticing how still he had become. Looking back, he could only imagine he had paled. Her mother? Then she could only be . . . He remembered his own cheeks reddening in mortification and how he had staggered across the room, barely managing to reach the far side before the bells chimed midnight and everyone in the room unmasked. As he'd slipped out the front door, his own mask still firmly in place, the resultant laughter had seemed to mock him and he'd fairly run all the way back to his hotel.

It had taken him hours to convince himself he hadn't gone mad. If his own father had been alive, he knew old Geoffrey Pentercast would have had his hide for even thinking what was on his mind. To fall in love at first sight with the one woman he could never have? His costume must have gone to his head. Even if the attraction lasted the night, he had no chance.

But the attraction had lasted. All through the miserable ride home on the posting coach. Through the weeks that followed. Each time someone returned from town with news to tell, and he could breathe a sigh of relief that she hadn't married. Each time he attended one of the weekly dances in Barnsley and found every lady in the room wanting. Yet he had convinced himself he had no chance.

But he had a chance now. Nine more days to let her see the man he had become. Nine more days to show her that he would make her the best of husbands. Nine more days to convince her that he wasn't the personification of Pentercast evil. He didn't much like the way her accusation still stung. He was his own person, not a reflection of all Pentercasts past. In fact, he'd never given a fig about his family's notorious reputation, except when it kept him from reaching for his dreams. He'd be damned if he'd let it get in the way now.

Her father had been so understanding that he was sure she wouldn't be infected with the famed Munroe prejudice against Pentercasts. He'd obviously been mistaken. Yet she was too intelligent to rely on the impressions of others to guide her, he was sure of it. She'd been the most clever student in the village school years ago. He'd watched her turn away dukes with a quip. Not that she'd noticed the times he'd come to London to check on her the last three years. Each time he'd gone, he'd been afraid of what he'd find—surely some other man had recognized her as a diamond of the first water. Surely someone else had claimed her hand and her heart. But much as she was in demand, he never saw any indication that she had fallen in love with any of her many suitors. It was that realization that had given him the courage to approach her father.

No, he wasn't being truthful with himself. It wasn't the fact that she was still unwed that had prompted him to hope; it was the fact that he finally saw he had something to offer her. She would never have considered him a catch, he was sure, because of the Pentercast name. However, in talking with her father and making inquiries about town, he had learned that the family was punting on the River Tick, without a paddle. And when it came to money, the Pentercasts had never had a problem, even if it meant working for it.

He glanced about the Manor house corridor, seeing his reflection glowing back from the polished wood paneling. The windows along his left gleamed in the sun, which made the green velvet drapes at their sides glow with an inner fire. The Aubusson carpets that lay scattered down the wide corridor echoed the greens and added the softness of sapphire and amethyst. In the Lawrence painting, his mother looked out of the gilt frame with a smile of complacency. No, the Pentercasts had no trouble with money. A shame the Munroes found that fact so objectionable. He smiled to himself as he remembered how firm Genevieve had been that he not use his wealth to win the wager, and her hand. She must know the difficulties her family was in. She must have realized she had but to crook a finger and any number of wealthy suitors would lay their hearts, and fortunes, at her feet. His smile froze on his face as it struck him that perhaps she had done just that—perhaps she had already accepted someone else's offer of marriage. He shook his head. No, she wouldn't have accepted his wager if that were the case. Whatever reason she had for refusing to wed, he would sweep it aside. He'd waited too long for any other outcome.

He was so caught up in his thoughts that he almost missed his brother trying to scoot around him. But Geoffrey bumped his shoulder in passing, and he reached out to catch his arm. "Easy there, my lad. Where are you going with dinner but a couple of hours away?"

His brother squirmed under his gaze, and Alan felt a prick of concern. Geoffrey spent entirely too much time at the local tavern. Scrumpy, the Somerset apple cider, had its own teeth. Already he could see the beginning of the red veining in his brother's ruddy cheeks and long nose that spoke of too many pints downed. The boy ought to know better, with their own father dead at forty-five and useless years before that. Still, he supposed, it wasn't surprising. The lad had entirely too much energy and no place to spend it. Alan had the estates to keep him busy, but Geoffrey had no interest in the land. He had had less interest in school, so Alan had reluctantly agreed not to return him to Oxford when he had begged off. A career in the military might have been a choice, but Alan wasn't sure he wanted his younger brother subjected to the horrors of the Peninsular campaign. Still, something would have to be done with the young man and soon, for it seemed to Alan that he was quickly moving down a path that had only despair at its end.

"I was only going down to the inn," Geoffrey all but whined. "The lads were talking about racing Dutch Mattison's three-year-old against that prime bit of blood Tom Harvey bought at auction in London. They were going to bring the horses round this afternoon so we could all decide who to wager on."

Alan let go of him. "Sounds like a lark. Don't let Tom talk

you into riding again, and try to be home in time to change for dinner for once."

Geoffrey grinned at him. "Thanks, old man. Oh, and do you think I could borrow a fiver? If I win, I'll double your investment."

Alan cocked his head. "I'll make good the wager, if you'll do me a favor in return."

Geoffrey looked dubious. "What?"

"I want you to go out hunting tomorrow morning. I don't care what you catch, as long as it includes four blackbirds."

"Blackbirds?" Geoffrey wrinkled his nose. "What on earth do you want with dead blackbirds? I'm told they make tough eating."

Alan didn't want to think about where he might have learned that. "Just get them for me and have them back to the house by ten if you can. I have an appointment in the village."

Geoffrey agreed with a shrug "All right. That's it?"

"That's it," Alan assured him.

Geoffrey looked up at him. "First cozying up to those Munroes, and now dead blackbirds. You begin to worry me, Alan."

Alan grinned at him. "Now there's a switch." As Geoffrey's look didn't waver, he felt his smile fading. "Cut line, Geoff. I can't believe my behavior is so aberrant. The Munroes are our neighbors, and it's high time we put this ridiculous bickering to an end. Do you truly have no use for them?"

"Not much." Geoffrey shrugged, but he dropped his gaze. "The mother has no more color than a whitewashed fence and the older daughter scares me."

Alan's grin was returning. "Does she indeed?"

Geoffrey shuddered as if in memory. "Oh, I know she's beautiful, but she has a way of looking at you with those deep blue eyes of hers that makes you think she sees right through you. She's too smart, Alan. No woman should be smarter than her husband."

"Depends on the husband," Alan quipped. "And I suppose you find the younger daughter no better?"

To his surprise, Geoffrey reddened. "She might have some promise, once she's had time to acquire a little town bronze. Now, if you're through with this oh-so-fascinating conversation, I really want to see those horses."

Alan cuffed his shoulder. "Go on, you makebait. Just don't keep Mother holding dinner again."

With a nod of a promise Alan wasn't sure he'd keep, Geoffrey trotted down the hall.

Alan shook his head. He'd have to give some thought to Geoffrey's situation, and soon. Right after he won his wager. This time his smile stayed with him a long time.

Six

Verse Four, Four Colly Birds

Gen tried to apologize to Chimes early the next morning, but the man was obviously still vexed with her, and in the end she stormed off to go hunting by herself. She knew her mother would be annoyed with her if she caught her out without a chaperone, but any of the other servants who were any good at hunting would be needed to serve breakfast. Besides, in her sturdy hunting outfit and boots and her Lepage at her hip, she doubted anyone would be willing to approach her anyway. As long as she stayed on their own land, she would be perfectly safe.

She decided to climb the rise behind the Abbey that morning, following the footpath that wound through the trees to the top. With the branches bare, she could see most of the land sloping away from her for miles around. Her father had taken her up the hill once when she was a child, she remembered.

"You see, Genny," he'd pointed out as she'd sat atop his shoulders, feeling like the queen of the world with everything spread out before her, "everything within the curve of the River Went once belonged to the Munroes. Maybe in your lifetime it will again." She could still see the curve of the river on the far side of the hill, followed its gray serpentine path through the tufted farm fields toward the village. Between the hill and the village lay the Manor, and closer to hand, the Abbey. Directly below her at the base of the hill nearest the Abbey bubbled the spring that fed the creek. With her eyes, she followed the creek along the base of the hill, watching it widen and deepen as other smaller rivulets joined it, until it emptied into the pond behind the Abbey. She shook her head, remembering how her father had had the pond widened each year until it was big enough to practice rowing upon. If only she'd known then how little money they actually had. She wondered whether she could have stopped him. Somehow, she doubted it. From the expenses that she had had to pay for him, it had taken him a long time to fathom that there wasn't enough money.

She forced herself to focus back on the landscape. She simply had to stop her negative thoughts if she were to be of any use to her family. She watched the black swans her father had purchased a few years ago floating serenely across the pond, heading for the rushes on the far side. One turned instead toward the far end, where the dam lay. Another piece of foolishness, she couldn't help thinking, although it at least had been her great-grandfather's doing. The swan waddled out on the bank, then strolled across the wooden planking of the dam. Something must have startled it, for it rose suddenly, neck outstretched, and flapped back toward the rushes. She could only hope nothing was wrong with the structure. The Lord knew, in the six years they had been gone, everything seemed to have aged twice that. The roofs in the gardener's sheds needed replacing according to Chimes, the bell tower her father had installed seemed to be listing, and at least three of the chimneys smoked. She had managed to convince her mother that these things could be taken care of when they returned to London, but she knew, most likely, her family would have to learn to live with them.

Her gaze swept down the empty creek bed, still a deep cleft in the hillside even though the dam let through a mere trickle of the former stream, down through the undergrowth that inhabited it now and across the stone wall to where the cleft opened on the Pentercast side of the property. Everything there looked neat as a pin, and a part of her wanted nothing more than to mess it up. She shook her head again. An unkind thought. For all Alan's faults, he seemed to have taken extraordinarily good care of his place. Truth be told, she envied him. With a sigh, she turned to see about her hunting.

Unfortunately, the game was no more cooperative than on Christmas morning. She had the woods essentially to herself, and although she stayed out much later than she had planned, she saw nary an animal worth the shot. The day was crisp and clear, though quite cold, and she wondered if they would yet get snow before the twelve days of Christmas were over. She tried not to think about what the end of those twelve days would mean to her or her family. And she refused to think about what it would mean should Alan win his wager.

She had gone down the hill and through the woods to come out into a small clearing on the far side of the estate nearest the Pentercast land. She had just about decided to give up for the day, when she heard a rustling in the undergrowth to her right. Darting behind a tree, she checked her Lepage to make sure the bullet was in the pan, then peered cautiously around the boll of the tree. About her, the wood had become quiet, much too quiet even for winter. The few birds she had heard earlier were silent. Even the morning breeze was still. Had she been spotted? Or was it a predator like herself? She leveled the gun at the offending bush, waiting. A moment later, Geoffrey Pentercast backed into view.

Gen scowled from her hiding place. She knew full well she was still safely on her own land. And he had to have crossed the wall to reach this spot. He was dressed in a deep red hunting jacket, belted at the waist, and black trousers tucked into boots. He had a game bag at one hip, a rifle in hand. The man was poaching! She was tempted to plant a shot between those mud-spattered boots of his just to teach him a lesson. Instead, she watched as he straightened, turning toward her. With surprise, she noted he held a ferret up by the tail. The animal was obviously still alive, for it twisted in his grip, snapping and hissing. She wondered if he had loosed it from one of Chimes' snares. Whatever the case, he grinned at the little beast, then carefully dropped it into the leather game bag at his hip. By the way the bag bounced around, the ferret found no more delight in his company than her sister Allison did. As he turned, settling the bag more carefully, she saw a brace of birds at his other hip. They were all black.

She frowned. Why would he poach blackbirds of all things? You couldn't eat them, and they presented little sport as the ridiculous birds were everywhere and hardly quietly hiding. Still, it galled her that he had had better luck than she had this morning, and on her own land to boot. She considered again leveling a shot at him as he made sure of his own rifle and turned to move on. Then his head came up, his eyes narrowing. She heard the sound too: something large was moving through the trees toward them at a fast clip. He had the advantage of being closer, with fewer trees between him and the approaching animal. But she was determined that he wasn't going to beat her this time. She leveled her rifle past him even as he brought up his own weapon. As a shape loomed up between the trees, the guns roared together, sounding like a single shot in the clear winter air. Someone screamed. Branches and leaves scattered as a large black horse erupted from the wood and galloped out of the clearing, reins trailing.

Geoffrey Pentercast dropped his rifle, paling, and dashed into the woods toward the scream. Gen froze where she was, her heart pounding in her ears. What had she done? Shaking, she lowered the Lepage to the leaf-strewn ground. Her feet refused to carry her forward. Her stomach heaved at the thought that she might have taken a life. She nearly cried aloud as Geoffrey reappeared, one arm around a woman who was weeping into his shoulder. As they reached the small clearing, the woman raised her head and Gen gasped as she recognized Allison.

"Are you sure you're unhurt?" Geoffrey was pleading, staring down into her eyes as if he couldn't quite believe it.

"I . . . I think so," Allison sniffed, and Gen sagged with relief. "It was just so sudden. And my horse just bolted on me, silly thing."

Geoffrey took out a pocket handkerchief and wiped the tears from her pale face. "I'm very sorry, Miss Munroe. I fired without thinking, I'm afraid. I've never been so thankful for being a poor shot, I assure you."

Allison blinked up at him. "You mean you did that on purpose?"

He stuffed the handkerchief back into the pocket of his hunting jacket, avoiding her eyes. "Well, I wasn't actually trying to hit you. I thought you were a deer."

Her face reddened, even as Gen bit her lips to keep from interrupting. Time enough later to tell her sister that Geoffrey's hadn't been the only shot. At the moment, she was almost enjoying watching a Pentercast get his due.

"Geoffrey Pentercast," Allison declared, "I always thought you were a loose screw, and now I *know* it! How dare you endanger my life with your paltry hunting? Come to think of it, why are you hunting on *our* land? You . . . you poacher!"

"If you want a poacher, talk to that Chimes fellow of yours," he sneered in return. "Seems I've seen his face in our woods often enough."

"That is beside the point! You tried to kill me!"

In the distance Gen heard Bryce, their abigail, calling for Allison. Geoffrey must have heard it as well, for his head came up, and he stepped away from Allison.

"Hush, now," he cautioned. "We both know that's not true."

"It is!" Allison maintained, refusing to be mollified. "And I shall tell the entire village what a villain you are!"

Geoffrey's hand shot out and covered her mouth, even as his other arm imprisoned her waist. Allison struggled against his grip. Gen, fearing the worst, reached in her pocket for another ball and began preparing the Lepage. She doubted she could actually shoot Geoffrey Pentercast, but she wanted to have a loaded, primed rifle in her grasp if she needed to defend her sister. Her hands shook on the powder, but she steadied herself, darting glances at the struggling couple.

"Hush, I said," Geoffrey ordered, and to Gen's surprise, Allison stilled. "Now, I don't want any trouble from your family, and I don't think you do either. Who knows, they might even force us to marry each other to make up for the scandal."

Above his large hand, Allison's eyes went wide.

"Yes, I didn't suppose you'd much like that thought, so before your abigail gets here, think hard. You say you're unhurt, and I'm quite willing to forget this incident. Let's come to an agreement." He shifted his grip, and the bag at his hip bumped against Allison. The ferret must not have liked the agitation, for the bag shuddered, and Allison's squeal came out muffled under Geoffrey's hand. Gen slid the ball into place and leveled the rifle, watching him down the barrel.

"Hush!" he insisted, clearly exasperated. "It's just a ferret. I know people who keep them as pets." His look brightened. "I have it—suppose I tame this fellow for your pet? The gentlemen in London will think you're all the rage. You just forget about this morning, eh?"

Bryce's calls were becoming more concerned, and much closer. Gen shifted her grip on the rifle, watching her sister. Allison appeared to think it over, then nodded. Slowly, Geoffrey removed his hand. Gen lowered the rifle.

"I agree with your plan, Mr. Pentercast, but only because I

wouldn't want to marry you if you were the last man on earth," Allison informed him, her head held high.

"How very delightful," he quipped. "Clichés at dawn. If you'll excuse me."

She grabbed his arm. "When will you bring the ferret?"

"Patience, infant. I've got to tame him first. You wouldn't want him to bite you, would you?" As Allison paled, he grinned. "I'm sure I can have him to you before you go back to London—say Epiphany? Now, I really must run." He snatched up his rifle and melted into the woods on the far side of the clearing just as Bryce cantered into sight on the right. Allison squared her shoulders.

"There you are, Miss Allison," the dark-haired abigail cried. She did her best to look stern, but the worry was all too easy to read in her dark brown eyes and her normally pretty face puckered "Why didn't you answer me?"

Before Allison could answer, Gen stepped from hiding. "It's all right, Bryce. I've been with her all along. She found me hunting and didn't want to scare away the game, isn't that right, Allison?"

Allison stared at her as if she'd grown horns and a tail. "Yes, of course."

Bryce looked between the two of them. "But what have you done with Blackie?"

Allison tossed her head. "That useless nag bolted when Gen made a shot. I cannot believe Father ever bought such a ridiculous beast as a country horse. I vow I will replace him when we return to London."

Bryce shook her head. "Well, next time you get away from me, you come when I call, hunting or no. And when it comes to that, perhaps next time you needn't ride so far ahead."

Allison pouted but said nothing.

Gen knew she and her sister needed to have a private talk. "Bryce, I'm afraid I didn't bring a horse, and it seems a shame for Allison to have to walk all the way back to the Abbey. Why don't you ride back and get Chimes to bring around the carriage? We could meet him at the head of the road."

Bryce frowned, and Gen wondered what she could possibly think they were up to. A woman only slightly older than she was, Bryce seemed to feel it her duty to protect her young ladies from some mysterious harm. She appeared to think danger and depravity lurked behind every bush. There were times in London when the trait had come in very handy. Here in the country it seemed unfounded. Well, she mused, in a few more days, it wouldn't matter, as they could no longer afford her watchful eye.

Finally, Bryce nodded, promising to return soon, and rode back through the woods. She was no sooner out of sight than Allison heaved a sigh and turned to Gen.

"How much of that disgraceful scene did you see?"

Gen smiled ruefully. "All of it, I'm afraid."

Allison blushed. "Well, I told you he was a reprobate."

"I think you do him an injustice," Gen chided gently. "I'm afraid I fired at the same time he did, and as he owned he was a miserable shot, most likely it was my bullet that nearly hit Blackie."

Allison's azure eyes widened. "Oh, Gen, no!"

Gen nodded. "I'm very sorry. And I promise you I've learned my lesson. I won't aim at what I can't see again. I'm just very glad you weren't hurt."

"It was rather scary," her sister admitted with a shiver. Then she brightened. "But I shall have a pet ferret for my trouble."

Gen laughed. "I wouldn't count on that if I were you. Geoffrey Pentercast doesn't strike me as all that dependable."

"True," Allison sighed, her smile fading. "A shame he isn't more like his brother Alan."

Gen gathered up her rifle and moved across the clearing. "Come along. We promised Bryce we'd be waiting."

"You're still quite put out with him, aren't you?" Allison asked, scurrying to keep up as Gen set off at a sharp pace through the bare winter woods. "Honestly, I think you're doing him an injustice as well."

Gen steadfastly refused to talk about the matter. There was nothing she could say that would not ultimately lead to the subject of the wager or their finances. They trudged through the estate woods in single file, their breaths puffing white in the cold air, until they reached the drive that wound through the land to the Manor. It was only a short time before Chimes picked them up in the carriage.

When they reached the Abbey's carriage house and Allison was safely on her way inside, Gen took him aside. "Chimes, I've been trying to apologize to you, but you're entirely too stubborn to listen!"

Her man grunted, moving away from the carriage to allow the groomsmen to unhitch the horses. "I'm less stubborn than some," he muttered, pulling her out of their earshot. "But I'll accept your apology, if you'll accept some good advice."

Gen narrowed her eyes. "What advice?"

"Don't get so uppity, missy. I know you've been trying to do your best by your sister and mum. Marrying Alan Pentercast would solve all your problems. Let the man win his wager."

She closed her eyes against the headache that was building. "I appreciate your thoughts, Chimes. But I must do what I see as best for all concerned."

He snorted, and she snapped open her eyes to glare at him. He held up his hands in surrender. "All right, I'll say no more on the subject. Just you think on what I said. It's the easiest way out, for all concerned." When her look turned darker, he scurried off, muttering under his breath. Gen threw up her hands and stalked back to the house.

She saw no more of Chimes that morning or at lunch. However, she knew he hadn't changed his opinion when afternoon brought a visit by Alan who was accompanied by the Reverend Wellfordhouse. She frowned as Chimes ushered them into the parlor where she and Allison had been helping her mother sort through dress patterns to use on some material they had found in a little used trunk. He winked at her before hurrying out. She vowed to have another talk with him later.

"William, Mr. Pentercast, what a lovely surprise," her mother offered as Allison simpered and Gen glowered. "To what do we owe this visit?"

William exchanged glances with Alan. "I was accompanying Vicar York on a visit to the Manor and . . . er. . . ."

Gen stiffened, afraid of what was coming. Surely William would not blurt out the facts of the wager in front of her mother?

"I suppose he was there visiting Fancy," her mother sniffed, and Gen relaxed slightly with the change of subject.

Alan frowned. "So it seemed. How did you know?"

"Your mother and I have discussed the matter," her mother replied archly, "and we are of the opinion that the vicar is courting Fancy."

"Is he indeed?" Alan intoned, leveling a glance at William, who fiddled with his cravat and paled.

"Yes, well, be that as it may," William sputtered, "I believe we came over here because the Squire had expressed a desire to see Miss Genevieve."

Gen bit her lip in chagrin. Her mother raised an expressive eyebrow, glancing at her. "Oh, and why would that be, pray tell?"

Gen released her lip, but felt herself blushing despite her best efforts. Before she could answer, Alan, who had wandered over to where they had spread the patterns in the sun filtering through the gauze curtains on the twin windows, spoke up.

"You know, Miss Munroe," he murmured, cocking his head to study the patterns, "I have the very bonnet to go with that one."

Gen frowned at the non sequitur. "Bonnet, sir?"

William coughed. "Yes, well, a bonnet of sorts. I believe Miss Wilkins in the village made it up for the Squire as a favor, isn't that so, Alan?"

"What *are* you talking about?" Gen demanded, feeling as if she'd somehow wandered in on the middle of a conversation. Allison was looking confused as well. Even her mother was frowning. Alan excused himself to go fetch a parcel from the entry hall.

"Well, my brother Geoffrey informed me that your hunting wasn't going as well as you'd wanted, Miss Munroe," he smiled, offering Gen the hat box with a bow. "I hoped this might make up for it."

Gen took the box, almost afraid to open it. What was today, the fourth day of Christmas? Wasn't that gift four colly birds? She had visions of four blackbirds flapping out of the box when she lifted the lid, like the old nursery rhyme of "Sing a Song of Sixpence." But Alan was grinning beside her, and Allison and her mother were eagerly awaiting a look. With a sigh, she untied the pretty blue ribbon and pulled off the lid.

Inside lay a mass of shiny black feathers.

She looked up at Alan, frowning.

"Pick it up," he urged.

Gingerly, she slid her hand around the feathers and found they were anchored to a frame of some kind. Scooping them from the box, she saw she held a slender straw bonnet entirely covered with black feathers. A ribbon of a vibrant shade of blue encircled the crown, and several of the feathers curved enticingly over the brim. "My word," she managed.

"Oh, if only you'd had that when you were in mourning!" Allison cried.

William bit his lip, and Alan smothered a smile.

Her mother pursed her lips, frowning at Allison. "I'm sure

your sister can put it to good use now as well, Allison. Isn't that right, Genevieve?"

Gen found it impossible to tear her eyes from the bonnet. "What, what is it made of?"

"Colly birds," Alan replied. "Four to be exact."

"Of course," she murmured. An image sprang to mind—Geoffrey Pentercast, four blackbirds at his hip. That's what he'd been doing out this morning. She wondered if she could disqualify Alan because his brother had poached them. Somehow, she didn't think William would allow that. She sighed, reaching up to settle the bonnet on her thick hair. "How charming, Mr. Pentercast," she murmured for his ears alone. "First you ask me to eat crow, and now you expect me to wear them."

Alan tilted back his head and laughed.

Seven

Verse Five, Five Golden Rings

Gen eyed the bonnet on her dressing table, the black feathers shining in the candlelight, still unsure whether she wanted to wear it or burn it. It really was rather fetching, with the blue ribbon, a blue that so closely matched her eyes, tied beneath her chin in a great big bow. She ought to be delighted with the man's ingenuity. Instead, she felt as if a noose were tightening around her neck. Like Geoffrey's ferret of the morning, she was being trapped, and she had no expectation of rescue.

She pulled the hairbrush through her thick hair, wondering again whether there was any way out of her dilemma. Perhaps she ought to sell the diamonds. No, it still wouldn't be enough for Allison's Season or another year in London. Whatever price they fetched surely wouldn't suffice to fix up the Abbey or allow her to sneer at Alan's wager. She winced as she hit a tangle in her curls. Tangles in her hair, tangles in her life. And it was only getting worse.

Someone tapped on her door, and she called for them to come in. Setting down the brush and turning, she saw her mother in the doorway. She smiled a welcome, and Mrs. Munroe moved into the room, pausing to straighten the portrait of Gen's father by the door, then crossing to tug the quilt back into place on the four-poster bed.

"Is there something you need of me, Mother?" Gen prompted.

Her mother paused behind her as she sat on the stool in front of the dressing table. Her gaze rested on the colly-bird bonnet. "I just came to say good night," she murmured.

Gen waited, sure there must be more. Her mother reached out and stroked the silky black feathers.

"This was an . . . interesting gesture for the Squire, don't you think?"

"Hmmm." Gen managed to make it neither an agreement nor a disagreement. She felt her mother's gaze on her and tried not to squirm.

Her mother sighed, crossing to the bed again and fluffing the pillows so that they rose a little higher against the carved headboard. "Genevieve, I am well aware that you and your father discussed your suitors far more often than you discussed them with me. I know I can be difficult to approach sometimes. But I hope you can speak to me when something is troubling you."

Gen blinked, a breath catching in her throat. Did she know? Had she guessed? "What . . . what do you think is troubling me, Mother?"

Her mother smoothed down the country quilt, her long-fingered hand lingering on the bright patterns. "You needn't be evasive. I'm speaking of the Squire. I hope you understand that he seems to have taken an interest in you."

Gen relaxed, turning to face her mother. "You are quite wrong there, Mother. The Squire is no more interested in me than were any of those other shallow gentlemen who flocked around me in London."

Her mother raised an eyebrow. "I see. You admit he is a suitor, then."

"No!" Gen argued. "I admit he seems to be taken with harassing me, annoying me, and in every way making himself disagreeable."

Now her mother frowned. "It does not seem so to me. This gift is a good example, and the hens he sent home with me the other day. In fact, he has been paying you the utmost of courteous attention. I take it you find that attention disagreeable?"

Gen felt herself reddening. "Oh, Mother, it's so difficult to explain. Doesn't he seem just a bit *too* attentive to you? Perhaps too kind?"

"He seems to me to be very different from what I had expected from a Pentercast, but then his father was like that as well. He appeared quite charming, but underneath . . ." She stared off into the middle distance, her face impassive, and Gen wondered what memory she was reliving. She blinked rapidly and returned her gaze to her daughter. "I have seen no sign that he is other than he seems; however, it is best not to overlook the fact that he is still a Pentercast, and a Munroe would never form a close association with a Pentercast."

Despite her concerns over Alan, the old litany bothered Gen. "But surely we should judge him on his own merits, Mother, not on those of his forefathers."

"There are tendencies, my dear, that run in families. I have no doubt that underneath his fine facade, the Squire is every bit as conniving and manipulative as his father before him. An acorn does not fall far from the tree, Genevieve. I can only hope that you have not offered him any encouragement."

Gen was forced to laugh. "Mother, I can safely say that I have not been the least encouraging. In fact, I have been actively discouraging to the Squire."

Her mother nodded, moving toward the door. "Good. Perhaps that is the best approach to take. I would not want you to lose your heart to someone unworthy. It can be a most painful experience. I must say I'm quite glad we'll be returning to London soon. I'm sure next Season we'll find you the proper husband."

Gen managed a smile. "Yes, Mother." Watching her in the doorway, tall, spare, distant, she found she had to try again to explain. "Mother, I thought you were happy here at the Abbey."

Her mother turned back to her, head cocked thoughtfully. "I suppose I am. I had forgotten how quiet it is here. You can hear the birds outside your window in the morning, even in the winter. And the church bells on the breeze. London is always so busy. I'm sure I could be quite contented here. But that would be very selfish. It is my duty to see you and Allison well settled, and we are unlikely to accomplish that here in the country."

"But surely there are dances here, social gatherings, picnics in the summer?" Gen persisted, encouraged by her mother's confession. "There must be other young men besides the Squire and his brother."

"None we would care to know," her mother sniffed. "Do not worry yourself over this, Genevieve. When Allison comes out next Season, you will have a whole new set of suitors to choose from. Surely one will be to your liking. Now, good night, my dear."

As her mother closed the door behind her, Gen put her head in her hands. She was trapped. Carstairs was right—she would have to tell them. She had wanted so much to give them a little time, a little peace, but she couldn't let her mother keep building dreams that would never come true. Squaring her shoulders, she looked up and saw the bonnet. She picked it up and hurled it across the room. It hit the bedpost with a rather satisfactory smack, and black feathers floated down upon the colorful quilt.

"Wonderful." She shook her head. "Now I'm supposed to sleep with them as well."

She didn't rest well that night and awoke the next morning feeling cross. Her mood was not improved when her morning's hunt turned up nothing again, even with Chimes' assistance. So much for being able to live off the land. Their only hope seemed to be those harvest tithes. Surely there was some way she could help Alan lose his wager. She thought over the gifts that would be coming, but she had no idea how he would accomplish them so could think of no easy way to thwart him. The more frustrated she became, the more her temper threatened. She was close to the boiling point when, after lunch, the entire Pentercast family arrived for a visit.

As on the day before, her mother and Allison were only too happy to play at being hostesses. Because her mother had agreed to put off mourning, both were dressed in gowns of sprigged muslin. Gen's dark mood hadn't allowed her to pick anything more festive than her lilac kerseymere. Even Mrs. Pentercast looked more fashionable in her gown of striped silk. Alan's dark coat and fawn trousers, and Geoffrey's attempt to match them, looked quite polished as well. She briefly considered pleading a headache, but a glance at her mother told her she would never be granted permission to leave. With a sigh, she prepared herself to do battle.

Battle, however satisfying it might have been to her nerves, was not easy to come by. Mrs. Pentercast and her mother were soon sitting in the two Sheraton chairs nearest the fire, heads close together in conversation, and Geoffrey was seated at Allison's feet on the chaise longue across the room, teasing her so that her face reddened in a blush and she giggled. The fire crackled in the grate. The bright brittle sun of winter sparkled on the window panes. It was all so nauseatingly cozy that Gen wanted to scream.

Her only consolation was that Alan seemed hesitant about approaching her. He stayed close to his mother's side until Gen could see the conversation was boring him to distraction, then wandered over to Geoffrey. But her sister and his brother immediately sobered at his arrival, and he was forced to leave them in awkward silence shortly after. She could almost feel his heartfelt sigh as he wandered in turn to the window.

Curiosity piqued her interest. Surely he wouldn't visit twice in one day, so he had to have brought her gift for the fifth day of Christmas. What would that be—five golden rings? She smiled to herself. Now, that would be a difficult one to accomplish without spending any money. Perhaps she would have him at last. The mere possibility made it worth a trip to the window to find out what was on his mind.

"You seem quiet today, Squire," she ventured.

He kept his gaze on the scene outside, where the brown winter lawn of the clearing stretched to the bare canes of the rose gardens and the sluggish pond beyond. "I appear to be *de trop,* Miss Munroe. Our families seem to have decided to get along quite well without us."

She glanced back at her mother and Mrs. Pentercast. Alan's mother was giggling over something her mother had said. She tried to imagine her mother saying anything humorous on purpose. She shook her head. "Yes, much better than I had ever thought possible."

He nodded toward his brother. "If I didn't know better, I'd say Geoffrey had developed a *tendre* for your sister."

She followed his gaze. Geoffrey was leaning closer to Allison, who was batting her golden lashes at him and smiling coquettishly. "Allison is practicing her wiles, Squire. She's too young to settle on any gentleman just yet." She looked back at him. "You do know that Geoffrey got those colly birds of yours off our land."

"No, he didn't mention that," Alan replied, raising an eyebrow. It disappeared into the lock of brown hair falling over his forehead. It made him look rather comical. She tried to ignore the fact that he also looked quite adorable.

"I don't suppose he mentioned that he fired at my sister either," she continued.

"What?" he frowned, both brows coming together over his

nose. If she had been hoping it would lessen his charm she was disappointed. He still looked handsome. "Are you sure?"

He looked so concerned, brows knit, eyes snapping fire, that she felt compelled to reassure him. "No one was hurt, sir. I saw the whole thing, although your brother didn't know I was there." His fierce look forced down her gaze in guilt. "In truth, I fired before I thought as well. In any event, he and Allison agreed to keep it a secret, so it seems there has been no harm done. I suspect the whole adventure is causing their giggles today." She couldn't help grinning up at him as his face relaxed. "However, you might want to keep an eye out for a ferret. Geoffrey caught one yesterday and promised to tame it for my sister."

Alan rolled his eyes. "I can only hope Mother doesn't find it first."

Gen chuckled. "I can imagine that wouldn't go over very well."

"I would not want to contemplate the results." He shuddered theatrically, then sobered. "I will speak with him. About the poaching, that is. I take it you think your sister's heart is safe."

"Quite," Gen assured him.

"What about yours?"

Startled, she looked up into searching brown eyes. "Mine, sir? What do you mean?"

He sighed. "If you have to ask, my dear, I'm obviously doing something wrong." Before she could compose herself to answer, he reached into the pocket of his navy waistcoat and pulled out a small brown velvet box, shoving it at her almost belligerently. "Here. Your gift."

She frowned at him, but accepted the box, which rattled in her grip. Prying open the lid, she saw the padded interior held a jumble of rings. She knew if she sorted them out and counted them, there would be five. They were all at least partially gold, some with stones that winked in the winter sunlight and sent reflections glittering across the gauze draperies. She couldn't give him any encouragement, she cautioned herself. She looked back up at him, schooling her face to impassiveness, waiting for an explanation.

"Engagement rings," he muttered, running his hand back through his thick brown hair and further disheveling it. "They belonged to various Pentercast women over the centuries. Surely one of them will fit."

He was doing it again, making something that should have been a precious moment in a courtship into something as common as trying on a shoe. She felt the tug of tears on her eyes and blinked, determined not to give in. Snapping the box shut, she handed it back to him. "One may fit or all may fit. It doesn't matter, for I won't be wearing any of them."

He refused to take the box from her hand. "Has nothing I've done changed your mind in any way?"

"Nothing," she snapped.

He started to speak, but his mother's voice interrupted him. "Ermintrude Munroe, that's a horrible thing to say! I always knew you were stuck up!"

Alarmed, Gen looked at her mother askance. Mrs. Munroe was sitting ramrod straight, lips tight, head high. "I can only say what I perceive to be the truth, Fancine," she murmured, ignoring the fact that Mrs. Pentercast's outburst had caused all eyes to turn in her direction. "You would do well to heed my warning."

"Warning, Mrs. Munroe?" Alan asked, crossing to his mother's side. "Is something wrong, Mother?"

Mrs. Pentercast struggled to heave her bulk upright. "She's just jealous, that's all. She always has been, and she always will be. She just *wishes* she had my power over men."

Gen's mother rose as well as Gen hurried to her side. "As usual, Fancine, you mistake my motives. I think it's time you left."

"I think it's *past* time," Mrs. Munroe sniffed, tossing her head so that the graying curls at either aide of her round face wobbled. "Of course, that ridiculous excuse of a butler of yours is nowhere to be found."

"Now, Mother," Alan began, all conciliation.

"Yes, Mother, really," Geoffrey put in, joining the group by the fire with Allison at his heels. "We were having a nice time here. We wouldn't want to spoil it."

Alan frowned at him, and his mother glared. "Certainly you're having a nice time. The Munroe women have always known how to be accommodating, with the right sort of man."

Allison gasped, paling. Her mother's eyes snapped fire. "Chimes!"

"Mrs. Munroe, please excuse my mother," Alan said firmly, glaring down at the little woman beside him. The fire went out of her, and her lower lip trembled. "And my brother as well." Geoffrey squirmed. "Perhaps it is time we took our leave. Miss Genevieve, would you be so kind as to show us to the door since your man doesn't seem to be free?"

"Gladly," Gen replied, leading them away from her haughty mother and distraught sister. By the time they reached the front entry, Chimes, looking harried, appeared with their wraps.

"I don't know what happened," Alan murmured to her as Chimes helped his mother on with her cloak and Geoffrey shrugged into his greatcoat. "But I want you to know it changes nothing. I still have seven more days of Christmas. Will you come riding with me tomorrow, providing the weather holds?"

It would have been easy to refuse. She was sure the request had something to do with the next day's gift, and if she refused she would make it that much harder for him to win. But looking up in his face, so open, with his emotions showing clearly that whatever the reason, he badly wanted her to agree, she found she couldn't refuse him. She sighed. "Very well, Mr. Pentercast. Say ten?"

His smile was almost her undoing. "Ten it is. Until then, Miss Munroe."

Gen didn't realize she still held the box of rings until he was out the door.

Eight

Verse Six, Six Geese a-Laying

Gen shoved the jewelry box into the sleeve of her gown and returned immediately to the withdrawing room, hoping that her sister and mother had calmed during her absence. If anything, things had only gotten worse. Her mother sat staring morosely into the fire, and Allison was curled up in the armchair sniffing. Gen paused in the doorway, hands on her hips. She knew she should be kind and conciliatory, but all she wanted to do was send them to their rooms like naughty schoolchildren.

"What am I to do with the pair of you?" she asked in exasperation. "I thought we had just gotten on friendly terms with our neighbors."

"One cannot be on friendly terms with those who are not in one's social circle," her mother sniffed. "They mistake every bit of kindness for condescension, or worse."

Gen shook her head, crossing to her mother's side. "Mother, you must stop this. The Pentercasts are not some vagabonds who happened into the neighborhood. Alan is considered a leading figure in the community. Mrs. Pentercast and you grew up together. How could she have suddenly fallen from grace?"

Her mother refused to look at her. "She has no refinement

of spirit. She never understood what wasn't right before her eyes, and then only when it was carefully explained to her."

"What did you say to her?" Gen persisted, kneeling beside her in a vain attempt to meet her downward gaze. Her mother kept her eyes on the fire.

"I merely cautioned her to consider Vicar York's motives. You knew he was courting her."

"Yes," Gen sighed. "So you mentioned yesterday."

Allison appeared beside her mother, obviously drawn by the gossip. She wiped a hand over her eyes to catch the last tears.

Her mother inclined her head in a nod. "He's over there every day, sitting with her for hours on end. And he rarely brings his Bible so you needn't think it's for her religious edification."

"I find it hard to imagine the vicar as a suitor," Gen ventured, smothering a smile at the thought of the rotund reverend roused to romance.

"I should think not," Allison sniffed. "He's much too old."

"Age has nothing to do with it," Mrs. Munroe replied. "Some do not find love until quite old, Allison. Though, mind you, I do not consider the vicar to be swayed by the dictates of passion."

Allison shuddered. "Imagine kissing him. Ugh!"

"That will be quite enough from you, miss," her mother scolded, raising her eyes at last. Allison quailed at the fire therein. "I'm sorry I ever brought up the subject, I can assure you. However, you both would do well to learn the lesson now— not every suitor comes out of love or admiration. Some have other motives entirely." She rose, shaking out her skirts, and Gen rose with her. "Regardless, I hope, Genevieve, that we have seen the last of the Pentercasts for some time. I could stand a great deal more of the peace we hoped to find here, and I do not think we are likely to stumble upon it in their company. Now, Allison, you will refine no more on what that woman said. It's well known that the Munroe women have always had the highest of standards. An extended practice session on the spinet should take your mind off this incident. Genevieve, please accompany her. I think now would be a good time to finish that embroidered slipcover you started last spring. I shall be consulting with Mrs. Chimes should you need me."

As their mother swept from the room, Allison sighed. "There goes all the fun we might have had. Just when things were getting interesting."

Gen eyed her sister as they made their way down the hall to the music room. "I trust this means you now find Mr. Geoffrey Pentercast a more congenial gentleman."

Her sister hurried to the spinet to hide her blush behind her music. "He can be quite enjoyable company when he puts himself out. I noticed you and the Squire seemed thick as thieves."

Gen picked up the embroidery from the window seat, where she had left it days ago, and jabbed the needle into the linen. "He can also be enjoyable company, although seldom in my presence."

"I think you mistake him," Allison said with newfound wisdom. "He seems to genuinely care for you."

Gen raised an eyebrow, needle poised in midair, heartbeat quickening unaccountably. "Whatever gave you that impression?"

"The way he looks at you when he thinks no one is watching. The way he brightens when he first catches sight of you. And he does keep giving you the most interesting presents. What was in the box today?"

"I thought you were absorbed in conversation with Geoffrey," Gen accused, narrowing her eyes.

"A lady can do more than one thing at a time," Allison informed her, head high. "Pray answer the question."

Gen studied the embroidery, wondering again if she should tell her sister what was happening. As before, other secrets got in the way. "It was just a box of rings he wished to give his mother. He wanted a woman's opinion."

Allison pouted in disappointment. "Is that all? I hope you picked a thoroughly disagreeable one, then. The old harridan deserves it. Imagine thinking I would tarry with a second son."

Despite herself, Gen laughed. "Oh, I see. If one is to ruin one's reputation, it should only be for someone of consequence."

"Certainly," Allison nodded, fingers curved over the keys. "A marquess, perhaps, or a duke. Anything less would be foolhardy in the extreme."

"I bow to the voice of experience," Gen teased.

Allison stuck her tongue out at her.

That afternoon when Gen changed for dinner, she was forced to remember the box of rings again, for it fell from her discarded gown with a rather loud thump. As she bent to retrieve it, she was glad that Bryce was still busy with her mother. She shoved it in the top drawer of her dresser and slammed the drawer shut. Her brushes and combs jumped, and the portrait of her father swayed on the wall. Glancing up into the smiling blue eyes so much like her own, she shook her head.

"Oh, Father, I hope I'm doing the right thing."

He smiled down at her, carefree, confident. The painter had definitely captured his gentle side, the side she had loved, the only side she and Allison had ever seen, until she had been forced to clean up after the messes he had made in life. She sighed. "Why couldn't you have listened to Carstairs, Father?" she murmured, feeling her headache returning. She turned away from the portrait, rubbing her temples. She caught herself in the act and froze. Was this what she had come to? Some melodramatic Society belle, mourning for her lost Season? Was Gen Munroe, toast of the *ton, whining?* She squared her shoulders. Not anymore. She had better things to do, much more important things. Things like helping her mother and sister have a happy Christmas. Things like making sure Alan Pentercast lost his detestable little wager. She put up her head and marched to the wardrobe to pull out her favorite pale pink silk evening dress. It was time she shook the cobwebs out of her mind and bent to her tasks.

Her optimistic mood carried her into the next day, right up to the point when she realized she would have to tell her mother about her ride with Alan. She fleetingly considered just sneaking out through the kitchen to the stables, but she knew propriety would demand that she take a chaperone, namely Bryce, who could not be counted on to keep silent on the matter. Then she realized that she could take Allison instead.

A whispered conversation in the corridor did the trick, and soon both girls were dressed in their riding habits and walking their horses in front of the Abbey in hopes of meeting their neighbors before they had a chance to knock at the door. Chimes had been enlisted to keep their mother busy, a task that was much to his liking. It was only a matter of minutes before Alan rode up. Allison brightened when she saw Geoffrey in his wake.

Gen had to admit that Alan was an impressive sight on horseback. The traditional riding coat was well cut to call attention to his broad shoulders, and the vivid red with its black velvet lapels looked well with his dark hair and eyes. Geoffrey's rumpled brown plaid jacket looked hopelessly outdated, but Allison didn't seem to care, fluttering her eyelashes as if she'd gotten dirt thrown in her face and simpering until Gen wanted nothing more than to tweak the curls that were artfully escaping her blue velvet riding hat.

"A bit eager, aren't you?" Geoffrey asked in greeting. Alan glared at him before turning to Gen and offering her a bow from horseback.

"My father used to say there is nothing so fine as a beautiful woman who knows the value of time," he smiled at Gen. Allison giggled. Gen managed a smile, thanking him as one of the grooms hurried forward to hand her up. In truth, she was finding it hard to be angry with him today. It was as if in determining she would no longer feel sorry for herself she had managed to wipe away all her negative emotions. She still was determined not to let him win, but that didn't mean she couldn't enjoy a quiet ride through the winter woods with a handsome gentleman at her side. When she and Allison were mounted, Alan led off back up the road toward the Pentercast side of the estate.

Allison easily maneuvered her horse beside Geoffrey's, leaving Gen no choice but to fall in beside Alan. From behind, she heard nothing but whispered conversation punctuated by giggles from Allison. She could almost regret not bringing the overly proper Bryce.

"I hope your mother is feeling more the thing today," Alan ventured beside her. "Although I was unable to get anything sensible out of my mother about their quarrel."

Gen grimaced. "I fear my mother can be a bit censorious in her opinions. She seemed to think it her duty to warn your mother that Vicar York's attentions cannot be honorable."

"What!" Alan reined in his horse so hard that the beast reared in protest. Gen guided her startled mount away from his until he could get the horse under control. Geoffrey and Allison gave their beasts the head and managed to ride past, taking the lead. His face coloring, in embarrassment or anger, Gen wasn't sure, Alan maneuvered his horse back in beside hers.

"I apologize for my reaction, Miss Munroe. I cannot have heard you correctly. Did you say the vicar is seducing my mother?"

"Good heavens no!" Gen exclaimed, careful to keep her surprise from her horse lest she repeat Alan's mistake. "Your mother seems to feel that he is genuinely courting her. My mother does not believe it. I really can't say why, although I must say the good vicar does not impress me as the importunate lover."

"I should say not," Alan murmured, staring forward over his horse's head. "Frankly, I had begun to wonder to what we owed such devotion of late. I had best speak with the man."

"And I had best speak with my sister," Gen frowned, scanning the empty road ahead. "The two of them seem to have outdistanced us."

Alan's brown eyes twinkled. "A difficulty we could soon remedy. Race you to the divide?"

Her spirits soared at the very idea. She didn't think to question them. "You're on," she cried, spurring her mount before he could even agree. They thundered down the road, Alan's brown pulling even easily with her dappled gray. She knew her horse was no thoroughbred like his; he could only have been holding the horse back to stay by her side. Still, the sense of flying sent the blood tingling through her veins as neck and neck, the horses sped through the cold winter air. Frost flew behind their hooves. Their breaths trailed clouds of mist. The trees blurred into a dark shadow alongside. She felt her mount hesitate and bent low over her horse's neck, urging her mount to greater speed. Beside her, she could hear Alan calling encouragement to his own horse. They burst out of the trees together and veered onto the road to the Manor.

Alan slowed his horse to a canter, and Gen followed suit. He grinned at her. "Well done. I concede the race."

"I don't accept what I don't fairly win," Gen replied. "You were holding back."

He raised an eyebrow. "I? Madame, Pentercast blood flows in these veins. We only play to win."

He realized his mistake too late. She could see his smile fading even as her own froze on her face. The best thing she could do was put her head up and ride, throwing her reply back over her shoulder as negligently as she would a dirty riding glove. "I would expect no less, sir. If you insist, I will call it a tie."

He spurred his mount enough to catch up with her, and put on his polite face once more as if nothing had changed. "A tie it is then. A shame we can't agree so easily on other matters."

She ignored the bait. "I still don't see my sister, or your brother. Do you think something could have befallen them?"

"Doubtful." He raised his voice to call for Geoffrey. Far ahead, a voice answered. "There, you see? We'll come across them in a few moments."

They continued on up the road, but it wasn't until they broke from the trees into the clearing around the Manor that she saw Allison and his brother, now moving around the back of the house. With a sigh, she followed Alan after them.

He managed to catch up to them near the herd of grazing cattle they had seen on Boxing Day. Skirting the herd, he steered them toward the outbuildings on the far side of the pasture near where the old creek, now a trickle that glittered with ice, had once disgorged onto the plain. For an hour, he proceeded to give them a tour of the various buildings and activities of the estate. Allison covered her mouth to hide a yawn several times, and Geoffrey actively fidgeted. Gen could understand their boredom. However, she had to admit she found the tour fascinating.

What Alan had created, she realized, was just what she had been envisioning when she had discussed with Carstairs moving the family to the Abbey. He had a excellent mix of pasture and tilled land, an orchard with apples and pears, and the beginnings of a vineyard. Besides the dairy cows, he had a respectable herd of sheep, a large flock of chickens, and over two dozen geese. He also had a score or more of people to help. She recognized some lads from the village threshing wheat in one of the barns. Tom Harvey was inspecting the cows in another. It wasn't until they reached the creamery, however, that she noticed the obvious deference to Alan.

As they entered the stone building, and her eyes adjusted to the darker interior, she spotted several women from the village hard at work before the churns. Spying Alan, they immediately rose. The paddles all settled into the cream with an audible thud. As one, the ladies dropped into deep curtseys, heads bowed.

"God bless you, Squire," one of them mumbled. She seemed to remember the woman's name was Jarvis, Mrs. Jarvis. Her husband had been a sailor who had never returned from Nelson's battle of Trafalgar. Her mother had said she was one of the needy. Apparently, thanks to Alan, she no longer had to rely on the occasional gifts of others. Alan smiled at them and went on explaining the process of separating the milk into butter and cream as if nothing untoward was happening. The women did not return to their work until he had left.

But the women were not the exception in their greeting, she soon realized. Everywhere Alan took them, men, women, and children greeted him with smiles and nods of welcome. To everyone he offered a kind word or answering smile. No one whispered after they passed, unless it was to nod toward herself or Allison. No one seemed the least displeased with the work being done. Everything was well run, well kept, and well organized. Despite herself, Gen was impressed.

When they finished the tour, one of Alan's grooms helped her to remount, and they rode through the old orchard back toward the wall, Allison and Geoffrey following.

"You've been quiet for some time, now, Miss Munroe," Alan murmured beside her. "I suppose I've bored you as well with all my farm talk."

"No, not in the slightest," Gen replied. "You have every reason to be proud of what you've accomplished at the Manor. I was thinking how much my own family could use such an estate."

"You have but to say the word," he murmured.

She managed to keep a smile on her face. "So you have said. I'm afraid you'll have to win your wager."

"I never intended anything less."

She tried to steer the conversation onto safer ground. "My father always wanted to see the place restored to its former glory. If only he could have seen this."

"He knew what I was trying to do," Alan reassured her. "He talked with me several times over the last few years on my trips to London. It was always an encouragement to me that he was willing to listen to my lofty plans."

"You talked with my father in London?" Gen frowned.

Alan reddened, but before she could question him further, there came a sharp crack behind them, and Allison drove her mount between them. Alan and Gen both managed to veer their horses aside to avoid a collision.

"I want to go home, and I want to go home now," Allison demanded, evidently oblivious to her actions. Her face was white, her eyes bright with anger or unshed tears.

Gen heaved a sigh. "What now?"

Alan reined his horse to a stop and Gen did likewise, forcing Allison to do the same. "I thought you and Geoffrey were getting along famously, Miss Munroe." He glanced back over his shoulder and shook his head. "Or perhaps not." Following his gaze, Gen saw that Geoffrey was galloping wildly away from them, in the direction of the village.

"Your brother is an arrogant, odious—" Allison began.

"That's quite enough, Allison," Gen interrupted with a quelling frown. "We understand your feelings on the matter. Squire, you'll have to excuse us. I think I should escort my sister home."

"I would be happy to escort you as well," Alan ventured, but Allison's lower lip was trembling, and Gen knew her sister wouldn't be able to keep from dissolving into tears much longer.

"That won't be necessary. We'll be on our own land, after all. We'll be home in moments. *Our* side of the estate isn't all that large." She gave him her best smile and saw him visibly relax. "Thank you for an interesting morning."

He turned his horse in a circle around them, and in doing so brought himself closer to Gen, lowering his voice for her ears alone. "You're quite welcome. I'll have some of my men bring by your gift for today."

"Gift?" she faltered.

"Six geese a-laying. I thought you might find them handier than shooting partridge out of pear trees."

"Gen, I am going home," Allison snapped, putting heels to her horse's flanks.

Flustered, Gen could only offer him a smile significantly less dazzling than her first and then urge her own horse to gallop after her sister's.

She forced Allison to a stop just before they reached the wall. "What on earth has gotten into you?" she demanded. "What happened?"

"I told you!" Allison wailed, tears falling. "Geoffrey Pentercast is the most toplofty, horrible, lecherous—"

"Lecherous?" Gen interrupted, her heart pounding alarmingly. "Allison, what did he do?"

"The blackguard tried to kiss me!"

Gen sagged with relief. "A kiss? Is that all?"

"Is that *all?* Isn't that enough?"

Gen shook her head. "My dear, you have been flirting rather outrageously. And you did let him lead you quite far ahead this morning. How did you expect him to act?"

"I expected him to behave like a gentleman," Allison sniffed, wiping her eyes with gloved fingers. "Now, if you're quite through ringing a peal over me, I should like to go home."

"Very well," Gen agreed, nudging her horse forward. "Perhaps this has served as a lesson for you. I don't think we need say anything to Mother."

Allison cast her a grateful look. "Thank you. I agree that the less said, the better."

Gen nodded, and they rode to a break in the wall, crossed to the Munroe side, and began the ride to the Abbey. She was congratulating herself on getting through the morning without involving her mother. Then it dawned on her.

However was she going to explain the six geese a-laying?

Nine

Interlude, Baritone Solo

"Can this family be counted on for nothing?" Alan demanded, striding into the Manor and tossing his riding gloves on the entryway table. Munson, their butler, crossed to retrieve them. "Where is my mother?"

"Mrs. Pentercast is in the library, Squire," Munson intoned. "Entertaining Vicar York."

Alan rolled his eyes. "It only wanted that. I'm going to change, Munson. Should the good vicar take it into his head to leave before I return, detain him. I want a word with him."

Even in his frustration he noticed the look of pleasure that quickly came and went in Munson's normally implacable gray eyes. That was one of the things he'd always admired about Munson, even as a child: distinguished gray hair, distinguished gray eyes, distinguished gray personality. Everyone who had ever remarked upon him, and they were few as Munson was as unobvious as a favorite piece of furniture, had said the same thing: "What a splendid butler." It was with an uncomfortable feeling of surprise that Alan heard him mumble with unbutlerish glee, "I'd be delighted, sir."

Could nothing go smoothly, he wondered as he changed from his riding gear to his usual dark wool trousers and coat. He couldn't seem to do anything right when it came to courting the incomparable Miss Munroe. He remembered just last spring, a scant two months before her father had met his untimely death, when he had ridden to town determined to stay the entire Season if that was what it took to win her. Her father had convinced him otherwise.

"Give her time," he had counseled. "We'll be home for Christmas this year, I promise. By then, she'll be heartily sick of this social whirl, if I know my Genny. You'll be the answer to her prayers. Trust me, my boy."

Like a fool, he had trusted the man, little knowing that fate was about to intervene. Once her father had been killed and the family was in mourning, he couldn't declare himself. It was only now, ironically during the Christmas Rutherford had promised him, that he could let her know his feelings at last. Then, just when he'd thought he was making headway, Geoffrey had to take it into his head to insult her sister! Not to mention his mother alienating her mother by taking up with the vicar of all people. That one at least he could nip in the bud. He had felt for some time that the gentleman was entirely too sycophantic. If this was another way for him to curry favor with the Pentercasts, he could jolly well stop now.

He was rather pleased to find the vicar awaiting him in the entryway when he descended sometime later: The gentleman was standing to one side of the mirror beside the door, making a show of not appreciating his profile displayed therein. Alan nodded to Munson, and motioned the vicar into the sitting room for a private conversation.

"Very good of you to see me like this, my boy, very good indeed," York began as a footman was closing the doors behind them.

Alan frowned. "I'm sorry, did you ask to see me?"

The vicar nodded, his double chins quivering. "Most assuredly, most assuredly. I believe it the shepherd's solemn duty to advise our sheep when one is about to fall by the wayside or run afoul of wolves, as the case were."

Alan tried to still his rising impatience. "Vicar York, I'm afraid I have no idea what you're talking about."

"Exactly my point, exactly my point," the older man sighed with a shake of his balding head. "I find the head of the family is usually the last to know in these kinds of cases, the very last."

"Has this anything to do with my mother?" Alan demanded.

"Good heavens, no! My dear boy, your mother is the very pattern card of virtuosity, the very pattern card. A finer lady is not to be found within a hundred miles, of that I am certain, quite certain. No, no, this concerns your brother, Geoffrey."

Although he knew nothing good could come of the conversation, Alan felt himself relax. "Oh? What about Geoffrey?"

Reverend York sighed, leaning back on the sofa on which he sat, folding his hands over his ample belly. Wide as they were, they almost hid the gap between his dark blue waistcoat and his darker blue trousers. "You've been preoccupied of late, Squire, quite preoccupied. Many have remarked on it. Courting, I believe?"

"I thought this was about Geoffrey," Alan murmured, his eyes narrowing. That usually was a sign to anyone around him to cease a particular topic of conversation, he knew from experience, but the vicar was not to be deterred.

"Geoffrey, most assuredly, did I not say so? It is your very preoccupation that has caused the difficulties, I'm certain, yes, I'm very certain. A man must put his own house in order before considering its expansion, if you take my meaning."

Alan rose. "Reverend York, I hope you don't take this amiss, but I don't understand a word you're saying. Without roundaboutation, if you please, what do you want from me?"

The vicar squinted up at him. "One mustn't be too precipitous, dear boy. Moderation in all things, I find, moderation. You might pass that lesson on to your brother as well."

"Out with it," Alan snapped.

The vicar started. "No need to be harsh, my boy, no need at all. I only go slowly to spare your sensibilities. But I cannot be silent when one of our own strays so far from the righteous path, so very far. It has come to my attention that your brother has been spending a great deal of time with a certain Tom Harvey, said person being known as somewhat less than a gentleman, I believe."

Alan shrugged. "Tom's been a bit on the wild side since we were children, but I don't believe there's any harm in him. Do you feel he's influencing Geoffrey?"

"I cannot say to that, my boy, I cannot say. I merely point it out as an example of the direction in which your brother seems to be heading. I further understand he's been frequenting the village tavern of late, following a rather predictable path home each night quite well to live, yes, quite well to live. Much as it pains me to have to tell you this, Squire, the last few nights, a variety of events has occurred along that path—fence posts uprooted, tree limbs broken down, barn doors let open for the animals to wander. My parishioners tell me these things, you see. It seems some think these events might be connected with your brother."

"That's ridiculous," Alan snorted. "Geoffrey's no vandal. Just because he's been spending time with Tom doesn't mean he'd do anything harmful. I know he's been spending time at the tavern. He's even come home a bit drunk once or twice. But I can't believe he'd damage anyone's property, even inebriated. Who told you these tales?"

The reverend heaved himself onto to his feet. "I am not at liberty to say. Sanctity of the cloth, you know, sanctity of the cloth. However, I thought perhaps you'd appreciate the warning.

Best look to your brother's well-being, my boy, and stay away from the likes of Genevieve Munroe."

Alan had been about to thank him, seeing as the reverend's thoughts had mirrored his own, but the last remark changed his thoughtful look to a glare, and York shrank under it. "Thank you for the warning, Reverend. And perhaps you'd take one from me. I understand you're courting my mother."

York paled. "Courting? Oh, no, no, my boy. You mistake me entirely, you surely mistake me. A charming woman, your mother, utterly charming. The most thoughtful, witty, sensitive woman in our county, haven't I said so repeatedly? A blessing to our fair village. A saintly—"

"Stow it," Alan snapped, his patience fled. "Just remember that the designation of your post resides with this estate. I think it would be a distinct conflict of interest should I become the son-in-law of the local vicar. Do I make myself clear?"

"Abundantly, oh quite abundantly," York assured him, nodding his head so vigorously that the hair on either side of his small ears flapped like the wings of a white dove. "Yes, certainly, I understand you completely. You needn't worry yourself on that score, no indeed you need not. Your mother is too fine a lady to ever consider someone as humble as myself. I would never encroach on her goodwill, which I hold in the highest esteem, as I do your own, Squire. I cannot imagine where you could have conceived such a notion as myself daring to even consider courting your mother. Why the very idea is laughable, entirely too laughable." To prove his point, he threw back his head and laughed.

"I am not laughing, Vicar," Alan pointed out when York finished, mopping his sweating brow with a lace handkerchief. "Thank you for sharing your concerns for Geoffrey, but I assure you they are unfounded. Now, good day, sir."

"Yes, good day, good day, Squire," the older man muttered, bowing himself toward the door. As Alan turned away, he caught a motion out of the corner of his eye and looked back to find the vicar eyeing him sadly.

"I do hope you'll heed my warning about that Munroe chit," he put in, easing one foot out the door. "They really can be the most disagreeable family, as I know you all realize from long standing. I hear she was quite the rage in London, quite the rage. No doubt she finds Wenwood a bit quiet for her tastes and can't wait to return. As soon as Christmas is over."

"I think you'll find, Vicar," Alan said quietly, "an entirely different outcome at the end of the twelve days of Christmas."

"We shall see, my boy, we shall see," he nodded, pushing his bulk through the door at last. "The acorn does not fall far from the tree, and I'm afraid Miss Genevieve is more comfortable in the forests of London."

Alan shook his head and the door closed behind the Vicar York. He could only hope the man was wrong, about his interest in Alan's mother, about Geoffrey's behavior, and about Genevieve most of all.

Ten

New Year's Eve, Verse Seven,
Seven Swans a-Swimming

"Geoffrey Pentercast is the world's greatest lout," Allison declared in the music room doorway.

Gen looked up from her place at the spinet, where she had been trying in vain to lose herself in a sprightly minuet. "And you claim *I* continue to harp on the same chord? I thought we exhausted that topic yesterday."

Allison flounced over to the window seat and threw herself down in a huff, only to leap to her feet with a squeal. She snatched Gen's embroidery out from under her and scowled at her sister. Gen offered a contrite smile.

"That topic cannot be exhausted," Allison told her, sitting more gingerly, "because he continually finds new ways to insult me."

"What has he done now?" Gen sighed, closing the lid over the keys in resignation to her fate.

"I was attempting to convince Reverend Wellfordhouse that he must come visit us tonight right after midnight—"

"After midnight?" Gen interrupted with a frown. "Whatever for?"

"New Year's, silly," Allison scolded with a shake of her flaxen curls. "We shall have good luck if the first person to set foot through our front door is a fair-complexioned gentleman, and William certainly fits that bill, unlike some others I could name."

Alan's dark head came to mind, and Gen forced it away. "I suppose he does. What does that have to do with Geoffrey?"

"I was getting to that, if you please. There I was, to the point of convincing William that he must be our salvation, when who should walk into the conversation as bold as brass but Mr. Geoffrey Pentercast. Oh, the absolute gall of the man! He teased me that he will show up instead of William, and that will ruin everything!"

Gen raised an eyebrow. "As if we would open the door after midnight anyway."

Allison clapped her hands with glee. "That's it! We just won't let him in. That will keep him from being our first footer." She jumped to her feet. "I will tell Chimes this very minute."

"Tell Chimes what?" their man of all work asked, appearing in the doorway with an armload of firewood for the rack. He hustled it into place by the little stone fireplace and stood back to dust off his hands. It did little good from what Gen could see—his entire uniform was coated with dust and grime.

"You'd better not let Mother see you," she hissed to him in warning as he paused beside her. He shrugged, offering her a wink, then focused on Allison. "Go on, Miss Allison, what was it you wanted to tell me?"

"You are not to let Geoffrey Pentercast into this house after midnight tonight," Allison announced grandly, head high. "I will brook no resistance on this issue, Chimes. Do I make myself clear?" When he merely eyed her with a frown, she dropped her pose and wrung her hands. "Please?"

He grinned. "Now, don't you worry, miss. I know we need a blond head in that door first off. Neither Mr. Geoffrey nor the Squire get through that door after midnight."

Gen nudged him with her foot. "I don't suppose you could begin that tradition a little early?"

Chimes turned his gap-toothed grin on her instead. "Now, don't you get started on that again. I thought you liked your goose eggs this morning."

"They were delightful," Gen agreed with a sigh, "especially the way Mrs. Chimes prepares them. However, I would just as soon not have to think about any more gifts from the Squire."

"Oh, I can arrange that, miss," Chimes assured her. She looked up with a cocked head, wondering at his sudden capitulation. He winked at her. "All you have to do is give up."

"Never," Gen swore, straightening her shoulders

"Give up what?" Allison put in, her blue eyes round with wonder.

"Nothing you need worry about," Chimes assured her, hustling back to the door. "Just remember that you come by your stubbornness honestly in this family." With a humph for good measure, he disappeared down the corridor.

"Has this something to do with that wager you don't want to talk about?" Allison persisted.

Gen snapped open the lid of the spinet. "Here, you probably want to practice. I promised Mother I'd help her make some salve for Mrs. Gurney." She fled the room before Allison could protest.

Once safely in her room, she wandered to the window that overlooked the back garden, pressing her forehead against the cold glass. New Year's Eve—she had almost forgotten that until Allison had reminded her. The twelve days of Christmas were half over. Six more days until she had to tell her mother and sister the truth about their situation. Worse, six more days and six more gifts until she was trapped into marrying Alan Pentercast. Despite her best efforts, her mood of despair threatened to return. She fought it back.

She couldn't let him win. There had to be some way to stop

him! What was today—seven swans a-swimming? Were there swans in England this time of year? She glanced again to the ponds at the back of the garden, her blood turning cold as she remembered the flock of swans she had seen from the hilltop days before. She shook off the chill. Alan could scarcely claim her own swans as a gift. He had to have something else in mind, but what?

He had been inventive so far, she'd give him that. She felt herself smile as she remembered the bonnet. French hens, colly-bird bonnets, what next, a swan's-down comforter? There didn't seem to be anything she could do but wait.

And wait she did, throughout the quiet afternoon and quieter evening. She took dinner with her mother and sister in the can-dlelit dining room and sat afterward before the fire in the with-drawing room, her mother embroidering, Allison reading aloud from Shakespeare. Watching her mother's calm stitching and listening to her sister's gentle voice, Gen knew she was the only one who was at all tense. The day was almost over, and Alan had not arrived with his gift. All she had to do was wait until the last stroke of midnight, now a little over two hours away, and she would be free of the cursed wager. She couldn't under-stand why the thought only made her more depressed.

They had agreed to stay up until midnight to see the new year in together, but by ten Gen was nodding, and by eleven even her well-bred mother was stifling a yawn. Allison, how-ever, urged them to stay awake. Gen knew she was still hoping William would heed her request and show up a few minutes after midnight. As for herself, she kept expecting a knock at the door, a knock that would spell the end of her waiting.

It was still only a few minutes after eleven when there came a fierce pounding on the front door, echoing down the long corridors of the Abbey, making her mother startle in her seat and Allison leap to her feet. Gen swallowed, rising to her feet despite herself.

"Chimes! Don't let him in!" Allison cried, dropping the book onto the floor as she dashed out into the corridor.

"Allison Ermintrude Munroe," her mother warned, also rising. "Moderate your tone."

"Yes, Mother," Allison nodded, already in the corridor, straining to race to the front door where the pounding had only intensified. "But you see—"

"I see only that you are behaving in a completely unladylike manner," her mother sniffed.

Gen's nerves snapped. "Chimes! Can't you stop that commotion?"

Her mother turned a frown on her. "Genevieve! Has everyone gone mad this evening?"

The pounding continued, with a voice behind it now, muffled, but urgent. Gen couldn't stand it.

"I'll go, Mother." She stepped out past her agitated sister, forcing herself to think about someone else's worries instead of her own. "Don't be concerned, Allison, it isn't even midnight yet."

Allison relaxed. "Oh, that's right."

"Allison, I think you had better explain yourself," their mother prompted, crossing her arms over her chest. Leaving her sister to her fate, Gen hurried down the corridor.

She reached the entry just as Chimes appeared from the back of the house. She stood aside as he approached the arched doors, which trembled under the furious pounding.

"Easy, now!" Chimes shouted through the wood. "I'm coming!" He fumbled with the lock as the pounding subsided, then swung open the heavy doors. Gen braced herself for she knew not what. To her surprise, Geoffrey Pentercast spilled into the room, eyes wild, greatcoat askew. His boots dripped water across the parquet floor. She recoiled, thinking him drunk, but as he glanced about and met her eyes, she saw he was more scared than anything else.

"The dam's broke!" he cried as Chimes scowled at him. "The water's pouring down the old channel. Do what you can, then for God's sake follow me to the Manor!" Turning, he dashed back out the door.

Chimes turned to Gen, shaking his head. "Bit early to be so drunk, if you ask me. Young men these days . . ."

Gen frowned. "I don't think he was all that drunk, Chimes. Get one of the groomsmen to investigate, would you?"

Chimes scratched his balding head. "Well, now, miss, I went and gave them the night off. It being New Year's and all."

Gen could feel the urgency left in the room from Geoffrey's plea. "Then you'll just have to go check yourself."

Chimes heaved a martyred sigh, moving toward the back of the house with an exaggerated limp. "And me with the lumbago that comes with the cold. Serves me right for opening the door, I suppose."

From the nether regions of the house came a cry of alarm. Chimes' limp disappeared as he hastened toward the sound. Gen raised her skirts to dash after him, her heart pounding.

Mrs. Chimes was standing by the kitchen door, wringing her hands. Water pooled at her feet. At first Gen thought she must have dropped the tea kettle that lay in the puddle, then she saw that water was seeping in under the door.

"By God, he must have been right," Chimes cried, pulling his wife away from the widening pool.

Gen grabbed some of the cleaning rags off the table and threw them into the water. "Here, Mrs. Chimes, stuff these in the gap. Chimes, help me with this table. If we wedge it up against the door so, we narrow the gap and help keep the water out." She strained to lift her end of the oak table, in the end satisfied to scrape it across the flagstone floor until it caught under the door latch.

Chimes backed away from their handiwork, wiping sweat from his upper lip with the back of his hand. "That will do it, miss. Best you go see to your mum and sister. I'll check the door by the chapel."

Gen nodded, dusting off her hands. "I can't think of any place else it might get in. The Abbey's somewhat on high ground, and the stables and other outbuildings are even higher. I suppose most of it will head toward the Manor." She started toward the corridor and froze. The Manor. Alan. She spun back and nearly collided with Chimes.

"Easy, miss," he cautioned, catching her arm to steady her. "We'll be fine, you'll see."

"It's not the Abbey I'm worrying about," Gen cried. "Go check the chapel door and meet me in the entry. I'm going to the Manor."

Chimes raised an eyebrow, but did as she bid without a word. She left Mrs. Chimes muttering about the mud on her kitchen floor and hurried to change into her hunting outfit.

She met her mother as she was returning to the entry. "There you are. What is going on?"

"The dam that held back the pond apparently burst," Gen told her, bending to tighten the laces of her half boots. "We have some flooding in the kitchen, but Mrs. Chimes is taking care of it, and Chimes is checking the chapel. I'm going to see if I can help the Pentercasts."

Even as she said the words, she knew she sounded belligerent. To her surprise, her mother nodded. "The water will run down the old channel, straight for the Manor. I imagine it could get rather high. They'll need all hands like the year the River Went flooded its banks and your father and I helped fill sandbags. I'll get my cloak."

Gen caught her arm. "There isn't time for the carriage, Mother, and the groomsmen are out. I'm going through the woods."

This time her mother did protest. "Nonsense. You can't go on foot, alone. It isn't proper!"

"I don't think propriety has much to do with a flood, Mother. Isn't it far more improper to ignore a neighbor in need, especially when we might be the cause of the problem?" She remembered the way the swan had startled at the dam the other day and cursed herself for not having had Chimes check the aging structure then.

Her mother frowned. "Our fault? How so?"

"There isn't time to explain now. I must go if I'm to be of any help with those sandbags."

Her mother shook her head in obvious capitulation. "Very well, but take Chimes with you. Allison and Mrs. Chimes and I will manage."

Gen gave her a quick hug, and her mother patted her awkwardly on the back. Then Gen hurried to find a lantern.

A few moments later, Chimes was leading the way through the dark woods, following the trail that led between the Abbey and the Manor. At some point in the evening, it had begun to rain, and drops continued to pelt them as they paused long enough to peer behind the house and confirm that the pond was indeed in turmoil, the water tumbling through the gardens and sweeping down through the woods. They stayed to the higher path, well above the waters, moving as quickly as they could through the dark and the rainstorm. Animals fled from their path, upset by the change in the woods.

"This will only make it worse," Chimes shouted as Gen pulled her hood closer about her face. The path beneath them grew slick. Gen slipped once, and Chimes caught her. When he went down a moment later, the best she could do was catch the lantern before it was dropped.

Chimes struggled back to his feet. "Crazy fool idea! What can an old man and a girl do against a God Almighty flood anyway!"

Gen held the lantern higher, checking to make sure he was unhurt. "We can be two more hands, Mr. Chimes. It doesn't take all that much strength to fill sandbags, or so I would imagine."

"Humph," Chimes muttered, snatching the lantern from her grip. He turned and stumped off toward the Manor.

Moments later they broke from the woods near the side of the Manor to find that the tide had arrived before them. The house was bright with candlelight inside, and outside people were scurrying about with lanterns trying to salvage what they could. By the light, she could see that water was foaming a foot deep around the outbuildings. Someone had opened the barn and let the animals free; the dairy cows were milling about in a pasture that was already well underwater. At least one of the trees was down in the old orchard. She urged Chimes forward toward the house.

Someone caught her arm as she reached the front steps, and she turned to find Tom Harvey from the village beside her. "Come around back," he told them. "We're filling the bags there."

She and Chimes followed him to the back of the house. Gen was stopped by the sight before her. The water had returned to the old ornamental pond behind the house, but the amount of water was so much greater, having been held in the enlarged pond behind the Abbey for so long, that it was already lapping at the steps to the terrace of the Manor. Several of the villagers had attempted to block its course with a wall of bags and rubble, but water was seeping through and pooling even higher. Tom led them up the side steps and across the terrace to where several more people were watching the approaching tide. Her heart quailed when she recognized the tallest as Alan.

"Is there nothing more that can be done?" she asked Tom Harvey. He shook his head, sending rivulets of water down his coat. "All we can do is wait. It's nearly spent now. If this rain will just let up, we might yet make it."

Gen surveyed the devastation below. "How could this have happened?"

"That's what I'd like to know," Alan said, beside her.

Gen glanced up, feeling guilty. "The dam broke—that's what Geoffrey told us."

"That's what I told you," Geoffrey agreed, appearing at his brother's side. "But it was no accident. It had been hacked clean through."

"What do you mean?" Gen demanded. "Someone did this on purpose?"

"No time for that now," Alan replied. "Looks like the rain's stopping. Let's just hope this subsides."

Gen turned back to the water below. The rain was indeed stopping, slowing until all that could be heard was the trickle of it draining off the Manor roof. In the distance, the church bells began chiming midnight. The clouds moved aside, and the moon came out, spilling light across what had been the Manor pasture, now a sheet of water several feet deep. Dark shapes glided across the moon to settle on the waters. Gen frowned, trying to make them out. Alan gave a bark of laughter.

"And I thought I'd failed. It seems luck is still with me, Miss Munroe. There are your seven swans a-swimming."

Eleven

Verse Eight, Eight Maids a-Milking

Gen stared at him as if he'd lost his mind. "What . . . what did you say?"

Alan waved a hand at the flooded pasture. "I always try to look on the bright side, Miss Munroe. I have to admit, this event is something of a challenge in that regard. However, it did bring me seven of your swans, and they do appear to be swimming."

Beside them, Tom Harvey guffawed. "Right you are, Squire. And just as the seventh day of Christmas is ending."

"Well, I for one don't see the humor in it," Geoffrey muttered. "This is one hell of a mess, if you ask me. I hope your people are up to fixing it, Miss Munroe."

"My people?" Gen gasped, turning on him.

"Yes of course, your people," Geoffrey snapped. "Who else caused this, I'd like to know?"

"Cut line, Geoff," Alan warned. "I know you think you saw the dam cut through, but it was dark. We don't know what happened."

"Whatever happened, you may be assured my family had nothing to do with it," Gen informed him heatedly.

"Of course not." Geoffrey sneered. "Quite innocent are all the young Misses Munroe, aren't they?"

"How dare you!" Gen began, feeling herself begin to tremble.

Alan cut in. "That's enough, Geoffrey. I suggest we spend our energies in trying to find a way out of this mess. Tom, I'm thankful you and the lads took me up on that offer to celebrate the New Year here, even if Geoffrey didn't think to join you. We'd have been lost without your help."

Tom, a large young man with thin sandy hair, shrugged. "The inn was likely a lot more boring than this. Looks like it's as high as it's going to get tonight. What else can we do for you?"

What could they do, indeed? Gen wondered as she gazed out over the new lake while Tom, Geoffrey, and Alan conferred for a moment. From what she could see in the obliging moonlight, Alan's pastureland was flooded, and his spring wheat crop was destroyed. At least some of the outbuildings had to have been damaged. She couldn't imagine how the water had been released, unless the dam had simply been too old to hold the weight behind it. If so, it was her own negligence that had caused this mess. She would have to see how she could help put it back to rights.

Beside her, Tom Harvey touched his forelock and strolled down the side of the terrace. Alan turned to her and she straightened, ready to hear how she might help.

"I'm afraid I'm not up to company just now, Miss Munroe. I take it you and your man can find your way home?"

His gruffness annoyed her, even though she knew he had good reason. "I hardly expect you to entertain me, Squire. I had been hoping Chimes and I might be of service."

"I appreciate the thought, but I don't know how you could help right now. I promise you we'll talk in the morning. You'll understand that I cannot escort you home."

Why was he so set on formalities when his entire farm was under water? "We'll be fine," she snapped. Then, to soften her words, she added, "I hope you know I was speaking the truth a moment ago. Despite our differences, we Munroes would never intentionally cause you Pentercasts harm."

"No, of course not," he replied, but without his usual warmth. "Now, if you'll excuse me."

Gen frowned as he brushed past her. "Is there nothing we can do to help?"

He stopped, turning to eye her. "Nothing, Miss Munroe. Just go home."

Snubbed, she yanked her hood back over her damp curls and stamped past Chimes toward the steps from the terrace. With a sigh, he turned to follow her.

This was what she deserved for trying to help a Pentercast, she supposed as she trudged back around the house. The proverb of casting pearls before swine came to mind. It was somehow satisfying. As they reached the front of the Manor, however, a call pulled her up short. Turning, she saw Alan hurrying after them. Her head came up, and she allowed herself a smile. About time the man came to his senses. He'd need every hand he could find to set things to rights. She promised herself she wouldn't even make him ask her forgiveness.

"Where do you think you're going?" he demanded.

Startled, she frowned. "Home. At your command, *Squire.*"

He threw up his hands. "I thought you had a carriage. I can't let you walk through the dark woods like this."

"How do you think we got here?" Gen demanded, hands on her hips, all thoughts of forgiveness gone. "I'm perfectly capable of taking care of myself, Mr. Pentercast. Now, if *you'll* excuse *me.*"

Alan caught her arm. "I'll do nothing of the sort. I don't have time to deal with this. You'll stay at the Manor tonight, and I'll see you home in the morning."

"Thank you for such a lovely invitation," Gen sneered, "but I'd rather eat mud. Come along, Chimes."

Chimes cleared his throat. "Might be a good idea, Miss Gen.

Moon's clear now, but them rain clouds could be back any minute. And it's getting colder too. Even in your fancy huntin' togs, you'll be catchin' the influenza for sure. You stay here with the Pentercasts, and I'll tell your mum to come get you in the morning."

Gen glared at him. "I've had enough of your interference, Chimes. Give me that lantern. I'll light the way myself."

"Of all the stubborn, willful," Alan muttered. Before she could open her mouth to protest, he swung her up in his arms. "All my life I've heard stories about how spoiled the Munroe women are, and now I've finally seen it for myself. Tell her mother I'll bring her home tomorrow, Chimes. Take care of yourself."

"Put me down this instant!" Gen demanded, kicking with both feet.

Alan grunted as she hit his hip. "If I do, you'll get your wish about eating mud."

"Right you are, Squire," Chimes chortled, backing away. "Good night, Miss Gen."

"Traitor!" Gen shrieked after him.

Alan hefted her higher on his chest, bringing her face on a level with his own, and she snapped her mouth shut. His brown eyes glared at her, his brows a dark thatch gathered in a scowl. A muscle worked in his lean jaw, which was peppered with stubble. It dawned on her that this was the first time she'd ever seen him angry. She licked her lips.

"If I apologize," she tried, "will you put me down?"

His frown eased. "No. Now lay still and be quiet."

He made it sound as if it were difficult holding her like this. From the strength of those arms she sincerely doubted it. She swung one booted foot experimentally. His frown returned. She stopped. "You needn't glare so. I really can take care of myself. Though it was thoughtful of you to be concerned."

The frown deepened. "Are you trying to turn me up sweet?"

She couldn't resist grinning at him. "Is it working?"

"No."

He started across the lawn at such a fast clip that Gen bit back a squeal of surprise. Her grip on his neck tightened as he took the steps to the Manor two at a time. He bumped open the door with his broad shoulder and swung her down to deposit her unceremoniously on the marble floor. She tried to catch her balance, but her wet feet slipped out from under her and she landed with a thud on her backside in a pile of sodden skirt. She glared up at him.

Alan sighed, offering her his hand. "I really can't afford this, Miss Munroe. I have cows to see to."

"Cows?" she fairly shouted, clambering to her feet alone. "Cows! First you tell me I'm too dim-witted to find my way home in the dark, then you carry me here as if I'm too frail to walk, and now you can't be bothered to find me a room! You may have grown up hearing about the spoiled Munroe women, sir, but the stories can't possibly compare to those I've heard about the arrogance of the Pentercast men! And you, I'm quite certain, are the prize of the lot!"

"Mother!" he shouted, the angry word echoing up to the high ceilings. "We have a guest." Lowering his voice, he offered her an ironic bow. "Good night, Miss Munroe. Always a pleasure." He turned on his heel and strode back out the door, leaving Gen wanting to throw something after him.

She had barely had a chance to calm herself before Mrs. Pentercast appeared, puffing, from the back of the house. "Alan? What's this about a guest? Oh, hello, Genevieve. Whatever are you doing here?"

Gen sighed. "I came to help with the flood, Mrs. Pentercast. But Alan doesn't seem to think I'll be of much use."

"Silly man," Mrs. Pentercast tisked, linking an arm in hers. "You look done in, child. Do you truly want to help, or would you like to just lie down?"

Gen found it impossible not to smile down at the little woman beside her. Mrs. Pentercast's round face was puckered with kindness, her tiny brown eyes warm. All fifty-some inches of her trembled with motherly concern. In every way, she was a direct contrast to the mother Gen had grown up knowing. "I really would like to help," Gen told her.

She nodded. "Good girl. Let's get you into dry clothes first, then we'll put you to work. Come this way." Keeping one arm linked with Gen's, she led her up the sweeping stair, chatting all the way. "You know, I always wanted daughters. They're so much easier to talk to than sons. And so much more helpful. Although, mind you, Alan can be a dear when he chooses. But girls, now, you can pamper and fuss over. And they'll be by you in a time of crisis. Yes, I always wanted girls. Your mother beat me there as well, I suppose."

Gen frowned, allowing herself to be led down a carpeted corridor past portraits of Pentercasts to a small bedroom in the corner of the Manor. There, Mrs. Pentercast pulled some clothes from a wardrobe and held them up to Gen.

"I was never as wonderfully thin as you are, my dear," she sighed, tossing several dresses onto the canopied bed behind her. "Although, like you, my figure was all the more noticeable because I was so short. Here, this ought to do." She held up an old-fashioned long-waisted gown of cobalt blue wool. With its long sleeves and high neck, it looked warm and cozy to Gen. She shivered as she reached for it, and Mrs. Pentercast clucked.

"You slip into this, and we'll get some hot tea into you. You'll feel much more the thing, you see if you don't. I'm sorry I can't send you one of the servants, but they're all a bit busy just now. I'll be right back with a towel for your hair." She bustled out of the room.

By the time she returned, Gen had stripped off the sodden hunting dress and pulled the cobalt gown over her head. Mrs. Pentercast helped her fasten the many tiny buttons up the back, nodding approval as she tugged it into place. It fit well enough although it was a little short for Gen; her wet half boots showed to their tops. Mrs. Pentercast insisted that she slip them off as well, bringing her a pair of leather slippers that were a bit big, but with an extra pair of wool stockings that felt good against her cold skin, they did well enough. Then Mrs. Pentercast led her down to the kitchen of the great house, where a team of servants was busy preparing some kind of meal.

"Soup and hot tea," Mrs. Pentercast explained as she caught Gen's look of surprise. "The men will be needing it, poor dears. Martha, is there something Miss Genevieve can do to assist?"

Martha Martin, the Pentercast housekeeper, offered Gen a smile from where she stirred a huge pot hanging over the blazing fire in the old-fashioned fireplace. "The loaves are just coming from the oven, mum. Perhaps the young lady could slice them?"

Mrs. Pentercast indicated an oak table not unlike the one in the Abbey kitchen, and Gen sat at it, sawing the serrated knife through the steaming loaves of oat bread set before her by one of the many maids. Her stomach rumbled at the savory smell. The maid grinned at her. Embarrassed, she quickened her efforts.

Some time later, she stood looking out the kitchen window, watching as Mrs. Pentercast and several of the maids made their way among the working men to hand out the bread, hot soup, and tea she had helped prepare. Over their torches, the far horizon looked a little lighter, and she realized dawn would be breaking soon. She yawned, leaning against the window frame. Beside her, the kitchen door swung open, and Alan thumped in to warm himself by the fire.

He hadn't even noticed her standing there, and she made no move to make him aware, preferring to watch him in silence. His dark hair was plastered to his head from the rain and his own exertions. His broad shoulders sagged with weariness as he slumped on the bench, stretching his long legs out to the warmth. A drop of water, shining in the firelight, slid down his nose, and he wiped it away with the back of his hand. Then he frowned as if feeling he was being watched and turned to her. Gen managed a smile.

He laughed, rising. "I knew I was tired, but not that tired. She's not yours yet, my lad. Save the dreams for your sleep." He stumbled back out the door before she could tell him he wasn't dreaming.

Dawn had broken before she found herself lying in the canopied bed in the corner room of the Manor. She awoke much later that morning to find her hunting dress freshly laundered and ironed and hanging in the wardrobe, along with her half boots, polished and with new laces. She felt guilty that the servants had gone to such trouble; they had surely been up as late as she had. Donning the clothing and boots and using the hairbrush she found on the dressing table to put her curls in some semblance of order, she then descended to the first floor. The footman there politely directed her to the breakfast room, where she found Mrs. Pentercast in a frothy white lace morning robe.

"Ah, Genevieve, up so early? I thought you'd sleep until noon after being up so late in the kitchen."

"What's this about the kitchen?" Alan grumbled behind her, and she hurried into the room to get out of his way. His hair was disheveled as always, but clean now shining in the light from the winter sun through the two multipaned windows. He wore rough wool trousers and a jacket, clearly ready for more work outside. She went to stand behind Mrs. Pentercast, gripping the top of her high-backed chair, suddenly unsure how to respond to him. Mrs. Pentercast rescued her.

"Sit beside me, Genevieve dear, and let me pour you some tea. Good morning, Alan. You look tired, my dear. I thought Gen's little meal should have helped last night."

"It wasn't my meal, Mrs. Pentercast," Gen heard herself say, taking the seat offered her. She accepted the tea from her hostess' hand and took a sip to steady herself.

"Well, perhaps not entirely," Mrs. Pentercast allowed. "But you were a marvelous help. Girls often are, you know, Alan."

"So I've been told," Alan quipped, going to sit on the other side of his mother. She obligingly poured him a cup as well. "I see you're dressed for traveling, Miss Munroe. I'll have the carriage brought around straight away to take you home."

Gen gathered her courage and met his eye. "That won't be necessary, Squire. The day seems to be bright. I can walk home."

"Let's not start that again," Alan growled.

"Walk home?" Mrs. Pentercast interrupted. "Oh, my dear, I don't think you'll want to. It turned quite cold last night. We'll finally have some winter snow if I'm not mistaken. Even the carriage is likely to be chilly. Make sure they put in the lap robes, Alan, and warm bricks at her feet."

"Nothing but the best for Miss Munroe." Alan almost sneered.

Stung, Gen looked away. His mother frowned.

"Alan, I cannot like your manner this morning. I know you're tired, but it isn't like you to be so gruff with a guest. Perhaps I should ask Geoffrey to see her home."

"Geoffrey is nowhere to be found this morning, I'm afraid," Alan replied, sipping his tea as if nothing were amiss. "I suspect he's investigating that broken dam."

"I hope he took someone from the Abbey with him," Gen snapped. "It *is* our property, after all."

"I'm well aware of that, Miss Munroe."

"What is that supposed to mean?" Gen demanded, setting down her cup with a clatter. "You suspect us of causing this mess, don't you?"

Mrs. Pentercast tittered. "Of course not, dear. Alan wouldn't be so silly. Imagine girls hacking through a dam."

"I have no difficulty imagining a certain young lady doing so," Alan replied, rising. "She has too much at stake, and I don't think she much relishes losing."

"Not as much as you relish winning," Gen countered, rising as well. He still towered over her.

"Oh, so now I'm the one who broke the dam and flooded my own farm, is that what you're saying?"

"You needed seven swans a-swimming," Gen sniffed, head high. "You said so yourself."

"If you really think I'd risk losing everything I've worked for to win a stupid wager, you value yourself much too highly, Miss Munroe," he sneered, tossing down his napkin. "Walk home if it pleases you. Good day."

"Alan!" his mother protested as he stalked from the room. Gen blinked back hot tears. "Genevieve, what is he talking about? What wager?"

Gen swallowed, holding onto the back of her chair with unsteady hands. "It doesn't matter, Mrs. Pentercast. I don't think your son wants to honor it any longer. Thank you for your kindness. I think I'd best be going now."

Mrs. Pentercast scrambled to her feet. "Nonsense! I'll have the carriage brought around myself. I won't have you walking home in this cold. Munson!"

Somehow, Gen managed to hold back the tears as the carriage was brought around. Mrs. Pentercast ushered her into it, and one of the Pentercast grooms drove her down the long road to the Abbey. She managed to hold them back while she was greeted by her mother and sister, then toured the Abbey with Chimes to make sure everything had survived the adventures of the night. She even managed to hold them back when he took her to see that the dam had indeed been hacked clean through. They found the ax still lodged in the remaining pieces. She didn't let the tears fall until she was safely ensconced in her own room that afternoon. Then she sobbed until her pillow was soaked.

It was because she was so tired, she convinced herself. She ought to be delighted that she had finally dissuaded Alan from continuing with his wretched wager. If he gave up, that meant she had won. The harvest tithes would be her family's for generations. They were saved, and she was no longer being forced into a loveless marriage. Then why was she so unaccountably depressed?

It was late in the day when Chimes tapped at her door, telling her she had a visitor. Her heart leapt, and she hurried to answer his knock.

"The Squire is at the front door to see you, miss," he bowed, and she frowned at his formality. "He has, um, something for you."

She wasn't sure whether to be depressed or glad. "You mean he isn't giving up?"

Chimes squirmed. "Well, miss, perhaps you ought to see it for yourself."

Frowning, Gen followed him to the entry of the Abbey. It stood empty. She turned her frown on Chimes. "Well?"

Chimes cleared his throat. "Outside, miss."

Shaking her head, Gen went to open the front door. And stared.

The small clearing in front of the Abbey was thronged with dairy cows. They bumped and shoved against each other, lowing pathetically. They scraped against the trees, shaking the slender branches; they trampled the brittle winter grass. She spotted one of the yellow winter pansies Mrs. Chimes had planted in the window boxes disappearing into a mobile mouth. She couldn't have stepped past the porch had she wanted to.

"What on earth is this?" she demanded of Chimes, who had come up beside her.

"This, Miss Munroe," Alan's voice rang out from the far side of the clearing, "is a herd of dairy cattle. A very small herd I might add. My other neighbors were kind enough to take most of my animals into their barns until my barns dry out, but I have nowhere to put these beasts. As my mother assures me you have the greatest desire to be of assistance, I'm leaving them with you."

"This is ridiculous!" Gen cried, standing on tiptoe to catch a glimpse of him. "What am I supposed to do with a herd of cattle! I don't even have a barn!"

"I don't care where you put them," Alan called. "They'll most likely survive a night or two in the clearing, as long as you keep them nicely packed together. I'll retrieve them in a day or so, as soon as the water subsides."

"You can't do this!" Gen shouted at him. But she knew it was in vain. She couldn't stop him from doing it. She couldn't even get out her own door! She threw up her hands, turning back to Chimes. "Gift, eh? Chimes, so help me, if I thought you were in on this . . ."

Chimes held up his hands in surrender. "I'm innocent, Miss Gen, I swear!"

She shook her head, gazing back at the lowing animals. "What are we to do with them?"

"Genevieve?" her mother called from inside the Abbey. "Chimes? I'm hearing the oddest noise."

Gen turned back to the entryway as her mother and sister appeared from one of the wings. "Good afternoon, Mother." She motioned to Chimes to shut the door. Unfortunately, one of the cows chose that moment to poke its head in. Her mother froze, and Allison gasped.

"Is that a cow?" her sister asked, moving cautiously toward the door.

Gen exchanged glances with Chimes and saw in his black eyes that she had no chance at bluffing. "Yes," she sighed. "I'm afraid so. And there are about thirty more like her in the front yard."

Her mother frowned. "How can that be?"

"It's a grand gesture," Chimes nodded, shoving at the cow in vain to get it back into the yard so he could shut the door. "Miss Gen offered to keep them for the Squire until his barns drained."

"Very thoughtful of you, Genevieve, I'm sure," her mother allowed, watching his struggles from the safety of the far side of the entryway. "However, I don't see how we can do so. What shall we do with them?"

"Hello the Abbey!" a voice called from the far side of the clearing. The cow, startled, pulled back its head, and Chimes made to snap the door triumphantly closed. Gen put out a hand to stop him.

"William?" she called back.

The curate's sandy head appeared over the backs of the cattle. "Yes. I heard about the flood and came to see how you were faring. I seem to have come at a bad time."

"Go around back," Gen called to him, motioning him around the side of the herd. "Chimes will let you in the kitchen."

She saw him wave and move off. She nodded to Chimes, who sighed with relief as he swung the door shut at last.

"Chimes," her mother intoned as Gen sagged with relief as well, "please send the Reverend Wellfordhouse to the withdraw-ing room when you retrieve him. Genevieve, I think we must talk."

With a heavy heart, Gen fell into step behind her mother and Allison.

In the withdrawing room, her mother motioned her to a chair opposite the fire, taking up her usual seat in the Sheraton chair. Allison curled up on the chaise.

"Now, my dear, please explain to me about these cows."

Gen managed a smile, her mind whirling as she sought to

think up a plausible tale. "Well, you see, Mother," she hedged, "as Chimes said, the Pentercasts were nearly flooded out last night, and since the dam was on our property, I thought it was only polite to offer to help."

"Help, certainly," her mother nodded. "But cows? What are we to do with them? We have no pasture, no place to house them. And we certainly have no food put up for them to eat."

"I'm afraid it's worse than that, Mrs. Munroe," William said in the doorway. "Pardon my intrusion, but I take it you've only recently been told you have a herd of dairy cows in your front yard."

"Quite recently," her mother sniffed.

"If you have any ideas on what to do with them," Gen told him, "we'd be delighted to listen."

William wrung his hands, offering her a wan smile. "I would be delighted to be of assistance as to the care and feeding of dairy cattle, Miss Genevieve. However, from my vantage point across the clearing, I believe you have a more immediate problem than housing or feeding them."

Gen frowned. "Oh? What would that be?"

"They seem to be, er, that is," William was turning several shades of red, but for the life of her she couldn't imagine what was discomposing him so. "Dash it all, they look like they need to be milked."

"Milked!" her mother and sister cried out with her.

William winced. "Yes, by your leave, just so. I don't suppose any of you have any experience with this kind of thing?"

"None whatsoever," her mother assured him, turning on her oldest daughter. "Genevieve, this really is going too far. We simply must tell the Squire we cannot keep them for him."

William cleared his throat. "Begging your pardon, Mrs. Munroe, but they'll never make it back to the Manor, even through the woods. I have had some little experience in these matters, having been raised on a farm until I was ten. I'd be happy to be of assistance. But you need to milk them soon, within the hour if I'm any judge."

"Surely they can be told to wait," her mother protested.

William shook his head. "I'm afraid not. If they are forced to remain unmilked, the milk gets quite hard and, er, I believe it is quite uncomfortable for them, not to mention the fact that they will eventually go dry, which would be quite a shame for the Squire, if you take my meaning."

Gen rose, determined. While she had no reason to wish Alan well, she couldn't imagine exacting her revenge through some innocent beasts. "It's all right, Mother. I got us into this, I'll get us out. William, if you could show me how to do it, I'll milk them."

He was turning red again. "I'm sorry, Miss Gen, but one alone won't make a difference. A skilled milker could do no more than ten cows in an hour, and I would imagine with this being your first time and the cows not familiar with you, you'll do far less. There looked to be about forty cows out there. You could never get to them all in the hour or so we have remaining. I'd say we need at least ten people for the job."

Gen sank back into her chair. "Ten people?"

Allison jumped to her feet. "I'll help. It will be a lark."

Her mother frowned at her. "I cannot like it, but very well. Since you have explained that it will cause the beasts pain if we refuse, I shall assist as well, William."

"We'll all have to help," Gen agreed. "Chimes, Mrs. Chimes, Bryce, and the other servants as well."

Her mother nodded.

Not much later, armed with tubs and buckets, the entire household of Wenwood Abbey descended upon the herd and set to work. William instructed the Munroes and Bryce, who had never been near a cow before, how to go about the milking. Mrs. Chimes and the groomsmen, it turned out, had had some experience and therefore proved the most adept, doing three animals in the time it took the others to do one. Gen found that if she followed William's instructions—touch the cow first to make sure it knew she was there, always milk on the animal's right side, and let them chew on the pansies if it seemed to help—she could manage the task. The animals' udders were warm to her hands, the milk soft as it squirted past her fingers. The smell was not unlike that of the horse stables—sweet and musty. After about the second cow, however, the novelty of the experience wore off, and she found each successive beast more daunting. By number three her arms ached; by number four her back hurt as well. It was nearly dark before they finished.

As Gen limped back toward the house, William fell into step beside her. "How often does this have to happen?" she asked him, almost afraid of the answer.

"Twice a day, I'm afraid," he told her with a gentle smile. "But you've got the hang of it now, Miss Genevieve. And it shouldn't be long. I'm sure the Squire's pasture will drain soon."

She nodded, too tired to do otherwise. Her one consolation was the tubs of milk, a good fifty gallons even with the amount they had spilled. Mrs. Chimes was already mumbling about the cheeses, butter, and clotted cream she would make.

"And with so many to help you, it will go much easier in the morning," William assured her. "Have the gentlemen carry the tubs for you, and as for the eight maids . . ."

Gen gasped, pulling him to a stop. "Eight maids! Oh, no, William, don't tell me!"

A slow smile spread across the curate's face. "Why, I believe you're right, Miss Genevieve. Eight maids a-milking. The Squire has done it again."

Twelve

Verse Nine, Nine Drummers Drumming

Since the pond was now reduced to a large frozen mud flat littered with dying pond lilies and threaded by a trickle of a stream, Genevieve decided to put the cows there the next morning after milking. Part of her feared the creatures must have frozen in the night, but they were apparently closely packed enough to generate sufficient heat for they greeted her family and servants complacently that morning when they all trooped out for the next milking. She was wracking her brain for what to feed them, besides Mrs. Chimes' pansies, when Tom Harvey arrived with a loaded hay wagon. She thankfully directed him to the back gardens.

"And did the Squire tell you when he planned to retrieve them?" she couldn't help asking as he turned the draft horses toward the back of the clearing.

He shook his head, trying unsuccessfully not to grin. "No, miss. The water's gone down some, but the problem is it seems to be freezing. The barns should be ready in a day or two, though."

"A day or two! Our garden won't last that long."

"Aye, but it'll be well fertilized."

She stomped back into the house to escape his chortle.

Her day didn't got any better. Her mother repaired to her room near the chapel to escape the smell that seemed to be permeating the Abbey walls. Even Allison no longer found the beasts so interesting. Gen joined her in the music room at the front of the house, where the lowing and odor were considerably lessened. They had decided a ride might be more the thing when Chimes ushered in Reverend York.

"Ladies, ladies," he nodded, panting and wiping his sweating brow. "I hastened here as soon as I could. A most unfortunate situation, most unfortunate. I understand your poor mother has gone into a decline because of it."

"Not at all, Vicar," Gen replied, rising to allow him the use of the sofa. Catching Allison's eye, she snatched up her embroidery as well. "She is merely resting from her exertions."

"We have been assisting the Pentercasts in their time of need," Allison put in from the spinet bench as Gen joined her there. "We have some of their cows in our garden."

"Yes, so Mr. Wellfordhouse gave me to understand. A most gracious act, most gracious. Rather unlike the Munroes of the past."

"How may we assist you today, Vicar?" Gen asked quickly as Allison bridled.

"You mistake me, Miss Munroe. You mistake me. I am here to offer assistance to you."

Gen smiled politely. "I fail to see how, sir." She winked at Allison. "Unless you'd like to take a turn with the milking?"

He stiffened. "Indeed not, miss, indeed not. I thought to give more spiritual comfort, as befits my station. Do you know yet who the culprit might be?"

Gen shook her head. "No. Truth be told, I haven't had the opportunity to do more than confirm it was not an accident."

"Do *you* know who did it?" Allison asked.

Reverend York blinked. "I, my dear?" he asked, pointing to

his wide chest. "Indeed not, indeed not. However, there are certain rumors going about the village, I am most sorry to say."

"Oh?" Allison prompted. Gen knew she should stop him; listening to idle gossip never did anyone any good. But she had to admit her curiosity.

The vicar leaned forward conspiratorially. "New Year's often prompts the youth to act in the most inappropriate manner, most inappropriate, if you take my meaning. I'm sure we all know a certain young man who is having a difficult time with his behavior."

"Who?" Allison breathed, her eyes wide in anticipation.

He leaned back and crossed his hands over his belly. "I cannot say, I cannot say, of course. But I have it on good authority that it was the younger brother of a certain prominent landowner."

Gen frowned. Geoffrey Pentercast? That made little sense. She hadn't time to ponder, however, for Allison leapt to her feet.

"I won't believe it! Geoffrey Pentercast may be a lout and a bully, but he's no vandal. You tell those fishwives in the village to find someone else to pick on."

"Allison!" Gen cried, appalled by her sister's vehemence. "I think you should apologize to Reverend York."

Allison glared at her, then dropped her gaze. "Sorry," she mumbled, paling as she sank back onto the bench.

"No harm done, no harm done," the vicar rumbled. "You are most kind to defend him, Miss Munroe. Considering the damage done to your property and the Manor, most kind indeed. I warned the Squire his brother's drinking would get out of hand, truly I did warn him. And now that the boy's run off . . ."

"Run off!" Gen and Allison chorused.

Gen was surprised to see what appeared to be a satisfied smile settle on the vicar's face. She found it hard to believe the man was enjoying their reaction to his tale. "Indeed, yes. I have it from dear Fancy that young Geoffrey hasn't been home since the night of the flood. Damning evidence, if you'll pardon the pun."

"It can't be," Allison insisted. "I will not believe he would endanger his own family's lives."

"With that I must agree, my dear, I must agree indeed. It is my opinion that in his drunken state he thought the waters would damage the Abbey. And what Pentercast could pass up the opportunity of causing a Munroe some difficulty, eh? However, once he realized his own family was in danger, he had no choice but to rouse you all in hopes you would help them."

Allison shook her head, opening her mouth for another protest, but Gen stepped into the conversation. "Has no one searched for him? The Squire and his mother must be frantic with worry."

"Ah, a devoted mother is dear Fancy, a devoted mother indeed," the vicar mused. "Even now she maintains his innocence. The Squire keeps his opinions to himself, but I believe he and some of the villagers have gone looking, to no avail." He dropped his voice, nodding sagely. "In my opinion, he's found someplace to sleep it off. He'll return when he must, only when he must. I only hope it will be in a less inebriated state, far less inebriated. Otherwise who knows what he might pick as his next target!"

"This is ridiculous!" Allison stormed, leaping from the bench once more. "I'm sorry, Vicar, but I cannot sit here and let Mr. Pentercast be maligned."

"No, of course not," Gen agreed, her mind whirling. "Reverend York, please don't think me rude, but I wish you would excuse us. We've been through a great deal the last few days."

"Certainly, certainly," the Vicar rumbled, rising. "I do apologize if my conversation upsets you. It can be difficult to face the flaws in one's friends, but that is how one builds character."

"Yes, well, we quite appreciate your desire to be of assistance," Gen replied, managing to steer him toward the door. Moments later, Chimes was seeing him out. With a sigh, Gen turned back to the music room.

"I won't believe it," Allison declared. "There has to be another explanation."

"I agree," Gen nodded. "The difficulty is, what? I can think of no reason why anyone would want to damage the Abbey or the Manor. Yet I cannot believe an ax just accidentally happened to fall from nowhere with sufficient force to chop through the dam."

"It is maddening," Allison declared, rising. "Let's take that ride. I cannot stay in this house another minute."

It took them some time to change into their riding habits, but within the hour they were on horseback and cantering through the Abbey woods. As if by mutual agreement, they avoided the path to the Manor, going instead first through the woods and then down the track toward the main road. It had grown considerably colder, Gen noticed. Her sister's nose was soon red, and she could no longer feel the end of her own nose. Their breaths, and those from the horses, froze in the air. The skies overhead were heavy with dark gray clouds. There'd be snow by tonight unless she missed her guess.

Allison was not disposed to conversation, so they rode side by side in silence. Although she had suggested the ride originally as a way to lift their spirits, she found the gray skies and cold wind little comfort. She was about to suggest to Allison that they return home when she heard the noise. From somewhere up ahead came a hollow booming, not unlike the sound of a large wooden drum. Beside her, Allison frowned.

"What could that be?"

Gen shook her head, reining in her horse. Allison did likewise. They listened as the sound echoed through the woods, steady, rhythmic. Allison's horse shook its head on the bit. She patted its dark neck and bent to whisper in its ear.

"Whatever it is," she told Gen, straightening as her mount calmed, "Blackie doesn't like it."

The chill that ran up Gen's back had nothing to do with the temperature of the air. "Perhaps we should go back for Chimes."

As if on cue, the noise stopped. There was a moment of silence; then the forest was rent by the creak and crash of a large falling object. Both horses shied, and Gen, like Allison, worked to calm her mount. "Allison, start for home," she ordered, trying to remain calm herself. "I'll be right behind you. We must get Chimes and the grooms."

"We can't run away like cowards!" Allison insisted. "It could be the vandal!"

"Don't be silly," Gen snapped, though she could feel her pulse racing. She managed to regain control of the beast at last and saw that Allison had hers in hand as well. "There's nothing here worth destroying," she added more patiently "The only thing of value in the whole woods is the—"

"Wenwood Thorn!" Allison cried. As one, they wheeled their mounts and kicked the horses into a gallop.

They pounded down the track, trees flashing past, cold wind whipping at their faces. Fear seemed to hang from every bare branch. It couldn't be the Thorn, she prayed. Allison had to be mistaken; it was only someone cutting down a tree for firewood; Alan widening the road for a new carriage; Chimes clearing away deadwood. A part of her knew how unlikely those events were; no one would cut firewood so far from town; she had left Chimes safely ensconced with his days-old paper before the kitchen fire; and Alan was surely still engrossed with cleaning up after the flood. Another part of her insisted that anything was possible. Indeed, any other explanation was preferable to the destruction of the Thorn. The Thorn had been her family's lasting gift to Wenwood; it was one of the few gifts from her father that could still provide comfort. It was her sign that this

Christmas would not be the end of her happy life, but the beginning of something new and possibly just as happy. She could not lose it now, not when she needed so much to believe in something.

They thundered into the clearing, and she was forced to rein in her mount sharply to keep from hitting the debris. Her heart seemed to stop beating in her frozen chest.

Lying across the clearing, its bare branches splintered and broken, lay the Wenwood Thorn.

"No!" Allison cried, turning her horse in agitated circles. Her hands as frozen as her heart, Gen barely managed to control her own horse. The beast hadn't completely stopped before she was sliding to the ground, stumbling toward the tree. Someone moaned and she knew it was her. She fell to her knees near the base of the tree. Trembling, she reached out a hand to the splintered wood. A sliver cut through the seam of her glove but she barely noticed. The old Thorn had been hacked apart low on its trunk, the sharp cuts still visible in the fractured wood. She wiped away the tears that were falling. She wasn't sure how long she knelt there before she saw the body.

As if from a distance, she heard her heart start beating again. "Allison!" she cried, climbing to her feet and scrambling around the wreckage. "Help me, quickly! Someone's been hurt!"

Hands still trembling, she dragged away the branches and debris that had fallen over the man even as Allison rushed to her side. It was an older man in a dark suit, large boned, heavyset.

"It's Reverend York!" her sister gasped just as Gen reached the same conclusion.

The vicar was lying facedown beside the tree, his hands cradling his head as if he had seen the blow coming. Miraculously, the larger parts of the tree seemed to have missed him, so that when Gen gingerly turned him over, she could find no injury. As Allison watched, wringing her hands, she patted his pale muddy cheek, calling his name. She was as terrified as Allison, but she didn't dare let her sister see it. She thought her heart would stop again, but then his eyes fluttered open, focused on her face. His arm shot out to grip hers. Gen jumped.

"Brigands!" he cried, his eyes wild. "Vandals! Run, ladies! Fetch help!"

"Please, Reverend York, calm yourself," Gen told him in what she hoped was a reasonable voice. Heaven knew she was shaking inside. "It's all right. There's no one here but the three of us."

He focused on Allison behind her, then back on Gen's face. "But the Thorn, the . . ." He caught sight of the wreckage around him and closed his eyes again with a groan. "Oh, no. Too late, too late."

Gen found his sorrow oddly comforting. "Are you hurt?" she prompted, putting a hand under his shoulder. "Can you sit?"

He eased himself up, patting his arms, legs, and torso. "Mercifully, I seem to be unharmed. Oooh." His hands had reached his head. "Perhaps I spoke too soon. I remember now. The brigands attacked me!"

There was nothing for it. Much as she would have liked to devote herself to finding out what had happened to the Thorn, the Reverend York's health had to come first. "Allison, you'll have to go for help," she told her wide-eyed sister. "I'll stay with the vicar."

"No, no," York insisted, struggling to his feet. Gen rose with him, alarmed. Allison stepped back out of his way. "I shall be fine. A minor wound. We must fetch the Squire. The brigands must be stopped."

"Reverend," Gen scolded, following him back over the wreckage of the tree with Allison at her heels, "you're in no condition to walk all the way to the Manor. If you must go, I insist you take my horse."

York had reached the edge of the clearing, and he paused to

lean against one of the larger trees, breathing heavily. "Nonsense. Can't . . . take . . . a . . . lady's . . . horse."

His gallantry amused her, especially under the circumstances. "But you are injured," she protested.

He shook his head and winced. "That is not the issue. I could not possibly use your side-saddle, and I lack the experience to ride bareback."

"Oh," Gen pulled up short, nonplused. "Then Allison must go and bring back help as I originally suggested."

"Yes," he sighed, straightening. "I suppose you're right." He turned his impassioned gaze back on her, and she was surprised to find that when he stood tall, he towered over her. "They must be caught, the brigands who did this. Desecrating the Thorn is bad enough, but to strike a man of the cloth as well! Such villainy cannot go unpunished."

"And it shall not," Allison promised, hurrying to her horse. "Help me mount, Gen. I'll be back straight away."

"Wait," Gen commanded, his words finally sinking in even as her fear rose anew. "Vicar, you keep saying brigands. How many were there? Where did they go? And how do you know they have gone?"

Her hands on the reins, Allison shivered, eyeing the nearby trees.

"Oh, they've gone, they've gone," York assured her with a wag of one plump finger. "They've done their vile deed. What need to stay? Nine of them there were, hacking at the poor tree like crazed drummers, like the most crazed of drummers. And I'm most sorry to say, Miss Allison, most very sorry to say that Geoffrey Pentercast was leading them."

"No!" Allison cried, and was forced to yank on the reins as her horse shied again.

Gen stared at the tree, feeling as if her lifeblood was draining even as the Thorn wilted. Nine of them? Drumming? It could not be. Even a Pentercast would not be so vindictive. Yet he had sent Geoffrey to do his dirty work before. Heat rushed up from her heart to her face. She stalked to her horse.

"Allison, help me to mount. You will stay with Reverend York. I have a few words to say to the Squire."

Thirteen

Interlude, Baritone Solo

Alan stared at the calculations on the paper before him, staggered by the results. He had had two days to assess the results of the flood, two days to review his plans for the estate and what impact it would have on them. He groaned aloud. His entire spring wheat crop was destroyed. The portion of the fall's harvest that was still being threshed, a good third of it, was gone as well. Two of his sheep had been trampled in the process of getting the animals to higher ground. One would have lambed in a few months. Several of his horses had come up lame. A neighbor reported at least a dozen cows dry. Tom Harvey reported that the Munroes were doing what they could for the cows he had left with them, but without barns to hold them, he might lose another forty head as well. Eight of the trees in the old orchard had been washed off their roots; another half-dozen were listing and might not last the winter. It would take him months to rebuild.

He slouched in the leather-upholstered desk chair and stared at the frescoed ceiling. And what had he accomplished for all these troubles? His worst fears about his brother had been confirmed—Geoffrey was a drunken wastrel with no regard to personal property or human life. He was everything anyone ever thought a Pentercast should be. And Alan had sworn when he became head of the family that he would not let his brother follow in their father's stead. He had failed miserably. He could only hope Geoffrey was somewhere safe and warm, and that he would return soon unharmed.

Worse yet was his relationship with Gen. He had done everything he could think of to change her mind about his acceptability as a husband. He glanced at the table beside the door, where lay her gift for the ninth day of Christmas—a set of tin soldiers, nine of which were drummers, for their first child to play with. *First child indeed,* he thought with a shake of his head. The last time he'd seen Gen, he'd taken his frustrations out on her, allowed his worries to make him snap at her. She was no closer to being his wife and the mother of his children than on the day he had started this game. In fact, she had every right to be completely disgusted with him.

He ran a hand back through his hair. Whatever way he looked at it, he had botched it badly. His farm lay in ruins, his brother was missing, and the woman he had chosen for his bride wanted nothing to do with him. And all by the ninth day of Christmas!

The door to his study creaked open, and he found himself scowling at the interruption. Then he rose to his feet, heart in his throat. "Geoff?"

His brother managed a weak smile, scratching at the stubble on his chin. "Hello, Alan. Do you have a moment?"

"Have a moment!" he roared, swinging around his desk and dashing across the room. "Is that all you can say for yourself, you cauker!"

He hugged his brother to him, wondering if it was only his imagination that said the lad was pounds thinner. Geoffrey submitted to the pummeling with a shrug. "What do you want me to say? I wasn't even sure I'd be missed."

"Not missed?" Alan pushed him out to arm's length and stared at him. His hair was on end, his clothes rumpled and filthy, his boots caked with mud. He was surely a sight, but Alan could not have cared less. "We had half the village scouring the hills for you. Have you seen Mother yet? She's been wild with worry."

Geoffrey refused to meet his gaze. "Sorry about that. I didn't intend to worry her. I just needed some time to think."

"About what?" Alan frowned, releasing him. He tried again to get his brother to look at him, but to no avail. His heart sank as he realized most likely he was about to hear a confession.

"About everything," Geoffrey muttered. "The last few days, the flood, my life." He sighed, looking up to meet Alan's eyes at last. He squared his jaw. "I didn't do it, Alan. I swear. I thought I might have, but now I'm sure."

Alan wanted to feel relieved, but somehow couldn't. He knew his frown had deepened with his confusion. "What do you mean, you thought you might have? Either you did or you didn't."

"Well," his brother hedged, "I had my reasons. You see, I was a bit well to live when I left the tavern that night. I remember heading home, but I got to thinking about what Miss Allison said to Reverend Wellfordhouse, about being their first footer for New Year's? And I was thinking how I had threatened to come instead and wouldn't it be a grand joke if I made good on that threat. Me being dark complexioned, that would serve her right for toying with my affections."

"Toying with your affections?" Alan couldn't help asking with raised eyebrow.

Geoffrey had the good sense to hang his head. "Well, perhaps toying isn't the right word. But you must admit she's been flirting rather outrageously practically since the day we met, and her not even out yet!"

"You still owe it to her to behave like a gentleman," Alan pointed out.

Geoffrey grimaced. "Dash it all, I know that. Only she is the most taking little thing. Anyway, I was thinking about her, and the next thing I knew, I was almost to the Abbey and my horse was shying away from water in my path. It took me a moment to realize what I was seeing. Then I realized that the water was going everywhere and rode to the Abbey to warn them. Next I came straight home, as you know. But you see, I couldn't really remember anything from the time I left the tavern until I reached the flood. And I thought, what if I did it and don't even remember it?" He blinked and looked away, wiping his nose with the back of his hand. "I thought maybe the drink was getting to me. You've hammered that into me, I suppose. And of course there was Father. So I decided to stay away from it and see what would happen. There was a nice abandoned barn over by Brightsfield. Good place to think." His brother grinned at him, and Alan found himself returning the smile. "You might try it sometime. Anyway, I'm still here. And I know I didn't do it, Alan."

Alan clapped him on the shoulder, feeling his own spirits lighten. "I believe you, Geoff. And I'm glad you're back. The question remains, however, if not you, who *did* break the dam that night?" He turned back to the desk and felt Geoff's eyes on him as he resumed his seat.

"I don't know, Alan," his brother shrugged. "I can't imagine why anyone would want to play such a scurvy trick—on us or the Munroes."

"You knew there have been other such acts?" Alan probed. Geoff frowned, shaking his head. "Reverend York told me. Barn doors let open, fence posts toppled, that sort of thing. It sounded to me like a gang of youths with too much time on their hands."

Geoff shook his head again. "Why haven't I heard anything about this? You'd think there'd be more gossip down at the tavern. Besides, I know all the lads for miles about and none of them would cause such trouble, unless . . ."

"Unless?" Alan prompted with interest.

"Nothing," Geoffrey muttered, looking away.

Alan had a suspicion as to where his brother's thoughts were leading. "You know, if there's anyone besides the Pentercasts with a reputation for wildness in this area, I understand it's our friend Tom Harvey. And I believe you mentioned once that he gets fairly unpredictable when drunk."

Geoffrey tried to protest, but Alan could see that he'd given his brother something to think about. "I suppose he could be our culprit, but wasn't he here the night of the flood?"

"He came in later, after the water started coming. I thought perhaps he was with you at the tavern."

Geoffrey shook his head. "I didn't see him there. I don't want to accuse anyone, Alan. Besides, Tom can be a very helpful fellow, as you've seen since the flood."

"Working off a guilty conscience, perhaps?" Alan asked with raised eyebrow.

"I can't believe it," Geoffrey insisted.

Alan frowned. "Then who?"

"I confess I'm at a loss," Geoff admitted.

Alan rose again, feeling the chair too confining. "Well, never mind that now. We should let Mother know you've returned." Putting his arm around his brother's shoulder, he steered him out of the study and down the corridor toward the center stair. Time enough later to determine exactly what had happened New Year's Eve. Although he had as much as accused Gen of causing the flood, he knew she could have had nothing to do with it. More and more he was becoming convinced there was a very real danger in their midst. Next time it struck, someone might be hurt. He very much doubted the solution would wait until the twelve days of Christmas were over.

Geoff had his foot on the bottom step when the front door knocker sounded.

"Go on," Alan urged him, falling back. "I'll see to it."

With a nod, his brother continued up the stairs.

Munson appeared from below stairs, crossing the marble floor with measured tread as the knocking came again, louder. Alan frowned, wondering what could have happened to put their unknown caller in such a pucker. Given the last few days, he was almost afraid to find out.

Munson swung open the door, and Gen brushed past him into the entry hall. Though her jaw was set and her vivid blue eyes snapped fire, he could see that she was pale. Her riding habit was rumpled as if she'd ridden hard, and pieces of dead leaves speckled her skirt from hem to knee. Alarmed, he took a step forward. "What's happened? Are you all right?"

She turned her glare on him, stalking across the entryway. Before he knew what she was about, she swung back her arm and slapped him across the face. "Murderer!"

He recoiled, more surprised than hurt.

"Oh, I say," Munson sputtered. "Squire, shall I call the footman to have this person evicted?"

Alan rubbed his cheek thoughtfully, gazing down at the tiny fury who stood with heaving breasts below him. Part of him wanted to demand her removal. The other part wanted to make sure she was all right. "That won't be necessary, Munson. I take it there's some explanation for this, Miss Munroe? Perhaps we can discuss it, in private?" He nodded toward the nearby drawing room, not sure she would accept his offer. To his relief, she swept back her skirts and stalked ahead of him to the door.

Alan eyed her as Munson shut the doors behind him, leaving them open just enough for propriety's sake and promising to go fetch his mother immediately. He wondered whether that was for Gen's protection, or his own. She was pacing before the windows, the sunlight glinting off her disheveled hair. As if she sensed his gaze upon her, she paused and eyed him in return. He wondered what she was seeing. Although he was fairly sure he was innocent of whatever she was angry about, he had to fight the urge not to squirm.

She sighed suddenly, looking away, as if the anger had fled. "How could you, Alan? I thought you understood what the

Thorn means to so many people, what it means to me. To cut
it down just to win the wager . . ."

He felt as if she'd kicked him in the gut. "The Thorn's been
cut down?"

She nodded, tears filling her eyes. "Allison and I found it
just now. It is quite destroyed." She gulped back a sob, and it
was all he could do not to take her in his arms. His mind
whirled—the Thorn destroyed? It could only be the work of the
vandal. The creature must be stopped!

"I promise you, Miss Munroe," he spat out, "the culprit will
not go unpunished."

She shook her head, wiping away her tears with gloved fingers. "What can you do to your own brother?"

"You suspect Geoffrey?" Before he could take umbrage, he
realized it made sense. The entire village seemed convinced
Geoffrey had caused the dam to break. He'd wondered himself.
But now he knew otherwise. "I assure you, Miss Munroe, my
brother had nothing to do with it."

She gulped back another sob, and he could see she trembled
with the effort to control her emotions. "Why do you bother to
lie? He was seen. Your plan is clear, sir, but I swear you shall
not win! Nothing would induce me to marry a man who would
stoop so low!"

He stared at her, feeling the blood drain from his face. "You
think I planned this? Why?"

She turned away from him, addressing her words to the winter
landscape beyond the window. "Reverend York said there were
nine of them and the sound was like drumming."

"And you assumed it was your 'gift' for the ninth day of
Christmas." He shook his head. How could he have been so
stupid to think he could win her despite her damned Pentercast
prejudice? Everything he had done had been for naught. She
could know nothing about him to accuse him of this. Something
inside him snapped. He strode to her side and grabbed her by

the shoulders, forcing her to turn wide eyes to his face. "That's right, look at me. Look at me, dammit! What do you see?"

She blinked, stiff in his grip. "I . . . I don't know what you mean."

He gave her a shake. "No, of course you don't, because you refuse to look beyond the end of your aristocratic little nose. Well, try, just this once, to see the man beyond. A man who'd give his life for you." He gave a wry snort of laughter. "A man who's already nearly lost everything he holds dear for the chance to win your love. A man who just happens to be a Pentercast."

She stared up at him, arrested, and a last tear slid down her pale cheek. Her eyes were misty, her lips parted. With a groan, he pulled her to him and kissed her.

His anger melted immediately, even as she melted against him. He had dreamed of holding her like this for so long, and for once the dream did not disappoint. She was soft in his arms; he could feel the curve of her pressed against his chest. Her lips beneath his were cool and salt-tanged from her tears. As he pulled her closer, his heart pounded against his ribs as if trying to reach hers. He could feel her heart's answering rhythm. And he knew in that instant that he would do anything, anything, to have her by his side forever.

He raised his head and looked down at her. Two bright spots of color stood out on her pale cheeks. He could feel her trembling. Her eyes were closed.

He had to laugh, releasing her. "You can't even look at me when I'm kissing you."

Her eyes snapped open, and she took a step back. "You should not have done that."

He laughed again, freely this time, his tension surprisingly gone. "You're quite right, Miss Munroe, as usual. However, I'm very much afraid that if you don't leave right now, I'm going to do it again."

She gasped and fled before he could make good his threat.

Fourteen

Verse Ten, Ten Pipers Piping

She raced the horse down the road from the Manor, heart pounding with the hooves, oblivious to the trees flying past, conscious only of the need for escape. She had gone some distance, driven in headlong flight, before she began to wonder what she was escaping from. Then she slowed the horse to a trot, breathing as heavily as it did.

No doubt it was his kiss that had her so rattled. None of her other suitors had ever dared to kiss her. She couldn't remember anyone kissing her, not even a brotherly kiss from William. Surely the first kiss was always discomposing. But this kiss! She closed her eyes, remembering the feel of his arms around her, the gentle caress of his lips, the firm line of his body. Her eyes snapped open, and she could feel herself blushing. Perhaps it was best *not* to think of his kiss.

But his words had been no less discomposing. Why, if she understood him correctly, he was in love with her. Just the thought would have once made her shiver with delight. Now she felt only confusion. She had dreamed so long of the handsome young man of her girlhood; then she had been crushed to find him no better than the Pentercasts she had been raised to despise. Which was the real Alan? Or was he someone else entirely?

She was so intent on her thoughts that she rode all the way back to the Abbey before realizing she had never fetched help for Allison and the vicar. She was rousing the grooms and Chimes when the Pentercast carriage pulled into the yard. Panic seized her at the thought of facing Alan again so soon, and she froze. What should she say? How should she act? And she must look a sight. The driver leapt to the ground and opened the door, assisting Allison in clambering down. Gen sagged in relief.

They all gathered around her sister, who, preening over her importance, sketched out the tale with evident delight, hands waving dramatically in the air.

"And then the Squire came with his horse and carriage to bring me home and take the vicar back to the village," she finished with a flourish.

"Lucky no one of importance was hurt," Chimes humphed. "Seems to me this vandal fellow has gone too far this time."

"Someone ought to plant him a facer," one of the grooms muttered.

"If you ask me, 'angin's too good fer 'im," another grumbled.

Chimes snorted. "Aye, but with the Squire behind him, not likely we'll see justice done."

Gen didn't like the way the conversation was going. However, before she could speak, Allison jumped in. "You all think Geoffrey Pentercast did it, don't you? And with no more evidence than gossip. Shame on you."

The groomsmen hung their heads.

"Now, Miss Allison," Chimes sputtered, "you yourself told us what the vicar said. Surely you don't think he'd lie about what he saw."

Allison pouted. "Of course he wouldn't lie. He's a man of God. However, he *could* be mistaken. Perhaps it was someone who *looked* like Geoffrey Pentercast."

"The only person who looks like Geoffrey Pentercast in these parts," Chimes replied with a snort, "is Geoffrey Pentercast. Pentercasts have always been trouble. We all remember the time old man Pentercast came home from the inn drunk and set fire to the hay fields. The acorn doesn't fall far from the tree."

"That's enough," Gen ordered. "We all have better things to do with our time than gossip."

Chastised, the servants wandered back to their duties. Allison and Gen turned back to the Abbey.

They found their mother awaiting them in the entry hall. "Welcome back, girls. What was all that commotion? Did I hear a carriage?"

"I'll let Allison explain, Mother," Gen replied, feeling craven as she slipped past her mother to the family wing. Her mother looked at her askance, but Allison launched into her tale and her mother focused on the dramatics. Gen escaped to the quiet of her room.

But she wasn't to be given time to ruminate. Bryce bustled in to help her out of her riding habit, tisking over its condition. She attempted to engage Gen in conversation, but gave up when Gen responded with unencouraging nods and unladylike grunts. Moments after Bryce left, her mother came in. Gen smothered a sigh of frustration.

"Most distressing news," her mother murmured. "Are you quite all right?"

"Actually, Mother," Gen replied with sudden hope, "I'm quite done in. I thought I might rest before tea."

Her mother nodded. "A wise decision. I will suggest the same for Allison. The Thorn will be a loss. I do hope the Squire can locate the perpetrator."

"I'm sure we all feel the same," Gen replied, her emotions warring. "I'll see you at tea, Mother."

A few moments later as she lay stretched out on her bed, alone at last, she found her mind a jumble of thoughts. Was

Geoffrey Pentercast the vandal who had flooded the Manor and destroyed the Thorn? If so, what was his reason? If not Geoffrey, then who would want to harm the Munroes and the Thorn?

If Geoffrey was the vandal as everyone thought, Alan was clearly shielding him, but was it brotherly love or a darker motive? And did he truly love her as he claimed, or was his declaration part of some plan that would bring her family pain? If he did love her, could she return his love? It would certainly make things easier for her family if she could bring herself to marry him. But was it only the lure of an easier life that made the idea seem palatable?

Needless to say, she got no rest and eventually made her way across the Abbey for tea. The package sitting on the entryway table caught her attention, but she refused to open it. She wasn't sure she wanted to see what else Alan could do on this ninth day of Christmas. She ordered Chimes to put it in her room and continued on to the drawing room.

Allison and her mother were there before her, her sister sliding over to make room for her on the sofa. She offered them both a smile and knew by the looks of concern on their faces that she was fooling no one.

"I have been thinking," her mother began as she poured and distributed the tea. "Perhaps, with this vandal about, it would be best if we returned to London early."

Gen accepted her cup, struggling to hold it steady. Not this, she prayed silently, not now. She had enough to contend with without having the specter of the end of Christmas hanging over her head. She wracked her brain to think of something to allay her mother's concerns.

Allison accepted her own cup with a shake of her head. "But Mother, you promised to remain through Christmas. And we still have two more days until Epiphany."

"Yes, I realize that. I was considering your safety, girls. From your story, Allison, I take it Reverend York was not greatly hurt, but we cannot be certain of the outcome the next time the vandal strikes. And it does not look as if the Squire will take action." She shook her head, sipping her tea. "Pity. I had expected more of him."

"I am quite tired of the way you all assume Geoffrey Pentercast is guilty." Allison sniffed. "I tell you, the Reverend York is mistaken. And when Geoffrey returns, he will prove himself innocent."

"Your loyalty does you credit, Allison," her mother replied. "But be careful not to mistake a handsome face with a kind heart. The two are not synonymous."

"Still," Gen prompted, having found her reason, "to allow anyone to drive us from our home seems to be cowardly in the extreme. I believe we should stay."

"Hear, hear!" Allison cheered, raising her teacup.

Her mother glanced between the two of them, and Gen held her breath. "Very well, since you both feel that way. But we will take a few precautions. You will not go out without one of the groomsmen or Chimes with you, not even to the village."

"Yes, Mother," Allison sighed.

Gen relaxed, sitting back against the sofa and taking a sip of her tea. Her mother nodded at their apparent agreement. The three sipped contentedly for a few moments. Then Allison reached for one of Mrs. Chimes famous scones on the tea tray.

"Given that we will be staying," their mother murmured, "I have decided to reinstitute the Munroe Epiphany party."

Allison clapped her hands with glee while Gen choked on her tea, hastily setting it on the table near the sofa. Could nothing go right today? "Mother," she managed to gasp, "you can't!"

Her mother pursed her lips. "Oh, I don't think it's inappropriate, even under the circumstances. I'm sure it will be expected with the Abbey open for the first time in years and us now fully out of mourning."

"But . . . but . . ." Gen sputtered, her mind whirling through ways to stop this latest threat to their finances. "You can't possibly plan a party in two days' time!"

Her mother complacently took another sip of tea. "Normally I would quite agree with you, my dear, but I had planned for such a possibility before we left London. I've been making arrangements since we arrived. And we will keep it tastefully small. I had Mrs. Chimes draw up a list of the best families in the area, and they number no more than thirty individuals, not including those children who are not yet out, of course."

Gen stared at her, stunned. "Thirty!"

"Oh, Mother, surely you'll let me come as well," Allison pleaded.

"Certainly, dear, since it will be in your own home. It will do you good to practice a little before we return to London." She took another sip of tea. "I believe we'll even have dancing. I wrote to the violinist from that lovely quartet Mrs. Bascombe had at her ball and they agreed to make the trip."

Gen felt as if a noose were closing around her throat. Outside, one of the cows scraped itself along the Abbey wall, lowing plaintively. She smiled. "But, Mother, what about the cows? The smell, the noise, and our obligation to milk them will certainly make the party a great deal less enjoyable for our guests."

Her mother allowed herself a frown. "You have a point there. They are quite a nuisance. Has the Squire determined when he will take them back?"

"I understand the barns will be open soon," Gen replied, trying to sound regretful, "but his pasture is still under water, and I understand the water has frozen. It certainly is cold enough."

Her mother's frown deepened. "This could present a problem. Since it was our dam that caused the damage, I cannot in good conscience demand he find another home for them. Still, I do not see how we can have the party here with them so near." As if to prove her point, another of the beasts pressed its muzzle against the glass of the drawing-room window and blew a gust of moist air, fogging their view.

"Pity," Gen agreed with a sigh of mock regret and true relief. "Perhaps next year."

Allison leapt to her feet. "No! We cannot give up so easily! We must at least *ask* the Squire if he can take back the cows. Would that be so awful? Surely he knows they are a burden to us."

Her mother set down her cup of tea. "I believe you are correct, Allison. Please ring for Chimes and ask him to have the carriage brought around within the hour. We will pay a call on the Squire."

"You go ahead, Mother," Gen told them as Allison hurried to the bell pull. "I'm still feeling a bit under the weather after this afternoon's excitement. I'm sure the Pentercasts will excuse me." And I don't give a care if they don't, she amended silently, sipping her tea. After what had happened, she didn't imagine Alan would be too pleased to see them, and he certainly wouldn't be in the mood to offer favors. She had a feeling his cows had found a new home for the winter. She'd deal with that after Christmas.

She should have realized she'd be wrong about Alan, as usual, she told herself at dinner that night as her mother and Allison hastened to gush over his generosity. Not only had he agreed to come get the cows the next morning, but he was sending his mother's gardener and staff to set their grounds to rights. In addition, at hearing they were hosting the party, he had offered the use of any of his servants they might wish as well as his mother's best china and silver. Her mother and Allison had been only too glad to accept his offers and had apparently spent the rest of the time before dinner plotting what else had to be done to make the party a success. If she hadn't known better, she'd have sworn they were trying to drive her mad!

She sat through the first course, listening to her mother and Allison's plans with growing concern. She wrestled with her conscience through several more courses, trying to convince herself that Carstairs could find a way to pay for the extravaganza. By the time dessert had been served, however, she knew she could be silent no longer. Much as she had wanted to give her mother and Allison one last happy Christmas, she could not allow them to spend the last of their savings on such a frivolity as a party. She set her spoon down beside the blueberry trifle Mrs. Chimes had prepared and cleared her throat. "Mother, Allison, we cannot have this party."

They turned surprised faces to her, their spoons in midair. She forced out the rest of the words. "I'm most sorry to have to tell you this, but we cannot afford it."

Her mother waved her spoon languidly through the air. "Do not fret, my dear. Mr. Carstairs can contrive, I dare say. The entire affair won't cost more than a few hundred pounds."

Gen was thankful she hadn't taken a bite of the trifle for she knew if she had she would now be choking. "A few hundred! Might as well be a few thousand! You have no conception of what you're saying, Mother. We are penniless."

Allison stared at her, frozen. Her mother frowned. "That isn't amusing, Genevieve."

Gen sighed. "No, Mother, it's not. And I've tried to find a better way to tell you than this, but the party has forced my hand. You must understand, both of you, that we are destitute. Father spent everything and beyond. All we have left is the Abbey."

"But my . . . my Season," Allison whimpered, her eyes tearing.

Gen reached a hand across the table and gave her sister's hand a squeeze. "We'll find a way, love, I promise. Only it probably won't be in London."

"This is ridiculous," her mother snapped, tossing down her

damask napkin. "You are obviously mistaken, Genevieve. I shall speak to Mr. Carstairs myself when we return to London. I will not have him filling your head with such nonsense. As if your father would leave us in such dire straits. The very idea is utterly reprehensible." She took a deep breath and seemed to collect herself, her voice returning to its usual murmur. "Allison, after dinner we should start addressing those invitations."

Now it was Gen's turn to stare: "But, Mother, haven't you been listening? We cannot afford this party."

"I do not wish to hear another word on this subject. I find I have no interest in this dessert. Allison, when you are finished, please join me in your father's study. We have much work to do. I shall expect your assistance as well, Genevieve."

Allison set down her spoon at last, glancing between her mother and Gen even as Gen tried to think of some way to break through her mother's resistance. "But Mother, if Gen is correct, we cannot . . . we should not host a grand party."

"That is quite enough!" Mrs. Munroe thundered, rising, and both of them started at her vehemence. "Your father was a good man. He would never leave us in such difficulties. There has been a mistake, you may count on it. I will write to Mr. Carstairs this minute and insist he wait on us here immediately. I will demand that he make an explanation for this outrage. And I will not hear another word on this subject, do I make myself clear?"

"Very," Gen clipped, sinking back against the dining chair in defeat.

"Good. Now, since you two seem to be fit for nothing but frivolous fretting, I shall have Mrs. Chimes assist me with the invitations. But I expect you will have thought better of this by morning." So saying, she swept from the room.

Allison sank against her chair as well. "I don't know what to think. Is it truly that bad, Gen?"

Gen sighed. "It is, Allison. You must believe me. Mr. Carstairs has tried everything these last six months, but to no avail.

She talks of returning to London, but we've already lost the London house and all its furnishings. The only horses we have left are the ones we brought with us and Blackie and Scott. We've lost everything but the Abbey. And if Mother insists on running up a mound of bills for this party, we may lose it as well."

Allison shuddered. "Then we must stop her."

Gen snorted. "Easier to stop the flood the other night. You heard her—she will not even speak of it."

"Perhaps Mr. Carstairs can explain it to her."

"If she'll listen to him. She never has. More likely she'll sack him instead. And then where will we be? No, there must be some way we can stop her." She stared off into the middle distance, sorting through possibilities. She could drop word of their financial straits in the village—that would effectively halt their line of credit. It would also shame her mother horribly. Besides, she was just as likely to purchase what she needed for the party from somewhere else where Gen would have no way to influence the shopkeepers. She might even have ordered the supplies beforehand, like the gifts for the servants on Boxing Day. Gen might be able to arrange for the invitations to mysteriously lose their way, but that wouldn't stop the party preparations, since her mother would still assume the event was occurring as scheduled. Short of physically restraining her mother, she could think of no solution.

"Oh, these ridiculous traditions!" Gen cried, rising to pace the room. "Why did I think living here would be any cheaper than London!"

"There is nothing for it." Allison sighed. "We must sell our jewels."

"Too late," Gen informed her, meeting her sister's shocked look with one of defiance. "How do you think I managed to save the Abbey? All of mother's jewels are paste, except for the Munroe diamonds. I was saving those for your dowry."

Allison's lower lip trembled. "Oh, Gen, how thoughtful! But what of your own? I know the Pentercasts are fairly wealthy, but won't Alan expect you to bring a dowry?"

Gen jerked to a stop. "What did you say?"

"I merely wondered whether you'll need a dowry when you marry Alan Pentercast this spring." Her sister had the audacity to giggle. "I don't suppose we can count the cows since he's taking them back tomorrow."

Gen sank onto her mother's chair at the head of the table. "Whatever made you think Alan and I are . . . that is, why would you ask . . . ?"

"Oh, honestly, Gen," Allison laughed, shaking her head, "anyone with eyes in her head could see it's bellows to mend with the two of you. And I must say, it will make short work of this penury situation. We have only to constrain ourselves until the wedding, after all. I dare say the Squire will care enough for conventions that he won't want his in-laws starving at his doorstep."

Gen stared at her, watching her sister's smile fade, and knew her emotions must be showing on her face. "I will not marry Alan to save this family, Allison. You have no right to expect it of me, any more than I would of you."

"Ohhh, you are so pigheaded!" Allison cried, jumping to her feet and throwing down her napkin. "The Squire obviously cares for you, and you once thought he was top of the trees, don't you dare deny it! But you won't marry him because it might benefit your family? Genevieve Munroe, that's the silliest thing I ever heard! I think I will help Mother plan this Epiphany party after all, just to run us nicely into Dun Territory. Then you'll *have* to marry Alan Pentercast!" Nose in the air, she stalked from the room.

"You're wrong, all of you!" Gen shouted after her, jumping to her feet as well. "Nothing will induce me to marry that man, so you may save your breath!" From outside came the lowing of cattle. Gen stalked to the window and threw up the sash. "And you be quiet as well!" In answer, the cold winter wind blew in the tang of cow dung. She snapped shut the window.

That night and most of the next morning, she fretted and fussed to no avail. Her mother refused to listen to her, Allison refused to listen to her, Chimes was too busy to listen to her, and even Mrs. Chimes scurried out of her way, looking vaguely troubled. The only time they worked together was on the final milking of the cows that morning, right before Tom Harvey and a group of young men from the village came to drive them back to the barns beyond the Manor. By late morning, she was sitting in the drawing room, at her wit's end, when Chimes ushered in the Reverend York.

"I'll go get the lady of the house," Chimes muttered at seeing her welcoming scowl. Left with no choice but to play hostess in the meantime, she greeted the vicar with slightly more warmth and saw him seated near the fire. She took a seat as far from him as was still courteous. When the silence stretched and she could no longer abide his complacent stare, she forced herself to make conversation.

"I'm a bit surprised to see you up and about today, sir, after your trials of yesterday," she ventured.

He shifted in his seat, and she wondered suddenly if she was making him nervous. Looking more closely, she noted drops of sweat around his jowled face, dribbling down to moisten the folds of his cravat.

"Indeed, indeed, Miss Genevieve, yesterday was a terrible day for the village, quite terrible. Have you quite recovered from your ordeal?"

"The Thorn's loss will be felt by all for some time," she replied in what she hoped was a conversational tone. She had no interest in letting the man see how she felt, for she was very much afraid her feelings would be the topic of conversation at his next stop.

"Quite, quite," he nodded. He leaned back and eyed her, fiddling with a large gold fob on the end of his watch chain. "Before your mother arrives, my dear, I thought to drop a fatherly word of advice in your ear. With your own dear father gone, you are all the more in need of male guidance, I'm sure, all the more in need."

Thinking of all the advice Chimes and Alan seemed to want to give her, she could hardly agree. Besides, she hadn't done all that badly on her own the last few months. Still, she supposed it was his duty. "What is it, Vicar?" she asked with what she hoped sounded like appropriate humility.

He leaned forward again, dropping his voice so that she was forced to lean forward as well to hear him. "I begin to see an interest developing between the Squire and you. I know you will understand when I say your father would hardly countenance such a match, hardly countenance it at all."

Surprised, she had to challenge him. "But Reverend York, surely you of all people would agree that we should end the feud between our families."

"Certainly, the peacemakers are always blest, oh most certainly," he nodded wisely. "But to make such a sacrifice as wedlock? No, no, that would be too much. I could not sit idly by and watch you throw away your chance at happiness merely to serve your family."

For a moment she sat stunned that, of all people, he would be the one to understand how she felt. Either she had severely misjudged him all these years, or her position was as misplaced as everyone had tried to tell her. "I . . . I don't know what to say."

He nodded again. "I could have guessed as much. He is an attractive man, the Squire—rich, powerful, and well thought of by all around. Especially by the ladies, I understand, most especially by the ladies. Perhaps a little too well by the ladies, if you take my meaning."

She frowned. "No, I don't."

He reached out to pat her knee and even though the touch was avuncular, she found herself flinching away from it.

"It is ever thus with the innocent," he sighed. "Far be it from me to sully the Squire's name, but I think you should be aware my dear that he has a reputation of tarrying with any number of young ladies in the surrounding countryside."

Gen shook her head, refusing to see Alan in that role. "No."

The vicar looked at her with evident pity. "I know this is difficult for you, my dear, but it is for your own good that you face these facts. The man is a renowned rake, renowned. Why, he's even been called out by one of the fathers, though, thank God, he was able to talk the man out of it before any blood was shed. The Pentercasts have always been good at talking their way out of scrapes. And I do believe he agreed to do right by the little by-blow."

"He . . . he sired a child?" Gen felt as if the room were spinning and gripped the arm of the chair.

"A child? Well, in that particular case I believe there was just one." He patted her knee again, and this time she was too stunned to move away. "I'm sorry to have to say this to you, my dear. But with your father gone and your mother known for her ability to avoid unpleasantness, I could see no other choice. I know how charming the Squire can be—giving extravagant gifts, cozying up to the relatives, praising a lady's beauty. I've seen it all before, countless times. I could not stand by and see it happen again."

She found herself on her feet, shaking. "Thank you for your concern, Vicar. If you'll excuse me, I find I'm not feeling very well after all. Mother should be with you shortly." As she stumbled from the room, she nearly collided with her mother, who frowned at her, a frown that quickly changed to a look of concern. Shaking her head, Gen could only hurry past her before her mother could ask her what was wrong.

So, it was true. Alan was a Pentercast through and through. Why did she continually fight to keep from believing it? She could feel the tears welling up. He'd never cared for her. She was just another of his victims, a game to while away the winter quiet, his Christmas diversion. She shuddered as she realized how close she'd come to trusting him, how much she had wanted to believe in him. After everything she'd been through, how she had longed for a champion—someone strong, powerful, in command. She'd have cheerfully made Alan into that champion. He had been right when he said she'd never seen him. But she saw him now. And she would never let him win.

She had to find William. There had to be a way out of this wager, surely she could make him see that. He would advise her how to free herself from this entanglement. She hurried to change into her riding habit. Ignoring her mother's dictate that she take a groom with her, she commandeered the watchful Bryce and rode toward the village.

It had been some time since she had been to the vicarage behind the little stone church. She remembered taking her lessons there with Allison and Geoffrey from the elderly curate whom William had replaced. It had been a small cozy house with a sunny parlor painted yellow. She was surprised to find it a great deal bigger than she remembered, with a separate wing housing the vicar's apartment and a covered walk connecting the house to the church. Leaded glass windows sparkled in the sunlight, and when she and Bryce were ushered inside by a housekeeper who was unknown to her, she found the walls hung in damask and the parlor windows in velvet. Life in Wenwood had definitely gotten better over the years. The Pentercasts were obviously generous patrons. No doubt it assuaged their guilt.

William met them in the parlor, his face wreathed in smiles. He was hastily shrugging out of a greatcoat as if he'd just come in from outdoors. "Miss Genevieve, and Miss Bryce, what an unexpected pleasure. Please, sit down."

"Bryce has a commission for my mother and cannot stay," Gen informed him.

Bryce, in the act of sitting near the door, froze, scowling at her. Gen knew she could scarcely call her mistress's daughter a liar in front of the young curate, but no more would she feel comfortable leaving her alone with William. Gen watched as Bryce visibly struggled over which rule of conduct she would honor. "Maybe we could go after you meet with Mr. Wellfordhouse," she tried.

"Oh, la," Gen trilled with a wave of her hand. "I would never be so selfish as to keep Mother waiting. Go along, Bryce. I shall only be a minute."

Left with no other choice, Bryce had to do as she suggested.

"She needn't worry," William smiled as Gen took a seat near him. "Mrs. Deems is just down the hall tidying up the vicar's study. If we leave the door open, I'm sure propriety can be satisfied." His smile faded as he took a good look at her. "But perhaps I should ask if there's a need for privacy. Is something amiss?"

She could feel the tears threatening and choked them back. "Oh, William, everything!"

Somehow she found herself sobbing on his shoulder, while William awkwardly patted her back and made soothing tisking noises. After a few minutes, she collected herself with difficulty, pulling away to fish in her reticule for a handkerchief. As she blew her nose, she could see William watching her, a concerned frown on his face.

"I'm all right," she assured him with a last sniff, "It's just been a rather difficult Christmas so far."

"Well, of course it has," he nodded understandingly. "First the news of your family's condition, then the flood, and now the Thorn. There must be times you wish you had never left London."

She sighed, rising to pace as was her wont. William politely rose with her.

"To be sure," she told him, "there are times I question the decision I made for the family. I thought the Abbey would be our salvation, that we would be able to rely on our neighbors to help us settle in. Now I don't know." She stopped to face him. "William, I've made a grave error with this wager. You must help me stop it, before something dreadful happens."

Outside came the sound of tooting, as if one of the village children had gotten a toy whistle for Christmas and was trying it out. William blinked as if trying to ignore it, focusing his eyes on her face. "Just what are you afraid of, Miss Genevieve?"

The whistle was joined by a second in ill-tuned chorus. Gen tried to ignore the sounds as well. "The gifts, for one thing. They are getting completely out of hand. My gardener's shed is now a coop for geese, our gardens may never be the same after penning that herd of cattle, and I don't even want to think about the Thorn."

William held up his hands as three more whistles joined the first two. "Now, I quite agree with Alan that that should not constitute your ninth gift. Unfortunately, since you seem intent on accepting it as such, I have decided to give in."

More whistles joined in cacophonously, and Gen was forced to raise her voice to be heard. "What do you mean, give in? Are you saying he's already lost? He's admitted defeat?"

William shook his head, but his answer was drowned out by the shrill sound from outside.

"Dash it all, what is that noise?" Gen demanded.

William took her arm and escorted her to the window, parting the sheer curtains with his free hand. Outside, a band of village children stood with sparkling eyes, each set of mittened hands wrapped around a wooden flute. As she watched, they finished

whatever song they thought they were playing together and lowered their instruments, grinning gleefully at each other.

"It seems the Wenwood Thorn still had a gift to give," William murmured in the silence that followed. "The Squire had
several of the lads help to carve one for every child in the village. I was just instructing our ten pipers here on 'While Shep-
herds Watched Their Flocks.' We thought to go serenading later,
particularly to the Abbey. So, you see, I cannot agree that his
gifts are so terrible."

Gen stared at her ten pipers, who had happily begun piping
again, and felt the tears returning. "Oh, William, I am so confused."

Fifteen

Verse Eleven, Eleven Ladies Dancing

Unfortunately, Gen's confusion was not alleviated by her conversation with William. Though he was her dear friend, or perhaps because of it, she found it hard to tell him her feelings about Alan Pentercast. Indeed, she wasn't sure she could put them into words even if she had felt comfortable doing so. In the end, she had let him think he had cheered her, then had collected a thoroughly disgusted Bryce and ridden for home, her concerns no more resolved than when she had left.

She got no release when she returned, however, as she found her mother, Allison, and Mrs. Chimes all closeted in close consultation for the party. She knew if she broke in she would be promptly consigned to duty or worse lose her temper over the cost they were incurring. In desperation, she retreated to her father's study, penned a hasty note to Carstairs, and gave it to Chimes to take it into town for posting.

She slept fitfully that night, plagued by dark, vague dreams. Awakening the next morning listless, she found it too cold for hunting and spent the hours wandering aimlessly about the Abbey. Everywhere she saw signs of her mother's handiwork—the unused ballroom at the far end of the house had been opened and dusted, the oak parquet floors waxed, the twin crystal chandeliers polished. The gilt-edged mirrors that hung at regular intervals along the dark wood walls, making the room seem larger and brighter, gleamed in their ornate frames.

In the kitchen, Mrs. Chimes and her helpers bustled about, putting together pies, pastries, cakes, and other luscious delicacies. Elsewhere, Chimes ordered about the footmen and the staff they had borrowed from the Pentercasts, sending them to carry silver, dishes, and glassware between the rooms, shuffle furniture and carpets, and fetch coal for the fireplaces. The maids were dusting rooms that hadn't been used for years, shrieking as they dislodged spider webs and bumping into each other as they scurried down the long halls.

Each sign of expense felt like another stone being added to the walls of Gen's prison. She was in such a foul mood by midday that she flatly refused to accompany Allison on a ride, consoling herself with the fact that the only horses left were thoroughly docile creatures more fit for harness than saddle. She was somewhat surprised, therefore, when Allison, with Bryce in tow, returned with their attendant groom sometime later, red cheeked and jubilant.

"Mother! Genevieve!" Gen could hear her calling from the entry, her excitement echoing down the long corridors. Curious, she roused herself from her place on the music-room sofa and went to see what was afoot. Her mother appeared from the opposite corridor just as she came in.

"Allison, moderate your tone," her mother scolded.

Allison giggled. "Sorry, Mother, but wait until you hear my news! The Squire's new pond has frozen completely over, and he's opened it for skating! They've a lovely brazier at one end to warm you, and some of the Squire's people are serving spiced cider and ale. Mrs. Pentercast told me to invite you all to join in the fun."

Her mother frowned, and Gen didn't know whether to follow suit or grin in delight. Part of her still wasn't sure how to face

Alan Pentercast after their last meeting, although she knew she couldn't avoid him forever. Another part of her longed to enjoy the sport she had loved as a child. Why did it have to be Alan that had the frozen pond? She would simply have to forgo the pleasure.

"Are you quite sure, Allison?" her mother was saying. "Mrs. Pentercast and I have yet to reach an agreement on a certain issue. And I thought she was too distraught over her missing son to be receiving. I cannot believe she wishes for our company."

"She most particularly asked for us all, Mother," Allison hurried to assure her. "Please may we go? I saw our old skates in the storeroom the other day. I'd so love to try them, wouldn't you, Gen?"

This was her chance to tell them she wanted nothing to do with Alan Pentercast, his mother, or his pond. "Truth be told," she heard herself say, "I'd love to go."

Their mother sighed. "Very well. Bryce, have Chimes bring round the carriage, then come help me change."

Gen tried not to notice that her spirits had lifted as she changed into warmer clothes. If she was feeling better, she reasoned, it was because she was going to have a chance to skate again. With any luck, a certain dark-haired gentleman wouldn't even be there. But she couldn't help darting a gaze all about the area as soon as they arrived just to make sure. And she was quite disgusted to find her spirits droop once more when she saw that she had been right.

Allison had been right as well. A number of the villagers had availed themselves of the Squire's hospitality. She spotted William on the far side of the roughly oval sheet of ice, helping one of the Mattison twins on with her skates. Near him, Mrs. Gurney and Mrs. Deems, the vicarage housekeeper, sat bundled in blankets, cups of hot cider in their gloved hands, enjoying a good coz. Farther along the shore Mrs. Pentercast, swathed in furs, sat in a large high-backed wooden chair that must have been brought down for her comfort. Beside her the Reverend York stood stiffly, bending solicitously to listen whenever she spoke. Glancing at her mother, Gen saw by her frown that she had seen the couple as well.

"There seems to be room nearest the fire," her mother observed, nodding to the opposite side of the pond from Mrs. Pentercast. Gen saw that a group of young men from the village were warming themselves near a large brazier of charcoal. Several held tankards of cider or ale. She started to follow her mother in that direction, and Allison darted ahead of them to claim a spot near the pond's edge. Gen took a stance next to her, glancing once again about the pond, looking for Alan. She scolded herself on her nervousness. It wasn't as if the man could accost her again, not with so many people about. And why was that thought rather depressing? With a shake of her head, she bent to help Allison on with her skates.

As she watched her sister stumble out onto the ice a few minutes later, arms windmilling for balance, she had to smile. She remembered a time when she had felt her form on the ice was far less important than the fun she was having. She was glad to see Allison agreed. With renewed enthusiasm, she bent to tackle her own skates, glad that her feet had not grown since she had last worn them six years ago.

She glanced up once at her mother's sniff.

"Some people, Genevieve, are simply not equipped for the role of suitor," Mrs. Munroe murmured with a nod across the pond. Gen looked to where William had brought tankards of cider to Mrs. Pentercast and the Reverend York. York pompously waved his aside with words that made William pale. Gen frowned. Then a few words from Mrs. Pentercast forced him to accept it. He held it awkwardly, shifting it back and forth in his gloved hands, scowling at the retreating William. Gen was glad her friend's back was turned so that he couldn't see it.

"No doubt he has difficulty holding his liquor," her mother

sniffed. Gen bent to her skates to hide her grin at the unconscious pun.

She had just finished cinching the final strap when she noticed a sudden quiet, as if everyone around the pond had collectively sucked in their breaths. Looking up, she saw with a pang that Alan had come out on the terrace, his brother at his side. Much as she was pleased to see Geoffrey alive and unhurt, she wondered how he could so easily show his face before so many of his accusers. Both Pentercast brothers were dressed for the weather in tweed greatcoats, leather gloves, and hessians. Alan wore a smile for his neighbors, but Gen could see the effort it cost him. Geoffrey's head was high, his chin jutted out defiantly, his shoulders were squared. To a person, everyone around the pond was staring at him.

"There you are, my dears," Mrs. Pentercast clarioned, digging a gloved hand from the furs to wave. "Alan, Geoffrey, come join the fun!"

They descended the stairs, moving down to the pond. Their guests all found it expedient to busy themselves in their activities. As Alan and Geoffrey reached the ice, people moved aside to make way for them. But it was no gesture of welcome. It appeared to be a desire not to come in contact with Geoffrey. His chin stuck out farther as he bent to strap on his skates.

With a spray of ice, Allison skidded to a stop just in front of them. Geoffrey looked up with a scowl.

"Good afternoon, Mr. Pentercast, Squire. How very nice of you to host this event for all your neighbors."

Alan inclined his head as Geoffrey straightened. "I'm glad you're enjoying it, Miss Munroe."

Allison bestowed on him a pretty pout. "I'd enjoy it a great deal more if there was a gallant gentleman to partner me."

Alan managed a smile, but before he could demur, she held out her hands to Geoff. "Shall we, Mr. Pentercast?"

A lopsided grin spread across Geoffrey's face, replacing the defiant scowl and making him look like a boy opening his first birthday present. "I'd be delighted, Miss Munroe," he proclaimed, taking her hands to swing himself out on the ice. Gen realized she had been holding her breath and released it. Around her, the pond returned to life.

"She has a good heart," her mother murmured beside her. "I only hope it will stand her in good stead."

Gen watched them racing across the ice, laughing, and suffered a pang of jealousy. How wonderful it must feel to be that free! She'd suffocated under the burden of their financial dilemma for months. Could she lift it so easily by skimming across the ice? Determined to put aside her doldrums, she stepped boldly out. One foot immediately shot ahead of the other, and she scrambled to regain her balance. As she felt her face heat in a blush, strong arms seized her waist and eased her back onto her skates. Her speeding heartbeat warned her who held her, but she didn't dare turn her head to confirm her suspicions lest she fall again.

"Easy does it," Alan murmured in her ear. "No doubt it's been a few years since you were up on these, but it will all come back to you."

The temptation to stay in his arms was remarkably strong, but she forced herself to straighten, sliding her foot slowly forward once more. She was pleased to see she did not slip. Alan's touch retreated as she found her balance. She turned her head to thank him and began to wobble once again.

"Give me a moment to put on my skates," he laughed, catching her again and setting her back on her feet. "I'd be delighted to tutor you in the finer points."

"That won't be necessary," she snapped, half afraid it was his presence that was causing her uncertainty to begin with. She concentrated on her wayward limbs, trying to regain the rhythm of skating. It was rather like dancing, if she remembered correctly. You balanced from foot to foot as if swaying to an unheard tune. Focusing only on her movements, she started along the shore.

"That's the way, Miss Genevieve," William called as she passed him, and she rewarded him with a smile. A few more steps and she felt her confidence rise. The shore began to speed by, the winter wind to whip her cheeks. Her troubles retreated with each step. She was free at last.

Allison and Geoffrey sped past, their laughter tinkling in the chill air. Two of the village children skated a circle around her, and she made a silly face at them. They giggled appreciatively, then turned to speed off for other games. Mrs. Pentercast raised her hand to wave as she passed, and she waved back, pleased that it caused no more than a momentary hesitation in her stride. She didn't much like Reverend York's beneficent nod, but decided it wasn't worth dwelling on. The day was clear, the air was crisp and she was once more in control. She felt so good she indulged in the luxury of a ladylike twirl. The village youths called encouragement and raised their tankards to her in salute.

She finished her circle, smiling and waving at her mother, who smiled quietly back. Emboldened, she quickened her stride and flashed past Allison, giving her sister's pelisse a playful tug. Allison squealed in delight, while Geoffrey raised a hand in threatened pursuit. She wrinkled her nose and wiggled her fingers at him, then sped off across the pond before he could follow.

This was how she had remembered her childhood at the Abbey—carefree, accepted, happy. This was what Wenwood and Christmas meant to her, this feeling of freedom, of simple pleasures, of friends and family. She knew she was right bringing her mother and Allison home. This was where they belonged. This was where her heart would always be.

Alan came up to skate beside her, and she slowed to take his arm. She saw his eyebrows rise in surprise, but just smiled at him. It felt right at the moment that he was here; she didn't want to question the feeling. No doubt she'd examine it at length tonight in the privacy of her bedroom, but now she only wanted to go on skating like this as long as possible.

Alan seemed to sense her mood, for he said nothing as they skated arm in arm around the oval of the pond. She could feel his strength beside her and wondered how it would feel to rely on someone other than herself again, a helpmate, a lover. She shivered at the thought.

"Are you chilled?" he murmured.

She shook her head, feeling herself blush. Perhaps she ought to focus on something other than his nearness. She forced herself to look past him to the shore of the pond. They were nearing the fires now. She saw Allison and Geoffrey had joined the other young people there and frowned at the tankard in her sister's hand. That had better be nothing more than cider Geoffrey Pentercast had handed her. Then her mother came into view, lips pursed in disapproval, and she found herself happy to look back at Alan again.

"It was kind of your sister to skate with Geoff," he said, as they turned. "I'm well aware that everyone assumes he's been responsible for these acts of destruction."

"I have to agree with Allison that he has no obvious reason to do them," Gen replied. "But the vandal's true identity eludes me."

"Then you no longer think I'm the one who put him up to it?" The question had an edge of belligerence, as well as hope. She really couldn't blame him after her recent behavior—But she found it difficult to answer, afraid that in answering she would open the way for the wager to continue. She glanced past him to the shore again, trying to marshal her thoughts. Mrs. Pentercast was grinning at her, but Reverend York was positively glowering. Belatedly she remembered his words of yesterday. She glanced guiltily back at Alan, trying to see the rake behind his gentle demeanor. All she saw was the frown of concern on his handsome face.

"What is it? You look as if you've suddenly discovered I buried my first three wives in the cellar."

She couldn't help but laugh. "Oh, nothing so grand as that, I'm afraid. As for your question, I must apologize for my behavior, Squire. I was so very upset at the loss of the Thorn that I lashed out without thinking."

"I quite understand," he replied, offering her a sad smile. "The old tree means a lot to me as well. I had Mother's gardener keep a few pieces in the hothouse. If they make it through the winter, Wenwood may yet have its Thorn."

Admiration and thankfulness welled up inside her. "Oh, Alan, I'm so glad!" She gave his arm a squeeze, then had to look away from the warmth of his gaze.

He slowed to a stop, and she was forced to slow with him. She glanced about the pond, afraid to meet his gaze. He sighed. "I won't make you face me, Genevieve. But you must know I haven't given up. I still have two more days left."

"I know," she murmured, steadfastly watching the other skaters.

"What do you see when you look out there?"

She was almost afraid to answer, not sure where the question would lead. Still, the thought seemed harmless enough. She looked around again, trying to see anything she might have missed that would be significant to him. Children chased each other about the ice, couples skated in quiet harmony, the village youths had convinced the footmen to bring another chair out onto the ice so they could push it around, Mrs. Gurney had managed to get Mrs. Deems to join her on the ice. "I see everyone enjoying themselves because of your kindness," she said truthfully.

"Thank you for that. But would you not say that skating is remarkably like dancing?"

She started, remembering her thoughts as she had tried the ice. "Yes, I would say they bear a great deal in common."

"And have you noticed how many ladies have taken the ice this afternoon?"

She licked her lips, seeing the trap being set. "La, sir, you cannot expect me to keep track of so many moving bodies."

She could feel him frowning. "You are quite capable of keeping track of any number of things, Miss Munroe. However, if you're determined to make this difficult, we can fetch the Reverend Wellfordhouse to do the counting."

Now she was sure. She felt her control, and her freedom, slipping. "That won't be necessary," she snapped. "Since you insist, I will do it myself. There's Allison, thank goodness, although I'm not entirely sure that chair they have her in is safe, Mrs. Gurney, Mrs. Deems, the Mattison twins, Charlotte Jarvis, Jane Henry, that young lady Tom Gurney is courting and her sister, and Mary Delacorte."

"And yourself," he prompted.

"And myself," she amended with a sigh. "You do not need to tell me that that makes eleven."

"Eleven ladies dancing," he murmured. "One more day until Epiphany, Miss Munroe. One more gift to end our wager."

Gen felt as if the burden she had carried had returned. Her back ached, and the skates pinched her feet. "Indeed," she acknowledged, turning away from him for the shore "A lot can happen in a day, Squire. You haven't won yet." She made sure she was halfway back to her mother before he could even think to answer.

Sixteen

Verse Twelve, Twelve Lords a-Leaping

Gen awoke the morning of the Eve of Epiphany feeling smothered. She pushed off the quilt and bedclothes and went to huddle before the fireplace, the Oriental carpet warm beneath her toes. The fire crackled in the grate, and from elsewhere in the Abbey she could smell the spicy aroma of the Epiphany cake baking. Outside the morning looked crisp and clear, and it seemed blessedly quiet. Alan's cows were safely home and being milked by people who were used to such activities. No doubt the cows were as thankful as she was for the move. She had a great deal for which to be thankful.

Still, the feeling of a weight upon her persisted, and she knew it hadn't been her bed coverings. It was the last day of Christmas. Tomorrow everything would change. She would have to dismiss the servants except for Chimes and his wife. Mr. Carstairs would likely answer her mother's summons, and she would have to admit she had been unable to convince her mother of the truth of their situation. She would have to watch as he took away the Munroe diamonds to pay for the party she had been unable to stop. And sometime today, Alan would bring his gift for the twelfth day of Christmas, winning the wager and claiming her hand in marriage. Like the fox she had hunted with her father, she could hear the hounds baying and knew it was only a short time before they closed for the kill.

She shuddered, rising to ring for Bryce to help her dress. She couldn't sit around moping all day. There had to be something useful she could do. But try as she might as Bryce helped her into her lilac kerseymere gown and she went down the long corridor to the breakfast room, she could not think of a way out of any of her difficulties. There was no more money for the servants, her mother and Allison were even now putting the finishing touches on the party preparations, and she hadn't been able to stop any present being given her by Alan, so she couldn't think of any way to stop him now. The feeling of helplessness intensified, and she fought it off once more. She was Rutherford Munroe's daughter, inventive, resourceful. She had to think of something.

She went to the music room to be away from the preparations and paced before the spinet, deep in thought. The more she thought about her situation, the more she became convinced that the answer lay with Alan. She might not be able to influence his gift for the day, and she almost shuddered to think how he might bring about his twelve lords a-leaping, but she could decide how she would face his impending triumph. What was she going to do when he won? Honor demanded that she accept his hand in marriage. Yet Reverend York had intimated that marriage would likely be the farthest thing from his mind. Surely he wouldn't have entered the wager with William of all people, if his intent was to seduce her. Therefore, he had to be serious in his intent to marry her. The question remained, why?

She remembered his kiss and felt herself coloring in a blush. The things he had said that day indicated that he loved her. If he had proven to be half the man she had once thought him, she could easily have returned his love. So many things he had done in the last twelve days showed him to have grown up to be as gentle and kind as she remembered. But other things pointed to a more harsh personality. How could she know who the real Alan was?

The crux of the matter lay with the acts of vandalism. If she could prove he had had no involvement in the flood and the destruction of the Thorn, she could believe in the Alan of old and accept his offer with some hope of happiness. If not, she would not feel guilty refusing him, regardless of whether or not he won his wager. That decided, she knew what she must do. She darted back to her room, donned her hunting habit, and slipped out through the side door in the Abbey chapel.

She spent the rest of the day gathering information. She re-surveyed the dam site, spoke with two men who would admit they had been with Geoffrey Pentercast on New Year's Eve, and interviewed several of the village mothers regarding their sons' activities of the last fortnight. She took tea with William at the vicarage and had a lively discussion of the possibilities. William, of course, could not imagine anyone in his parish doing anything so vile as to destroy the Wenwood Thorn, but Gen was able to get him past his initial indignation into a thorough discussion of the reasons behind such as activity. By the time she returned home, she had much to think about.

As she stood beside her window that evening, waiting for the bustling Bryce to help her on with her finery, she looked up into the clear winter night at the stars sparkling above the bare trees. A single star shone brighter than the others, and she was reminded of the night—Epiphany, the night when the wise men had given their gifts to the baby they had searched so long to find. They had come so far only to find a poor child, wrapped in swaddling clothes, lying in a manger. Yet their faith had al-lowed them to see a king. After all her ruminations and discus-sions, that was what it all came down to, the simple act of believing. Somehow, in her father's death and all the unpleas-antness since, she had lost that. A tear fell and she dashed it away with the back of her hand. Resting her forehead against the cool glass, she took a deep breath to calm herself. If she wanted to find her king, she would need to find that belief once again.

The entry hall was already thronged with guests when she joined her mother and sister in the receiving line sometime later. I must seem festive, she told herself firmly, pasting a smile on her face. Every wood surface, from the paneled walls to the parquet floor to the rosewood bench and matching hall table glowed with a fresh coat of wax. Every spot of brass and gilt gleamed from polishing. The candles in the sconces glowed. The corridors leading off the entry hall were draped in evergreens, with roses sent from the Pentercast hot house sprinkled among the green. Now she could see why Bryce had insisted on her wearing the white satin gown trimmed with rouleaux of roses along the hem. With the Spanish sleeves of pink tucked with white, and the scalloped neckline, she looked like one of Alan's roses come alive.

She took her place beside her mother and Allison to welcome their arriving guests, returning her mother's nod of approval with her own smile. It seemed to her a good omen that her mother had chosen a simple, elegant gown of rose satin with a ruff of white ruching at the throat and white lace at the cuffs and hem. Beside her, Allison was in a pink sarcenet gown that complemented the pink of excitement in her cheeks. Even Chimes had found time to have his coat pressed and his hair combed, although he still ushered in their guests with considerably less aplomb than the normal butler. In fact, Gen could only call his expression gleeful as he brought Mrs. Pentercast and her two sons forward to be received. It cost her a lot to keep the smile on her own face.

"You girls look lovely." Alan's mother smiled in approval, reaching out to give Gen's arm a comradely squeeze. Gen steadfastly focused on Mrs. Pentercast, knowing that if she looked directly at Alan without fortifying herself, she would be undone.

She did notice, however, that Geoffrey Pentercast had set a large box on the hall table, shoving aside the greens that were decorating it.

"I've never seen the Abbey look more festive," Mrs. Pentercast continued, then paused to peer up at Gen's mother's face thoughtfully. "I'd tell you that color quite suits you, Trudy, but I know you're not talking to me."

Her mother inclined her head. "Perhaps that can be remedied tonight, Fancine."

Alan's mother clasped her hands. "Oh, good! For I have much to tell you. Come find me when you're done here, and we'll have a good coz." As if she couldn't resist, she reached out to squeeze Mrs. Munroe's arm as well. "I've missed you, dear!"

Gen's mother stiffened at the touch, and Gen made ready to jump into the breach, but her mother managed to keep a smile on her face. "I'd be delighted to discuss the matter further. Please enjoy the party."

Even as Gen straightened herself to face Alan, Geoffrey pushed his way in front, giving her mother the briefest of nods before seizing Allison's hand. "Promise me at least two dances," he commanded.

Allison tossed her head. "One dance is surely all that is proper, Mr. Pentercast. Er, isn't that right, Mother?"

"Allison is still learning the dance steps, Mr. Pentercast," her mother intoned, eyeing them both as if she'd found a worm in her apple tart. "She hasn't been properly presented. I'm sure you understand."

"In other words, I ought to thank you for sparing my feet," Geoffrey grumbled. Allison brindled, but he slumped past her into the corridor leading to the ballroom and she was forced to face forward to greet the next guest.

"My brother is still learning as well," Alan chuckled, stepping forward. "I hope *you* understand, Mrs. Munroe."

Gen commanded her stomach to stop doing acrobatics, to no

avail, even as her mother inclined her head in understanding. "Some gentlemen, like a good meal, require more seasoning than others."

"Why, Mother, that was almost poetic!" Allison chimed in.

The faintest of pinks arose on her mother's cheeks. "Nonsense. Squire, you are most welcome."

He bowed over her mother's hand and Allison's. Gen took a deep breath as he reached for hers. She was almost afraid of what would happen when he touched her, but he held her hand the briefest of moments before straightening. She nearly sagged; with relief or disappointment, she wasn't sure. He cocked his head, eyeing her, and several locks of dark brown hair fell onto his forehead.

"I suddenly feel as unseasoned as my brother. Dare I request at least two dances?"

She ought to say no as easily as Allison had. She ought to find some excuse, any excuse, to keep him at a distance until she was sure of him. But all she could see was the light of hope in those dark brown eyes and the hint of a smile around his warm lips. "Make it three, and you have yourself a partner," she heard herself say. She was quite thankful that the next guest claimed her attention before she had to respond to his look of surprised delight.

She survived greeting the rest of their guests, although her heart sank when she counted considerably more than her mother's first estimate of thirty people, and was pleased when William offered her his arm to escort her into dinner. She was quick to note that her mother while carefully following etiquette as to seating arrangements, nevertheless had found a way to separate Allison and Geoffrey by putting them on opposite sides of the table with a very large silver epergne of greenery between them. Fortunately for Gen, the arrangement also put her and Alan on opposite sides of the table of the offensive epergne, leaving her to converse with Mrs. Pentercast on her right and

Geoffrey on her left. Although Geoffrey managed no more than a grunt to her sallies, she could tell by the other conversations around the table that dinner was going to be a much more successful affair than their first night with the Pentercasts. The neighbors laughed, wine flowed, and the food was superb. Gen tried not to count the cost of the oysters in aspic or the curried ham slices, and she didn't even want to know how much it must have cost to get fresh strawberries for the trifle Mrs. Chimes had prepared for dessert. The gentlemen did not tarry long over their port, and soon the entire company was gathered in the ballroom for the entertainment.

William claimed her hand for the first dance, and although she was disappointed it wasn't Alan, she was pleased to note that her mother had agreed to partner him. Tom Harvey stood up with Allison, who was beaming with obvious pleasure. Gen caught a quick glimpse of Geoffrey Pentercast glowering before she was forced to give her attention to the various steps of the lively country dance her mother's imported quartet struck up.

From then on, her hand was claimed by every gentleman in the room, from the Widower Jenkins who owned much of the land on the other side of Wenwood to Mary Delacourte's younger brother Charlie who was appearing, like Allison, at his first grownup dance. Every gentleman in the room but one, that was. Alan seemed to be equally busy doing the pretty with every lady in the room, and actively insisting that the other men do the same. Much as she could admire his chivalry in partnering her mother, his own, and even the elderly Widow Tate, she found it difficult to watch him cavorting with Mary Delacourte, whose figure-hugging blue silk gown with the low décolletage matched the color of her eyes, neither of which appeared to be wandering. That could not be said of the eyes of most of the men in the room as she laughed at something Alan had said.

Gen was sitting on one of the chairs arranged along the side of the room to catch her breath later in the evening when she first noticed their guests' attitudes toward Geoffrey Pentercast. Just as they had at the pond the day before, none of them seemed willing to be in his company. When he approached a group, it grew silent or disbanded. When he asked a lady to dance, she refused. Even the young men of his own age, bumping into each other in their attempts to reach the refreshment table at the far end of the room, suddenly lost their appetites when he joined them.

"Something has to be done about this," she told her mother, nodding to where Geoffrey stood with fists at his side, scowling at no one in particular.

Her mother shook her head. "It is a shame, but I'm afraid he brought it on himself if he truly is the culprit. The Thorn was an important part of Wenwood."

"Oh, let's not start that again," Allison snapped, throwing herself down on a chair to join them. She waved the young man who was attending her off to go fetch her a cup of punch. Gen smiled, thinking how well her sister would do in her upcoming Season. Then the smile faded as she remembered there would be no Season. She forced herself to focus on the present.

"I know you think him innocent, Allison," her mother was saying. "But that does not change the fact that he is the most likely candidate."

"I disagree," Gen put in, winning her a beaming smile from Allison. "I'm beginning to think he is innocent as well. If that is true, it seems most unfair for everyone to ostracize him like this. And while they do, no one thinks to find the true culprit."

"Exactly!" Allison cried, jumping to her feet. "We should be launching an investigation! Calling in the home guards!"

"Moderate your tone, Allison," her mother sighed, motioning her to return to her seat. "If he is innocent, I agree that we must find the real vandal. However, I do not see how that can begin here tonight, at our party."

Allison lowered her voice conspiratorially. "I've already

launched my own investigation, and I cannot find a single one of the villagers who will admit to being with Geoffrey when he cut down the Thorn. You will remember Reverend York said there were nine of them."

Gen's glance was drawn to the far side of the room where the Reverend York was paying his usual court to Mrs. Pentercast. The lady in question seemed to be less enthused than usual with his devotion, mostly, Gen suspected, because the gentleman refused to dance, and the lively Mrs. Pentercast was forced to keep him company on the side.

"It does not signify," Mrs. Munroe sniffed with resigned tolerance. "None of them wish to admit they were with him and suffer his fate, that is all."

Allison shook her head so vehemently that her flaxen ringlets bounced in wild abandon. "I think not, Mother. When Gen and I first heard the noise that day, it sounded like a single hollow booming, much as one might bang a large drum. I doubt nine young men, intent on destruction, would make such a sound."

Gen looked at her younger sister in admiration. "You are quite right, Allison. It *did* sound like a single woodsman. But who?"

Allison sighed, slumping in her seat with a scowl. "That I have not been able to determine."

"Regardless," her mother put in with a nod toward the refreshment table, "it appears Mr. Pentercast has decided to take his leave."

They looked to where Geoffrey was indeed stalking toward the door, shoving aside those who stood, even remotely, in his way. The other guests stared at him as he passed, and quickly bent to whisper when he was safely out of hearing. Gen shook her head, rising. "This is unfair. I'm going to tell him he is welcome to stay."

Allison sprang to her feet. "I'll come with you."

With a nod of acceptance from their mother, they hurried

across the room. Before they could reach the door to the corridor, however, Alan intercepted them.

"Ladies," he bowed, "I believe you are needed for the next set."

Gen glanced quickly over her shoulder, where a number of their guests were lining up for another country dance. She counted eleven couples. "If you ask our mother, sir, I'm sure she'll be happy to complete the set with you."

He frowned, but she darted after Allison before he could detain her.

The corridor was empty as she stepped into it, but she thought she heard voices from the farther end of the entry hall. She started down the corridor and heard a footstep behind her. Halting, she found Alan beside her.

"Is something wrong?" he frowned at her.

"Nothing at all," she lied cheerfully. "Please return to the party, and I assure you my sister and I will rejoin you shortly."

His frown deepened, and he matched her purposeful stride. "It seems odd you'd want to leave such a successful party. Might I be of assistance?"

She stopped to face him, ignoring the warning pounding of her heart. "Squire, you are being very kind, but I assure you, there is nothing to be concerned about."

He cocked his head, eyeing her as he had when he entered. "Why don't I believe you? There have been too many strange events this Christmas, Miss Munroe, for me to feel comfortable allowing you to wander off by yourself."

"This is my own home, sir," she informed him, throwing up her hands. "What could possibly happen here?"

Down the corridor, Allison screamed.

Alan thrust Gen protectively behind him before dashing toward the sound. She lifted her skirts and raced to follow. Ahead of her, Alan cursed and slid sideways on the polished floor. From under him scampered a terrified ferret.

Gen skidded to a stop and backed up against the walls as the furry creature darted past her. Alan had regained his footing and was immediately at her side. "What the devil?"

Allison appeared in the mouth of the corridor, hurrying toward them. "Did you see it? Where did it go?"

Gen pointed down the corridor toward the party. "How did that thing get in here?"

Allison put up her head. "You needn't get waspish. It was a gift for me from Mr. Pentercast."

Alan groaned. "It only wanted this. Geoffrey!"

His brother appeared, grinning. Gen fought the desire to knock the smile off his face. "Sorry about that. I guess it just slipped out of my hands."

"How dare you!" Gen managed through gritted teeth. "And to think I thought you innocent!"

His grin disappeared into a scowl. "I am innocent, but since all your fine guests have given me the name, I thought I might as well play the game."

From down in the ballroom came shouts and screams.

"I'll deal with you later," Alan swore before turning to dash back down the corridor. Gen favored her sister and Geoffrey with a scowl of her own before hastening to follow.

The ballroom was in an uproar when she entered. Every lady who was able had scrambled up on one of the side chairs. Others stood huddled in a trembling group in one of the corners. Even the quartet had managed to elevate their instruments off the floor. The older gentlemen were attempting to calm their agitated wives while the younger men were slapping their knees and laughing over the joke. She caught a glimpse of a furry black tail disappearing under the skirting of the refreshment table.

"It's just a ferret," Alan was calling in explanation. He motioned to Tom Harvey, William, and several of the other men to join him. "We'll have it caught in no time."

Allison hurried into the room, a small homemade cage in her hand. "Here," she cried, thrusting it at Alan. "Use this. And please don't hurt him."

"Allison Ermintrude Munroe," her mother said quietly from behind her. "If this is your doing you may rest assured that you will not be permitted to another party until you are old enough to be a spinster."

Allison swallowed, stepping back out of Alan's way. "Yes, Mother."

"It was my fault," Geoffrey Pentercast offered, stepping up to join them. "I'm afraid I took the general snubbing in character and decided to get even. I'll help catch the beast. He knows me now."

"He's under the table," Gen pointed out. With a nod, Alan and the other men set out.

It took considerably longer than Alan had claimed to subdue the beast, who proved very good at darting away at the last minute and quite inventive at finding dark corners in which to hide. Unfortunately, these corners included the sofa on which Mrs. Pentercast and Reverend York sat, the skirting on the raised dais that held the musicians, and the hem of Mary Delacourte's dress. They finally ran him to ground against the French doors to the garden. Geoffrey managed to grab the little creature by the scruff of the neck and pop him back into the cage. As they carried it past her, Gen saw that the little animal's ribs were heaving as hard as her mother's.

"Well, that was quite a little adventure." Alan laughed as the women were assisted back down off the chairs and the room was set to rights. Her mother was hurrying to encourage the musicians to begin playing again, and Allison was boasting of her bravery to a group of young men. Looking up at Alan, Gen found she couldn't be angry. His hair was in complete disarray, his neckcloth had come undone, and there was a piece of cake stuck to one corner of his chin. She reached up a hand to dislodge it. "You go to great lengths, sir, but I do believe William would agree with me that there were twelve lords a-leaping here tonight."

He stared at her. "Are you saying . . . ?"

She deposited the cake onto a side table, her heart pounding even harder than when the ferret had escaped. "I'm saying I haven't been asked to dance. You had indicated you wished to dance with me, hadn't you?"

"Above all things," he murmured, reaching out to take her proffered hand. His glove was covered in strawberry jelly. Laughing, he pulled it back. "But perhaps I'd better clean up a bit first."

Gen smiled at him, suddenly sure of her feelings. "You never looked more handsome, Squire. But I'll have Chimes show you to one of the guest rooms. Perhaps by the time you return, they'll be ready to start the next set."

Seventeen

Interlude, Baritone Solo

Alan was glad Chimes led him to the guest room instead of merely pointing the way. He'd never been very good at following the twists and turns of the Abbey's corridors, and right at the moment he was too bemused to know where he was, let alone where he was going. Chimes made sure he was settled, then, chuckling, left him with warm water, soap, and towels that a footman hastily brought so he might perform his ablutions, promising to return shortly with fresh gloves and neckcloth.

She was conceding defeat. He could scarcely credit it. He'd done everything he could to maneuver the various guests into a set with twelve couples so that he could attempt to claim his twelve lords a-leaping, but he knew full well she could have disagreed with his interpretation had she wished. He hadn't even mentioned the gift, and here she was ready to grant it to him. He knew he ought to accept the offering gratefully, but after all her protests the last twelve days, capitulation had seemed so unlikely that he found it impossible to comprehend. Not for the first time he found himself wishing he understood what was going on in that beautiful blond head.

He had scarcely shrugged out of his coat and rolled up his sleeves when there was a hesitant knock on the door. Frowning, he reached for his coat again, wondering who could need his services so soon. Before he could call for the person to enter, the door opened and the Reverend York slipped inside, closing the door carefully behind him.

Alan set the coat back down again with a sigh, reluctant to have his time to think so easily interrupted. "Good evening, Vicar. Are you in need of refurbishing as well?"

The man shook his head, crossing to ease his bulk down onto a chair beside the fire, from which vantage point it seemed he intended to watch Alan's work. Alan frowned at the familiarity, but his frown went unnoticed. The vicar settled in and leaned back.

"No, no, my boy, luckily I was spared your, er, valiant attempts at catching the creature. I thought it best to remain at your mother's side. Women are so easily upset by such events, indeed, indeed."

"Indeed," Alan quipped. "Then you'll excuse me while I continue."

"Certainly, certainly." York waved a meaty paw. "You wonder at my presence, I'm sure. I thought this a good time for a fatherly word of advice."

Alan smothered a groan. "Vicar, please don't take me wrong, but I was never very good at listening to fatherly advice, even from my own father."

"Ah, but your father wasn't exactly known for dispensing good advice, I believe."

Alan, in the act of soaping his hands, paused and glanced again at the vicar. Was it only his imagination that the last words were less than his usual sycophantic bluster? The man was regarding the fire, hands clasped over his belly, as if nothing untoward was happening. Shaking his head, Alan returned to his task.

"I see you haven't heeded my warnings about Miss Munroe," York put in.

Alan paused again, eyeing him. "No more than you have heeded my warnings concerning my mother, sir. I guess we can both say that love knows no caution."

"Ah, well said, well said," the vicar nodded. "Yes, well said indeed. So, you fancy yourself in love with the chit, I take it."

Alan finished washing his hands and toweled them dry. He knew his annoyance showed in his every quick move, but he couldn't seem to muster up the desire to care. "Vicar, I continue to fail to see what business this is of yours."

"It is my business as the shepherd of this flock," York asserted, puffing out his chest. "I cannot sit idly by while the leader of our fair community does himself such a great injustice."

"If you are referring to the famed Pentercast/Munroe feud, you may save your breath," Alan told him, shrugging back into his coat. "I don't believe in that nonsense."

There was a timid tap on the door, and the footman scurried in with fresh gloves and a neckcloth for Alan. Alan accepted them with a nod, and the footman scurried out again, leaving the door ajar as he did so.

"I had hoped to spare you this, my son," York rumbled with a melancholy shake of his head. "But you hold the evidence in your hands and you cannot see it, you cannot see it at all." He heaved a martyred sigh. "It has come to my attention that Miss Munroe is, how can I put this delicately, less than pure?"

Alan turned to stare at him, the neckcloth gripped tightly in his hand. "I cannot have heard you correctly."

York couldn't meet his eyes. "I know this is difficult. You must understand it is no easier for me to admit I have failed one of my flock. Of course, I can take some comfort in the fact that she was led astray by the wicked life of London and not in my own village. Still, to have taken lovers at such an early age cannot speak well of the lady's constancy."

Alan crushed the neckcloth in one hand; it was the only way

he could keep from putting his hands around the man's neck, and throttling him. "How dare you sit there and calmly spout such lies?" he managed to grit out through his rage. "You will apologize at once."

York blinked, his jowls quivering, whether in fear or righteous indignation, Alan couldn't be sure. "I only thought to spare you, my son. Consider, if you will, that as lovely as she is, she has had three whole seasons without marrying. There must be a reason. And the servant—they haven't lived here for years and yet they have a pair of men's gloves and neckcloth handy? Does it not strike you as odd? Love may know no caution, as you said, my boy, but surely you have not abandoned all logic. Think of your family, your dear family. Think of how important it is to pass down the family name. You wouldn't want to bring home a heifer and not know which bull has sired her calf."

"Enough!" Alan shouted, hurling the neckcloth to the floor. "I will hear no more of this, do I make myself clear? You may thank God you are a man of the cloth, because if you weren't I'd call you out. Now get out."

"No need to become belligerent, sir," York sniffed, though Alan could see he had paled. "I came only to help. I've always been a staunch supporter of the Pentercasts, as well you know. You can count on my discretion." His eyes narrowed, giving him a decidedly crafty look. Alan wondered why he hadn't recognized it before.

"Of course, were I to lose my place at Wenwood, I would have no course but to explain to others why I was thrown out for speaking the truth."

Alan stared at him. "Are you attempting to blackmail me?"

York held up his gloved hands. "Oh, heavens no, dear boy, heavens no. I just want you to understand the possible repercussions should anything untoward happen to my position. A man of my age cannot be too careful, you see. Such livings are not easy to come by, not easy at all."

"And harder to keep, I warrant," Alan snapped in reply.

"Ah, you do understand." York nodded, rising. "I'm glad we had this talk, my dear boy. We seem to have reached an understanding." He moved toward the door, then turned back to Alan, his eyes once more narrowed. "Oh, and if you do decide to go through with this marriage, there will be no special license. I'm afraid you'll just have to wait while I read the banns over the next few weeks. That is, if I remember." He sighed. "She really isn't the right one for you, you know. I've done all I could to prevent your heartache."

"That, sir, is another lie," said Reverend Wellfordhouse. Alan looked up in surprise to find the curate bristling, standing in the doorway, Gen, Allison, and Geoffrey crowding close behind him. "Pardon this interruption, Squire." William bowed to Alan before leading them into the room. "You see, we've been comparing notes on the mysterious destruction of the Thorn, and we've come to a conclusion that I could scarce credit, until I heard Mr. York's last speech." He frowned up at his master. "If I didn't know better, Mr. York, I'd say you were threatening the Squire."

York beamed beneficently. "Not at all, my boy, not at all. Squire Pentercast and I part on the best of terms, isn't that so, Alan?"

Alan gritted his teeth, but the look of concern on Gen's face kept him silent. Above all else, he felt she mustn't know the lies the man was spreading. "The Vicar and I understand each other."

Wellfordhouse shook his head even as York nodded. "Mr. York, these good people seem to think you cut down the Thorn yourself. And worse, that you've been behind all the vandalism. I'd like to be able to prove them wrong. May I see your hands?"

Alan started. York? The vandal? He narrowed his eyes as he considered the possibility. York was certainly large and strong enough to have broken the dam and cut down the Thorn.

Alan found it harder to believe that he would wander about the countryside destroying property, but then he remembered that York had been the one to tell him of the acts to begin with. Perhaps there had been no other acts. The man had merely lied to cover his tracks. He would not have given it credence had he not heard the bile the man was spouting a few minutes earlier. He glanced at Geoffrey and saw he wore an equally fierce look. Miss Allison stood with arms crossed over her chest, a pretty pout on her face. Gen was watching his brother closely, and he nearly groaned aloud. It seemed she still thought Geoffrey might be behind all this.

"My hands?" York echoed beside him. "What is this nonsense? A man of my maturity, my social standing, my place in the community, a common vandal? Really, sir, you of all people should know the danger of listening to idle gossip."

Wellfordhouse looked sad. "I do, Mr. York, believe me, I do. That's why I would very much like to see your hands."

"This is ridiculous!" York snapped, pushing his way past him. "I will not . . . ump." He glowered at Geoffrey who barred his way. "Stand aside, sir! I will not listen to such accusations."

Alan moved forward to catch the man's arm. It was time for the truth to come out. He could stand that look of doubt on Gen's face no longer. "Why shouldn't you listen?" he growled, grabbing one of the man's hands even as York attempted to shrink away from what he saw on his face. "The rest of us have had to hear enough from you." He held up his hand, looking past York to Wellfordhouse. "What exactly do you think to find, William?"

Wellfordhouse cleared his throat. "Well, sir, for all he's a fine strong gentleman, Mr. York doesn't generally do much manual labor. It really isn't fitting for a man of his station. Cutting down something as large as the Thorn had to have been a major effort, especially as it followed shortly on the destruction of the dam. I expect he'd have given himself blisters."

"Do you indeed?" Alan mused, gazing at Gen. She stood wide-eyed as if holding her breath.

York struggled, and Alan tightened his grip. "Nonsense, I tell you! What possible reason could I have for such dastardly deeds?"

"I have no idea," Alan replied. "Let's find out." He wrenched the glove off his hand. Across the palm lay a bandage, stained with blood. York groaned. Allison clapped her hands. Geoffrey grinned. Wellfordhouse looked troubled. Gen let out her breath, and Alan could see her slender frame relax. He glanced back at the bandage.

"So you did it," he breathed. "Why?"

"Fools!" York snapped, yanking his arm away at last. "You all think you're so bloody smart! The Munroes are better than the Pentercasts, and the Pentercasts are better than the Munroes. Well, I'm better than the lot of you put together! How do you think I got this post, eh? You're all too young to remember when I was just the visiting clergyman. You don't know how condescending they all were. 'Not very bright, that York,' they all said. 'But useful now and then.' Well, I was useful all right. Even then, the Munroes and Pentercasts were always out to show each other up. And old Geoffrey Pentercast, your father, he was out to woo Rutherford Munroe's sweetheart. I saw them one day, out in the orchard kissing, most unseemly. I threatened to go straight to Munroe with the news, but it seems old Pentercast had a heart after all. Swore me to secrecy. Put me in this plum position. Let Rutherford marry the chit after all. Said she was better off. I knew she suspected, but she was too proud to say anything. All these years, I've been quite nicely off, thanks to the Pentercasts' generosity, though it's been a bit thin since your father died. You were always too much the gentleman to leave secrets behind. And you didn't seem to have much use for me. So I made sure your mother approved of me. But that wasn't good enough for you, was it? No, you have to take up with a Munroe! Do you honestly think I'd let you marry one of them, a brazen hussy whose first act would be to give me the sack? Positions like these are hard to come by. I did what I had to do to keep it. Just remember, I know all your secrets, every one of you. You wouldn't dare turn out Thaddeus York!"

In a fury, Alan balled his fists at his sides. He didn't need to look at Gen to know the story had to have made her as sick as it did him.

"That is quite enough," said Reverend Wellfordhouse, surprising everyone. York clapped his mouth shut and scowled. "I don't think the Deacon will think much of your interesting little career. You, sir, are a sorry excuse for a clergyman."

Gen laughed suddenly, and Alan started at the sound. Everyone turned to look at her. "Oh, William," she chuckled, with a shake of her head, "what an understatement."

William blushed, but Geoffrey bustled forward. "Understatement or not, you've cost me my reputation, Mr. York, and I'm not going to stand by while you—"

Alan laid a hand on his brother's shoulder. Thank goodness Gen's outburst had broken the tension. "Easy, lad. He'll get what's coming to him. I can promise you that. Miss Munroe, didn't you once tell me your father had a quite extensive wine cellar in the Abbey?"

Gen grinned at him. "He did indeed. Allison, if you'll ring for Chimes, I think he'd be more than delighted to give Reverend York the full tour."

Allison scampered to the bell pull with evident pleasure. William stood looking at his master with saddened eyes. Geoffrey was rubbing his hands together gleefully. York had no choice but to keep up his malevolent scowling. Gen linked arms with Alan.

"I think," she murmured, looking up at him with a light in

her vivid blue eyes that quite took his breath away, "it's time you and I had a good talk."

Bemused, he left the reverend to his brother's good graces and allowed her to lead him from the room.

Epilogue

The Twelfth Day of Christmas

It wasn't as easy as Gen had hoped to get Alan to herself. Now that she finally understood, she felt she needed to apologize to him for all her harsh words and lack of faith. She wanted to explain to him her reservations about marrying until she was sure of her love. But as she led him back down the hall, looking for a place where they might have a private word, she found many of the rooms cold and dark and others being used by various party guests to freshen up before the midnight supper that would be announced at any minute. She could feel his surprise and wonder at her behavior, but found it impossible to explain until she knew they were alone. She wasn't about to take the chance that, like her mother, someone like the Reverend York might overhear and use her confession to his advantage and her sorrow.

Before she could find her room, however, her mother found them. "Genevieve," she frowned. "I've been looking for you and Allison everywhere. It is most unseemly of you to leave the party like this." She spared a frown for Alan as if intimating it must be his fault, but he merely offered her his best smile.

"It was quite rude, Mrs. Munroe," he acknowledged with a bow. "However, given the circumstances, I thought you would rather we unmask the vandal away from prying eyes and spare the Munroes the scandal."

To Gen's surprise, her mother paled and swayed on her feet. Gen grasped her arm, even as Alan slipped an arm around her. "Are you saying we are the cause of this destruction?" she gasped, staring up at him.

"Oh, Mother, of course not!" Gen cried. She helped her mother to a large decorative armchair that was set beside a suit of armor along the corridor alcoves. "Whatever made you think any of us would do such terrible things! We certainly lack the motivation, as well as the strength."

Her mother bowed her head. "Of course I realize that, Genevieve. I just thought someone might have been trying to scare us away, to keep us out of Wenwood."

"You aren't far off, Mrs. Munroe," Alan told her gently. "We can talk of this later. All you need to know for now is that the culprit has been apprehended and everyone's reputation is intact. Now, may we escort you back to the ballroom? I'm sure the party cannot continue without its gracious hostess."

She rose, accepting his arm, and Gen had no choice but to follow behind them to the ballroom.

Even as her mother entered, Chimes reappeared from his duty, beaming, and hurried immediately to orchestrate the opening of the midnight supper buffet. Allison and Geoffrey appeared shortly thereafter, with Geoffrey shoving his way into the line and graciously making room for Allison beside him. Alan shook his head and offered Gen his arm. "Shall we?"

She sighed, but nodded, and they took their place in line.

Gen found she wasn't in the least hungry, but nodded absently as Alan indicated particular delicacies that he then heaped on a plate for her. Ahead of her she heard Allison squeal in delight, and craning her neck, she saw that Mrs. Chimes had produced yet another favorite Munroe Christmas tradition—the Twelfth Night Cake. Chimes was presiding over it, clench-fisted in his parceling out of the confection. He went so far as to frown Allison away from a particular piece and to nod in agreement when Geoffrey snatched up one of the larger pieces. When Alan reached for a piece for Gen's plate, however, Chimes brought up his serving knife like a foil.

"None of that, now, Squire," he warned with a wave of his cutlery. "You let the lady pick her own piece."

Gen frowned at him. "Really, Chimes, I think you go too far."

"I ain't gone nearly as far as I need to go," he chortled. "Now there's a nice ladylike piece right there, much better than this man-size piece the Squire was eyeing."

Defiantly, Gen reached across his arm and plucked out the larger piece, depositing it on the plate Alan held.

Chimes glared at her. "Don't you come running to me when it doesn't work out," he muttered, whacking off three more pieces of the ring-shaped cake in quick succession. Gen stuck out her tongue at him and Alan laughed, propelling her safely out of reach of the knife.

They found a seat near her sister and his brother at one of the round tables her mother had had erected in the next room. Around her, everyone was hurrying to start in on the cake, hoping to find one of the treasures within.

"I hope I find the bean," Allison exclaimed, taking a big bite.

"Bet I know who you'd choose for consort," Geoffrey bragged, taking a mouthful of his own cake.

Allison tossed her head. "Don't be so sure of yourself, sir. I have many beaus."

Geoffrey snorted. "Sure you do, moonling. All the teenies in Reverend Wellfordhouse's scripture class think you're a real beauty."

Allison tossed down her cake. "I *will* have beaus when I'm brought out next Season. You wait and see, Geoffrey Pentercast. And *they* will be gentlemen."

"No doubt," Geoffrey began; then he choked. Rudely fishing

in his mouth with his finger, he produced the clove. "Damn, the knave. I knew I should have saved that piece for Reverend York."

Gen joined Allison in laughter. Alan laid his hand on hers, and she looked up, startled.

"You haven't tried yours yet," he chided gently.

Gen eyed him. "Neither have you."

"What say we try together?" he nodded, picking up his piece in one hand. Gen considered using a fork, then gave up the pretense of propriety. She seized her cake and held it up. Together, they took a bite, he of his, she of hers. She then set her piece down, laughing.

"Nothing in mine, just cake," she shrugged.

Alan took another bite. "Keep eating."

Gen frowned, but did as he bid. It wasn't until the third bite that she felt something solid in her mouth. Daintily pulling it out, she saw she held a bean.

"The queen," Alan smiled, putting down the rest of his cake. "Are you as sure as Allison about your consort?"

"Completely sure," Gen told him, pushing the rest of the cake aside. "There is no one I would rather have by my side than you, Alan."

Gen met his eyes and saw the answer to all her questions written there. If only she'd had the courage to look sooner, she might not have spent the last twelve days in such turmoil. Yet she couldn't be sorry. She smiled and opened her mouth to tell him what she felt.

"Oh, my word!" At the table next to theirs, William gasped. Everyone around the room swiveled to watch as he fished out a pea.

"Well," Mrs. Pentercast smiled. "The king. How very fitting, Reverend Wellfordhouse. Geoffrey tells me there will shortly be an opening at the Wenwood church. I do think it's time we had a change of vicars, don't you agree, Alan?"

Alan pulled his gaze away from Gen with obvious difficulty. "I quite agree, Mother. And I'll tell the church fathers the same when they meet on that other matter, William."

Blushing, William could only stammer his thanks.

"This is all well and good," Allison put in with determination. "But you missed the more important question entirely." When she was sure she had everyone's attention, she continued. "Who will be your queen?"

Geoffrey started laughing, and the others joined in. In the joking that followed, with several moving closer to William's table, Alan seized Gen's hand and pulled her up and away from the tables. Everyone was so busy, in fact, that they managed to slip out into the entryway unnoticed.

"I believe you wanted to tell me something," he prompted.

"I?" Gen faltered. "But you were the one to bring me out here."

He sighed. "Madame, you've made some rather damning statements this evening. Will you keep me in suspense?"

She gazed up at him, finding it hard not to chuckle. Even though he had taken the time to refresh himself, his hair was once again falling down over his forehead, his cravat was askew, and there was a piece of Epiphany cake lodged in the upper button hole of his waistcoat. "I love you, Alan Pentercast."

He took a step back, staring at her. "What . . . what did you say?"

She took a step toward him, closing the distance he had made. "I said I love you. I believe such a declaration on the part of the lady is usually followed by some acknowledgment on the part of the gentleman."

"I . . . I," he stammered, "I don't know what to say."

Gen put her hands on her hips. "Alan Pentercast, you've pursued me against all odds through the entire Twelve Days of Christmas and you don't know what to say now that you've won?"

He snorted. "Twelve Days of Christmas, nothing! I've been pursuing you since you were sixteen and refused to stand up with me at your come-out, you little minx. And I can tell you, that was rather lowering since I was under the impression you'd had a crush on me for years."

"Oh, I did," she informed him blithely, sure of herself again. "But I couldn't very well come out and admit it, now could I? Miss Genevieve Munroe, smitten with a Pentercast? Perish the thought."

"And so you became the belle of London instead. It was a rather convincing act."

She smiled, remembering. "It was rather fun. And I did try very hard to please my family and find someone I could love more than you. It simply wasn't possible."

This time he stepped forward until only inches separated them. "Madame, much more of this blatant flattery and I warn you I will not answer for the circumstances."

Keeping her eyes on the mistletoe hanging from the chandelier above them, she stood on tiptoe and threw her arms around his neck. "You've won your wager." She smiled up at him. "It is Epiphany, and I'm ready to declare that I would like nothing so much as to be your bride."

"Hang the wager," Alan murmured, bending his head to hers. "The mistletoe has to come down tomorrow. Let's not waste another minute of it."

Author's Note

There are many versions of the song "The Twelve Days of Christmas." In one of the more frequently sung versions in modern-day America, the last few verses have nine pipers piping, ten drummers drumming, eleven lords a-leaping, and twelve ladies dancing. It is also common to find Americans singing of "four calling birds" in the fourth verse.

However, in Regency England, the song was more often used as a memory game, similar to games played in twentieth-century America, in which someone must remember a growing number of unrelated items, and the first one to forget is out. In addition, the Regency version of the song told of "four colly birds" or blackbirds. The Regency version was also slightly different in the last few verses—nine drummers drumming, ten pipers piping, eleven ladies dancing, and twelve lords a-leaping.

Although many American readers may find the Regency verses unfamiliar, I chose to use the version that Gen and Alan would have known, since "The Twelve Days of Christmas" is, after all, much more than a song to them.

BOOK YOUR PLACE ON OUR WEBSITE AND MAKE THE READING CONNECTION!

We've created a customized website just for our very special readers, where you can get the inside scoop on everything that's going on with Zebra, Pinnacle and Kensington books.

When you come online, you'll have the exciting opportunity to:

- View covers of upcoming books
- Read sample chapters
- Learn about our future publishing schedule (listed by publication month *and author*)
- Find out when your favorite authors will be visiting a city near you
- Search for and order backlist books from our online catalog
- Check out author bios and background information
- Send e-mail to your favorite authors
- Meet the Kensington staff online
- Join us in weekly chats with authors, readers and other guests
- Get writing guidelines
- AND MUCH MORE!

**Visit our website at
http://www.zebrabooks.com**

ROMANCE FROM JANELLE TAYLOR

ANYTHING FOR LOVE   (0-8217-4992-7, $5.99)

DESTINY MINE   (0-8217-5185-9, $5.99)

CHASE THE WIND   (0-8217-4740-1, $5.99)

MIDNIGHT SECRETS   (0-8217-5280-4, $5.99)

MOONBEAMS AND MAGIC (0-8217-0184-4, $5.99)

SWEET SAVAGE HEART   (0-8217-5276-6, $5.99)

ROMANCE FROM FERN MICHAELS

LOOK FOR THESE REGENCY ROMANCES